Praise for *Tore All to Pieces*

"Powerful. Fun. Real. The characters feel like different kinds of people in a real world. I believed them. I believed in them. And the stories? Good-ass storytelling. Hammer down."—Robert Gipe, author of *Trampoline*

"Willie Carver is brilliant. *Tore All to Pieces* continues the work of exploring Appalachia as it is and not as it is poorly imagined. Too often Appalachia is collapsed into a degrading polemic of 'those people' to soothe the soul of the wealthy and powerful when they are confronted with poverty in the region, or it is forced into an uplifting ascension narrative that is more uncritical cheerleader than honest engagement. Carver rejects both rhetorical ruts, and we are the richer for it. Appalachia, and regional literature, has found a poet worthy of the task of telling a slice of our many stories honestly, tenderly, and compassionately."—Wesley R. Bishop, managing editor of the *North Meridian Review*

"Through Willie Carver's words, the stars have sound, cabbages speak love, and there is compassion for all."—Ann E. Kingsolver, director of the University of Kentucky Appalachian studies program

"A wild emotional ride—I laughed, I cried, I wanted to smack certain characters. I couldn't wait to finish it and didn't want it to end. Poignant, funny, and full of humanity."—Karen Taylor (1961–2025), late associate professor of French at Morehead State University and editor of the *Kentucky Philological Review*

"Carver renders Appalachia with a loving light that isn't afraid to unearth the rusty needles behind the Go-Mart. This is a drama of the everyday, written with fearless compassion and structural brilliance."
—Justin Wymer, author of *DEED* and *Let the Forest Go*

"To read *Tore All to Pieces* is to take a warm bath in the stillness of Appalachia, without anxiety about what this stillness might signify. Carver beckons us to submerge ourselves into what bell hooks calls 'the Kentucky backwoods,' understanding Kentucky's hills and hollers as both a location of flight and the promised land of return. A site not of shame but of belonging, Carver's Appalachia is home to all."
—M. Shadee Malaklou, director of the bell hooks center, Berea College

TORE ALL TO PIECES

TORE ALL TO PIECES

Willie Edward Taylor Carver Jr.

Published by The University Press of Kentucky

Scholarly publisher for the Commonwealth, serving Bellarmine University, Berea College, Centre College of Kentucky, Eastern Kentucky University, The Filson Historical Society, Georgetown College, Kentucky Historical Society, Kentucky State University, Morehead State University, Murray State University, Northern Kentucky University, Simmons College, Spalding University, Transylvania University, University of Kentucky, University of Louisville, University of Pikeville, and Western Kentucky University.

Editorial and Sales Offices: The University Press of Kentucky
663 South Limestone, Lexington, Kentucky 40508-4008
www.kentuckypress.com

Map illustration by Robert Gipe

This is a work of fiction. The characters, places, and events are either drawn from the author's imagination or used fictitiously. Any resemblance of characters to actual persons, living or dead, is coincidental. Some of the characters are depicted using homophobic slurs and other language that may be upsetting to readers. Discretion is advised.

Cataloging-in-Publication data available from the Library of Congress

ISBN 978-1-9859-0370-8 (hardcover)
ISBN 978-1-9859-0371-5 (paperback)
ISBN 978-1-9859-0372-2 (pdf)
ISBN 978-1-9859-0373-9 (epub)

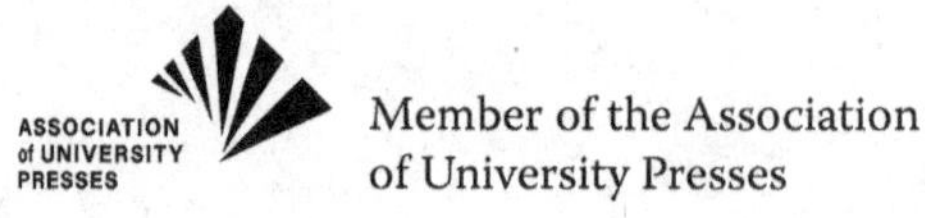

Member of the Association
of University Presses

To every Kentuckian born south of the Mountain Parkway

Write about the truth. If you write about the truth, somebody's living that. Not just somebody, there's a lot of people.

—LORETTA LYNN

THE PIECES

PEOPLE

Ashley. She's one a them Fox Creek Slones. Belongs to Clay's boy, I think.

Big Jason. Randall Mullins's oldest. Drunkard up Cow Creek. Swarps ever day a the week.

Brandi. That's Connie's little girl. One played pee-wee baseball with the boys.

Caleb. That's Marvin's boy—the one that dated that drag queen from Battersburg.

Chris. Henry and Katie's boy. The quiet one who got all fancy and moved to Lexington.

Crissy. That little girl that cooks over at the grade school. Ain't bigger'n half the kids.

Dan. Vicky Case's son, Reverend, the one whose sister married Ed Hall from Cow Creek.

David. He's that preacher from over on Ice Plant, the one who rewired Kim's house.

Doug. Good ole boy from over in Knott County. Farms and fishes. I bet you met him.

Eugene. Pastor over on Big Branch. Lord, he's dead now going on fifty years.

Henry. That bigheaded Tackett used to work over at the mines near the head a Big Branch.

Jamie. From over on Big Branch with the black Maverick—the one Sissy hung with. Queer.

Jason. Jason Miller played forward at Mosely forever. Courthouse even hung his picture up.

Jerry. Jerry Jenkins. Mud and Lori's daddy. Used to do the auction out on Cow Creek.

Joyce. She's the preacher's wife at that church over at the head of Ice Plant.

Katie. Henry Tackett's woman. The one that worked at the nursing home.

Keesha. Mandi's young'un—that mean little ginger one.

Keith. Bush Spurlock's boy. The one that ain't no count, not the other one.

Kevin. Middle boy a Greg and Sissy. They said he's a manager now at McDonald's.

Little George. One a them Johnsons with the guns. Big feller that lost his wife to cancer.

Lonnie. You know him. Connie's oldest young'un. Always down at the garage.

Mandi. She's a Gunnell from up Cow Creek, lives up past Ed Hall, the bedridden feller.

Mark. Bush Spurlock's oldest boy. Moved out to Parkersburg, WV, for that woman.

Melissa. Jimmy's girl. That big one who married that tattooed biker from Canard County.

Mud. Jerry Jenkins's boy with the long hair that Chigger sold that old lemon Honda to.

Nathan. He's one a them Hackworths on Fox Creek. One who studied car motors.

Patrick. The one that Chris hung around. Vicky's grandbaby. Dan's son. Love his heart.

Patty. Patty don't take shit. She's been working at the Fast-n-Fill as long as I can remember.

Paula. She's the blond and with the brother who . . . you know. She works over to the schools.

Pauline. A Johnson. You'd know her if you seen her. Walks like a man. Pure crazy and a cheat.

Rayeanne. That's Dan Case's little girl. That one who whooped them boys on the bus.

Simon. Ain't that the little boy kin to Joyce and them did that poem on the radio?

Tammy. Works over at the Dollar Store. Managed Martin's before it closed down.

Trina. Shew, that wild Johnson girl who lost her mommy. Family lives over near Mosely.

Vicky. Walt's wife. Walt from over on Big Branch. She's Dan Case's mommy.

Walt. Walt was a decent man. He probably helped build half the houses up this holler.

Wanda. Widow a Bush Spurlock. Does the food over in Mosely at the school.

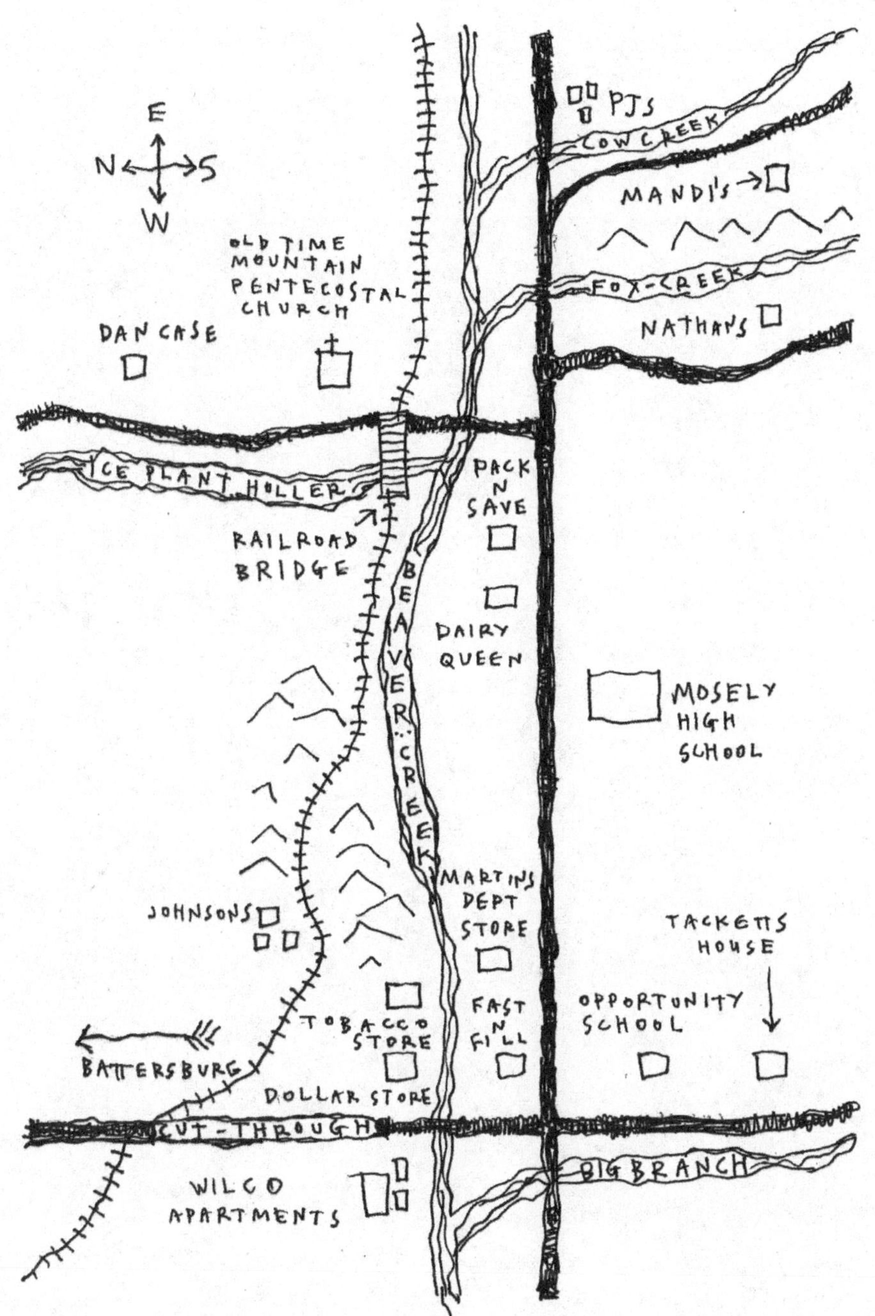
E
N
S
W
PJS
COW CREEK
MANDI'S
FOX-CREEK
NATHAN'S
OLD TIME MOUNTAIN PENTECOSTAL CHURCH
DAN CASE
ICE PLANT HOLLER
PACK N SAVE
RAILROAD BRIDGE
BEAVER CREEK
DAIRY QUEEN
MOSELY HIGH SCHOOL
MARTINS DEPT STORE
JOHNSONS
TACKETTS HOUSE
OPPORTUNITY SCHOOL
FAST N FILL
TOBACCO STORE
BATTERSBURG
DOLLAR STORE
CUT-THROUGH
BIG BRANCH
WILCO APARTMENTS

THE FAT TRUTH

I could use adverbs and maybe even begin
my sentence with some limp preposition
even smother my *who* with an *m* that tucks
around the lips of *o*, that folds around the hole
until only folks whose hanging indent is a
clean measured half inch might feel brave
enough to put my words in their mouth

but restraint ain't that sexy
to folks who use real butter

may my words be full fat and high cholesterol
may they flare out, plump with meaning's cream
saturated in color and light and cheap pork rind
the taste of which will matter, I promise you
since I want the weight of me coating mouths
and whether they swallow me or spit me out
their tongues will be thick with my lingering lipids

GAS STATION PROLOGUE

Mosely. Summer 2023.

"Soft pack or box?"

She asked it like there was a right or wrong answer.

"Gimme a soft pack if you got it."

Rayeanne didn't indicate if she approved of his choice. She heaved the fat of her stomach onto the counter so she could reach for a soft pack of USA Gold Lights from a large plastic cabinet positioned above her. The midday sun was firmly clear of the hill line, now coruscating in thick swaths of light off the gas pumps onto her position behind the register. She flipped her sunglasses down to see well enough to choose the right pack of cigarettes, then pulled them back up on her head to keep her long hair off her face. She would have known the placement of the cigarettes by heart, having worked at the Fast-n-Fill for going on twenty years after replacing her brother Patrick, but they hired new boys every other month for the third shift, so the stocking was never consistent.

"$5.88."

Rayeanne eyed the customer in front of her, a short and stocky thirty-something worker man in a neon safety vest, as he unfolded neat one-dollar bills. His arms were covered in suntan and thick, dark hair. Behind him to the right, a motley throng of five or six bottlenecked an aisle, looking at their phones or chatting. To the left, in the corner, a pinecone-helmeted woman attacked scratch-off tickets, leaning against a plastic Kentucky Lottery podium wedged between stacks of pop and the drink cooler. She surveyed the line of customers from her perch, waiting for just the right moment to jump back in for more tickets.

A creaking and sizzling advanced from behind Rayeanne, and she reflexively squeezed herself to the left. Patty Ross, mid-sixties, wiry and only slightly hunched over, contrasted Rayeanne's largeness and relative youth, as Rayeanne's fat protected her face from age. Patty balanced a heap of soft fried bacon on top of a deep metal buffet pan. For a brief moment, as she walked, she passed through the stretch of light burning in through the windows of the gas station, and the steam from the deep pan ascended like thick, translucent smoke.

Patty opened the backside of the glass heating cabinet that held breakfast foods. She slid the fresh bacon onto an older pile, then dropped the deep pan into place. "Sorry y'all's been waiting. We'd done run out a gravy earlier." The hungry customers fell forward in anticipation.

The man in the neon shirt lifted a bank card. "I only got five ones on me. Can I use this?"

"Yeah." Rayeanne flipped a device around and squeezed the fatness of her pointing finger along its outside curve. "Slide it here."

Patty began to take orders. She opened a Styrofoam container and broke up two soft and lightly browned biscuits at their thick cloud centers and then smothered them in white cream gravy and pieces of spiced sausage glistening with oil and pricks of red pepper. She closed it and turned to the next person.

Rayeanne handed the worker man his receipt. Patty was already ladling out another order.

The man hadn't moved.

Slight irritation welded together Rayeanne's next words. "Buddy, you need something?"

The man swept his head around like he was checking to see who was paying attention; most folks seemed worried about food. "Yeah. I was wanting to know if, uh"—he clacked the short edge of his card three times against the counter—"if you might wanna go do something with me sometime." His gaze oscillated, starting up at her face and then falling down to the receipt in his hand as he spoke to her, like he might find some revelation or answer between the date, location, and sales tax.

Rayeanne shifted her weight and stepped forward, away from the light, so she might size him up with greater ease. She liked that he didn't mind making people behind him wait. Her answer was neither soft nor sharp: "Depends. You ever consider switching to Marlboro?"

Before he answered, the entrance on the other side of the gas station, the doors farthest from the register, blew open and a giant man, easily closer to seven feet than six, came into the door frame. Standing halfway in, halfway out, he hollered up onto the oval platform that separated the workers from the customers. "Patty, you working?"

Patty, layering a plate with paper towels so the ham and cheese rolls she was packing up wouldn't slide in their oil, answered without turning away. "Yeah. What you need, Little George?"

"There's a whole flock a young'uns out there praying in a circle up yonder in the Dairy Queen parking lot. Something going on?"

She shook her head and closed the container. "I ain't heard nothing. But hell, might be the end of time as far as I know. It'd be my luck, too. I just cussed out this pan a gravy little bit ago." She stirred the gravy instinctively when she referenced it.

The scratch-off-ticket lady edged herself up against the front door, the closer one in front of the register, and peered with her hands above her eyes. She spoke with authority, waving her arm downward as if to say there was nothing to see: "Why, that's just them folks from that church up Ice Plant. I recognize the van."

Reassured, the giant entered the store and clomped toward the coffee, the lottery woman joined the end of the line of customers, and the man with the receipt was still looking at Rayeanne, who had yet to respond. She spoke flatly. "I'll think about it. I'm here bout ever day. Come ask me again sometime."

The man nodded at her, looking satisfied with her answer, stuffed his receipt, card, and cigarettes into his shirt pocket, and headed out. Patty served up food and Rayeanne rang up customers. When the line was cleared and the lottery-ticket woman took ten one-dollar scratch-offs back to her corner, Rayeanne declared she was taking her thirty-minute break. She filled a container with what remained of the morning's breakfast, grabbed a pop, and stepped outside. She didn't see anybody praying—kids or otherwise—just the same old parking lot and the same old cars and the same old roster of humanity she always saw.

She sat at a wooden bench perched out on the grassy area near the bathrooms. Behind her was the road that led toward the cut-through and out of Mosely. In front of her was a long and unending span of hills that rose into the sky like old fences, so many trees crowding together that they bled through each other and ceased to be separate, just a skin of green and brown dividing town from sky. In front of them, the Martin's building, the old high school, the Dairy Queen, Nathan's Garage, and various houses, trailers, businesses, and buildings stretching out as far as she could see, which in the winter was as far as Fox Creek but now, with the green swell of summer swarming the landscape, was just a double-wide trailer in the distance opposite the mouth of Ice Plant Holler.

Rayeanne watched the parking lot flood with people. A big-headed bald man and a woman with a giant purse fought at each other while a patch of young'uns cried to leave the backseat. A woman with short purple hair on a motorcycle was buying gas for herself and another lady in a silver SUV. A woman with big blond hair walked out with three bags of ice. A skinny man in a tight pink shirt pulled up in a black truck, looked brand-new, and talked across rolled-down windows to a couple of young men in a thirty-year-old, four-door sedan; the passenger seat man's eyes were fixed on the road. Rayeanne ate. She had two biscuits sweating butter and ripped into thick chunks, a half dozen strips of chewy pepper bacon, two soft fried eggs with bright yellow yolks. Everything was smothered in thick white gravy. She chewed each bite until the flavors merged into something pure and meant to be together, relishing the harmony washing around her tongue. She brought it all down with heavy swigs of full-sugar pop.

She was only halfway through her break when she heard hollering from the store entrance. The lottery woman stood in front of the door, looking at her. "Hey, sissy, you bout through? Patty's done got a line backed plumb out to the coffee machines." She threw her head back in the direction of the coffee machines as she spoke, and the sun fluttered across the silver frames of her old eyeglasses, which glinted around her head like a cheap halo.

"Shew. Yeah, I'm coming." Rayeanne rubbed a fingertip through the last vein of gravy clinging to the side of the container, then licked it clean, holding it on her tongue for a moment to consider the taste, and in her contemplation looked lost in either prayer or devotion. She swallowed, then tossed the empty container in the trash by the door as she went back inside the store, sacrificing the second half of her break to rescue her overwhelmed colleague.

BATHTUB FAITH

Mom gathered us
	like we were the godless crowd
	like she bore the good news
	like the sun was now shining
in light made of new colors,
and we convened, a throng of three,
crowding the public space
between the commode
and washing machine
in that single-wide trailer
as she kneeled before
a beaming white bathtub
transformed by cleaner
and her work.

I got out that old grime
scrubbed through soap scum
and just washed away
them well-water iron stains.
Don't it look brand-new?

Unwilling to dirty her tub
with children's words,
we simply stood
in witness.

Now if you young'uns
can just rinse around the rim
with some new hot water
and any old rag
after you wash yourselves
it will always look like this.

The multitude took leave.
The light grew faint.
The sun twisted.
Iron stains crept back.
Grime cleaved unto the ceramic.
Dirt and grot hovered and clung
beneath our bathwater.

Every month, a bathroom sermon.
The same faithful speaking in tongues
        this time we would feel the spirit
        this time we would keep it clean.

Y'all just gotta do your part
and starting today
and every day after
we're gonna have a bright, clean tub
and I won't have to work so hard.

We saw the miracle and believed
but we never once ran new hot water
never once rinsed around the rim
never once wiped with any old rag.
And the sun set ten thousand times.

. . .

I am forty
in my own tub.
I take a bath.
I pull a plug.
I watch water
orbit its drain.
I run new hot water
over the same rag
that made me clean.
I anoint the rim
and rinse the scum

and the past
with the rag
just like you
always prayed
we would.

SERIOUS

Battersburg. Big Branch. Mosely. Fall 2023.

Chris Tackett eased into the mostly abandoned parking lot at six minutes after eight in the morning, taking one of many empty spots near a glass door he had known since childhood. The door hid behind a peeling sign reading *Appalachian Outpatient Surgery.* It was written in large blue letters intentionally reminiscent of the colors of the University of Kentucky Wildcats, just close enough to draw in customers who choose surgery centers based upon college athletics and just different enough to avoid a lawsuit. Below the facility's name in white script splattered by mud kicked up by the tires of people leaving those surgeries were the words *Where You Matter!*™

The entire facility was pushed back against a hillside, so close that as he pulled in from the road, the sky disappeared from his windshield, trees and dirt from the slope taking its place, flooding the view and giving Chris the momentary impression that he was driving toward the earth from somewhere higher up, descending rather than rolling horizontally. It had been so long since he had lived here, belted by hills, that he was overcome by the distinct feeling that he should look to make sure the sky was still there. He didn't check to see. He cut the engine. Removed his keys. Surveyed the familiar landscape. A clinic against the hillside, joined on the right by a painted cinder block car wash and on the left by a pizza place that doubled as a bar. A couple of stray dogs sniffed around a garbage bin hidden behind a wooden gate. Otherwise, an empty road squeezed along the hillside, and slate-colored fog swung up in curls from the creek beside it, a creek that fed into the lake. A lake Chris swam in often as a kid. A lake that Chris knew well.

He took a deep breath. He now lived two hours away, in Lexington, the closest big city to his parents' home in eastern Kentucky. He didn't return often, partly due to circumstance and partly due to a small prickling of anxiety that shadowed him each time the road stopped being a road and started being an extension of his childhood, a setting that merged with his history and memory. A whispering skin that threatened to hold him here.

His dad's appointment was at eight o'clock, but six minutes wouldn't be too late. Still, Chris prided himself on punctuality, a rare trait in his family, and made a mental note to leave earlier next time he needed to come down. He imagined his parents, Katie and Henry, in the waiting room. Henry would be talking up strangers, most willing and wooed by his rough-lumber charm, and Katie would be looking through an oversized handbag, frazzled and determined, still filling out paperwork with information that the hospital surely had taken from them hundreds of times already.

She would rummage through her large purse, swear violence against unwatched grandbabies who had taken her pen, and then steal one from the nurses' station.

Chris tossed his coat into the backseat and headed in.

He found his mother in the waiting room, balancing a clipboard against the waxed arm of a wooden chair covered in cracking apricot vinyl. Her leggings bore cats in Santa hats tucked into faux fur boots, paired with a neighboring county's high school boys' sports T-shirt and oversized camouflage men's coat. She sucked on the writing end of a cheap blue pen and then scratched it furiously across the top of a hospital form until it began to streak haphazard lines across the page.

She looked her age in the uncertain fluctuation of the cheap fluorescent light. Chris's dad wasn't with her.

"Y'all been here long?"

Katie looked up and handed the clipboard and pen to her son like she was giving up a crying baby. "Shew. I'm glad you're here. See if you can make out them tiny letters. You reckon they'd print this bigger since half the folk come here's old enough to sing Bocephus." She gestured to a white-haired woman, half asleep, at the other end of the waiting room, both her head and rolling oxygen tank propped against the wall. "But just make sure you check *diabetes* and *heart condition.* It might just say cardiac and not heart. Good drive in?"

Chris looked over the form, checking the boxes marked *diabetes* and *overweight.* His mom's large square print, her choice to capitalize all nouns, and even the cautious precision of her signature all pinged him with unexpected nostalgia. "Ain't too bad. Slow start and I-64 was crawling cause of a accident. Am I supposed to choose *cardiac arrhythmia* or *congestive cardiac failure*?"

Chris flipped the clipboard and pointed to the only two options listed under *Cardiovascular History—Conditions.*

Katie rolled her eyes up and sleeves down. "Well, now, if they listened to me, you'd check em both, but they said he ain't got heart failure." She gestured at the nurse's desk, her closed fist exploding open as she finished the sentence, fingers splaying out with frustration as if to condemn not just the distracted nurse but perhaps the clinic, adjacent hospital, or the entire medical establishment. "You think it's cold in here? Shew. I'm freezing. You ain't gotta be a doctor to see he does. The man can't walk to the bathroom without smothering so bad he's gotta take a break, and his stomach's so swelled up he can't eat. Looks foundered."

The white-haired woman sleeping against the wall coughed herself awake. Pain shot across her face and she gripped the arm of her chair. She looked in need of help, but there was also something serene in the slowness of her post-cough breathing. Chris tried to catch her gaze to see if she needed anything, but she repositioned herself and closed her eyes again.

Katie continued.

"But they don't listen to me. Just write 'symptomatic' off the edge and then half check it—it might make them look for it. Buddy, I wouldn't drive on that interstate. You never know these days. They's so many wild people out there. And you couldn't pay me to drive up there in Lexington. It's about to where I won't drive down here, neither."

Chris motioned to the nurses' station, and his mom nodded, so he handed the clipboard to a nurse who took it politely but without looking up from her phone. The tips of her hair, pulled back in a messy ponytail, were dyed green.

"Sit here a second." Katie motioned toward the seat across from her. Chris sat. She checked her purse for something, appeared reassured it was there, and then zipped it closed. "Now, don't judge me for my outfit, but by the time I got the babies and your daddy out the door it was pushing 7:30, and they'll cancel an appointment as sure as look at you here. Took two months to get this one. I guess they might be mad we ain't made the co-pay for the last one, yet."

"You need any help?"

"Why, no. Let em stack up. What they gonna do, repossess?" A phone buzzed, a distant machine wheezed, and the nurse coughed. Katie nodded. "They done took him on back."

Chris looked to the door leading into the small rooms where nurses and assistants prepped patients. "Why ain't you with him? They already take him into surgery?"

She said, "No, I left so I wouldn't get mad at him. That's what I was gonna tell you."

"Why was you getting mad?"

Katie shook her head in mild frustration, her eyes running the length of the room and landing at the nurses' station. "You know exactly how that man is. He's back in 'ere cutting up with the nurses and now they don't believe he's sick. I done told him, I said, 'Henry, right there's why they don't believe a word you say. You're back here laughing and hooting and can barely breathe and they won't take you serious.' And right there's why they don't believe me when I tell em he's got heart failure."

"Well, at least he's in a good mood."

Katie eyed Chris.

Chris shifted tactics. "Well, Mom, you know how he is. We probably ain't gonna change him at this age."

"Well, I ain't gonna listen to him neither, not when I'm the one has to take care a his ass when he gets to smothering." She shifted her weight to her other hip. Her forehead showed a flash of pain that dissolved quickly into something calmer. She paused. "Well. Sorry for cussing. But I told him a blue million times and he won't listen." She paused, like she was weighing the potential consequences of finishing her thought, then added, "Not like anybody ever does."

"You ain't gotta apologize to me."

"No, but I do need you to go on in there and sit with him. He'll be happy you're here. It's only one at a time now, you know. New government rules."

The nurse's phone chirped a video game congratulatory sound, a little trumpet followed by cheerful applause.

Chris said, "Well, Lord, I don't want to take your place. You go on back in with him."

"No, now, I ain't going. I'll get mad if I go back. And if he dies me cussing at him, I won't be able to live with it. Ain't no safe surgeries, not even little ones. But promise me you'll make sure he's serious. And make sure that he tells em he's on blood thinners but he ain't had none since Monday night. He don't know what he takes and what he don't. But make him act right. He'll listen to you."

Chris sighed. "You sure about that?"

She closed her eyes, then exhaled. "Yeah. I'm gonna sit here, get out my checkbook, and start writing out the bills. I'd like to get to the grocery before the end a the day if I can."

Chris walked up to the nurse and said he'd be going back.

She sang "To your right" like it was an old church hymn lyric, her lilt rippling in the soft vowel of her final word. Chris let the sound echo in his mind, pleased with it. She pressed a button on the wall and went back to her phone.

Two doors opened, and Chris walked through.

Henry felt the thinness of the threadbare hospital gown painting a chill across his thighs. He had run hot his whole life, especially lying in beds, capable of drenching pillows with sweat in his sleep. When he was a child, his mom would accuse him of having fevers, but the problem was never the temperature of his body, just the largeness of its heat, like he was walking around leaving a trail of his aliveness sticking to the air and furniture. Even when he worked in the mines in the dead of winter and he and the other men would stumble out of the narrow mouth of the coal mine and light up their cigarettes, while the others bitched about the cold under the naked limbs of the winter tree line, the coalblack on their faces absorbing the chill of the evening, Henry had only ever felt fresh. The cold felt good, carrying away the rumbling churn of his body's heat.

In the last few years, he had started to feel cold. At first, he'd blame the feeling on his being wet from a drainage pipe project or from sweating too hard hauling hay, or he'd reason he'd had a couple of beers too many, but it soon became undeniable. His inner furnace had slowed. He had gone and become an old man without knowing it. And now, sitting in the hospital bed waiting for some doctor to widen his throat, only his dignity prevented him from shivering.

Katie didn't have to walk out in a huff. He was being funny, and the nurses were laughing. Ain't that proof enough they weren't bothered? She'd be beating herself up about it, Henry knew. He imagined her storming away, checking the corridors for the fastest way out to get to a cigarette, remember she hadn't smoked in ten years now, and then find some place to just sit and brood. On the one hand, he felt a little frustrated with himself, if not guilty, for getting her upset, but on the other hand, he was envious of the fact that Katie wasn't shivering yet. Her fire was still raging hot, ready to blow, ready to burn itself a new path. She was still very much alive. Henry was at least satisfied to give her that, a reminder that she was still burning.

Yes. She was burning, and it was good.

The promise of coffee bobbed across the room. Weak, watery, overly sanitary. Henry's stomach lurched. He shifted himself and tried to pull the gown further down his exposed thighs.

You burn when you've got fuel. A man's fuel is work to provide for others if he's a good man, is taking what he can from the world while giving it back as little as possible, if he ain't. Henry had been both, but once the kids came along, he was mostly the former, working however many jobs or hours it took to give them the best chance not to have to do the same someday. But a man's fuel only lasts as long as his body can do that work. Henry was running on reserves, on whatever was left in the tank. There'd be no more stops at the gas station.

Now a woman, that's a different story. A good woman like Katie has unlimited stories when she's young. Katie was a beautiful girl. Henry met her in '75 at a bonfire his cousins were burning. They were sitting around telling lies at each other. She came walking up the lane with his girl cousins, who left her standing alone, holding high school books in the grass by the barn. He had dropped out in eighth grade over a decade before. Her long, straight hair fell down most of her back, just a river of blond splashing against her body. Henry jumped up, leaving the boys to their stories, swaggered across the yard, and walked straight up to her and told her she was too pretty to be standing by herself. She, a high school senior, looked at him, a twenty-five-year-old man in his prime, dead in the eye and said, "Well, I'm too pretty to stand beside most of the old drunks laying around here." She said it so matter-of-factly that he had to look away. A woman like that could have any story. Henry knew that even then.

A nurse's aide walked in and handed Henry a clipboard. "Can you tell me your birthday?"

"Why, honey, y'all offering whiskey?"

She did not look Henry in the eyes as she spoke and instead focused her vision on some machines behind him. "No, we're plumb out of liquor. I got some liquid charcoal we might give you later if you're good though."

"Well, damn. You oughtta be a salesman."

"Saleswoman. Now, can you tell me your birthday?"

"Fifth of December. '49."

"You got somebody picking you up? Wife or kids?"

"My wife, but she's probably out with the kids right now buying extra insurance on me. None of em bothering to come. She's a terrible woman. Raised awful kids, too. Every one of em looks like the mailman . . . and that's a complicated one, cause the mailman's a woman."

The aide scanned a tag on the bed with a small device, tapping buttons on the screen as she talked. "Well, she sounds smart to me." She handed Henry a clipboard. "Make sure you sign and date there on the bottom. These will follow you into the operating room." She aimed a kind smile at Henry's head. He signed. She laid the papers at the foot of his bed and pulled the divider curtain back, walking out without closing it behind her.

The paper listed Henry's birthdate at the top. She must have wanted to make sure he wasn't already senile or something, that he was in his right mind enough to answer questions she knew the answers to already. The pulled-back curtain intensified the cold in the room. Henry put one of his pillows across his legs.

He had spent many nights around those bonfires and had seen many girls hanging around his cousins. But Katie was different. The dignity in her response. The possibilities just itching to grow planted deep down in her intelligence. Henry knew that night that if he could make her story into his, then his purpose would be elevated, his meaning more important. And through dumb luck and cockiness, he had made that happen.

They played house. They fought. They made up. He worked in the mines. She worked at the nursing home. She was the first woman in her family to open her own bank account. She wrote checks even though she had cash in her pockets just to show the world that she was its equal. He was the first man in his family to rise to foreman. He would walk into poker night or a rooster fight and men would tip their caps and say, *Evening, Foreman.* They bought brand-new cars right off the lot. They ate at restaurants and went to bars and drank beer. Men flirted with her. He fought them over it. She looked displeased as it happened, but then later made love to him with a passion equaling his bruises or, once, his broken collar bone. They took vacations, once driving all the way to Myrtle Beach just because she had never seen the ocean and he had the weekend off.

After a few years came the children. Then the stories revealed themselves. The first baby to cry, to present a need, just rewrote Katie. That young girl caught fire and was never quenched. Henry would provide resources and she would meet needs. Less beer. More milk. Fewer visits to the beach. More visits to the dentist. She stopped hunger, anger, fear, sickness, doubt, and any number of challenges a child and the world might conjure together—and Henry would take the back burner to her mission, would lay down what he had to give, watching her make magic while they both grew fatter and stronger under the warmth of the purpose she gave them. A couple of strokes and a bad fall, and Henry's fuel was gone. But babies keep on needing whether you've got the means to help them or not, and with grandbabies replacing babies, children were an unlimited truth in their lives, so as Henry's fire slowed, Katie's began to take on new shapes and flare out in glory and purpose.

A man in blue scrubs walked into the room. He held a tiny half-can of pop in his hands. "Where'd your wife go? I thought she might want one a these, maybe a coffee?" He sat the can on a small, rolling table next to Henry, then lifted a cartoonishly large remote attached to the bed. He pushed a button on it that lifted Henry as Henry answered the man, "You was too slow. She done run out. Said I wadn't worth waiting on if she didn't have something to drink. She's a mean old woman."

"All the more reason to give her coffee, then, I reckon."

Chris could hear his dad before he could see him. Henry was reclined in a hospital bed in one of eight or so spaces cut off from each other by long yellowing curtains. His were pulled open. He had lost weight but otherwise looked the same as the last time Chris had seen him a few months back. His head was reclined on his right arm, and his feet were crossed on top of a pillow that some nurse or aide had clearly placed under them. Another sat over his thighs. On the table to his right was a small, unopened can of pop next to a pile of folded clothes—blue jeans and a gray T-shirt, the only thing Henry wore unless he was going to a wedding or a funeral—and the gold-plated watch that his brothers bought him as a gift when his second stroke convinced him to finally quit working. He was mid-conversation with a big-armed man in blue scrubs who appeared to be in his fifties or sixties and was holding a clipboard.

Henry spoke first. "You didn't have to come all the way here just for this. I know how busy you are. They're just gonna put a little stent in my throat and be done with me. Just a little pissant surgery."

Chris took the only seat, a hard plastic blue chair sandwiched between the wall and a pole suspending an IV bag. "Well, I got off a whole day a work for it. Figured it was worth it just for the day off."

The big-armed man in scrubs gave a chuckle. "Yeah. I got me a whole week coming up. We're planning on going to California to see our daughter, took some computer job out there. Got us tickets to a 49ers game."

Henry slapped his knee playfully. "California! All them pretty girls on the beaches. You won't come back here. Fellers like me cain't compete with that."

The man in scrubs made some scratches on the clipboard. "Well, I won't be seeing much of em, not if my wife has any say in it."

"Well, see, there's your problem," Henry replied. "Now, me, I wouldn't take my wife. That's just asking for trouble."

"I know, but mine's just as dangerous if you don't take her. Probably more so." He flipped to the next page on his clipboard.

Henry nodded in agreement. "Now, I'll tell you. I did basic training out in San Diego and did some hitchhiking in the sixties. I was excited—thought it would be all girls in bikinis and Raquel Welch fighting over me in my uniform. Funny thing is, I didn't see a damn thing like that. Spent three days thumbing around southern California and all that tried to pick me up was a bus full a teachers and a couple a gay guys. They had nice cars, though. The gay fellers, not the teachers. One of em had a little blue '67 Dodge Coronet. You ever seen one a them? Jesus, that was a nice car."

The man in scrubs said, "Well." He pressed a button on the machine attached to the pole holding the IV, offered a tight head nod, then stepped out of the room, which grew quickly quiet.

Chris broke the silence. "What time did they say they was doing the surgery?" He leaned forward and wrapped the palms of his hands around his knees, then tapped them with his fingers. His shoes were the whitest thing in the room. "Do they put you out for it or they gonna make you do the cutting yourself?"

Henry said, "That part about gay guys picking me up hitchhiking, that wadn't offensive, was it?"

Chris pretended to scratch the back of his neck for a second. "Lord, no. You're fine. I was just wondering if they do it while you're awake or if . . ."

Henry stopped him. "Cause I wouldn't say nothing to hurt nobody's feelings or nothing. Hell, I probably said all kinds a stupid stuff when you was a kid, Chris. And I remember what happened to that Case boy from over to Ice Plant. I wish we woulda known y'all was, you know. We just did it all wrong, is what I mean. I just wouldn't want you to think . . ."

Chris's face paled for a moment as his father spoke, then he interrupted him in a sudden rupture of energy. "Ain't nothing offensive. No. I'm just glad some gay feller somewhere has a nice car. God knows my transmission ain't long for this world. Hey, is somebody drinking this pop?" Chris lifted the half-can off the table.

"No. They brought that for your mommy. Go ahead and take it. I ain't allowed to drink nothing." The can popped open, then the sound of fizz and Chris taking a sip. They waited a moment in silence, which Henry broke. "Well, anyway, I just wanted to be sure. I mean, I didn't care that them guys was gay. Course, they wadn't no Raquel Welch, neither."

Chris looked at the beeping machine, sat up straight again. He moved the tab on the can of pop back and forth. "Well, I mean, heck, ain't nobody a match for Raquel Welch. I ain't too gay to say I'd choose her over random guys with nice cars."

Henry said, "Well, now, I bet she's still a looker."

Chris said, "Maybe. But I just meant she's probably still rolling in it."

They both laughed.

A nurse whisked into the room. Her scrubs bore a repeating ichthys pattern and her bright yellow sneakers perfectly matched her hair. She wore a blank name tag and enough makeup for three of her. The nurse studied a machine without talking, then smiled at them both and said in exaggeratedly loud clarity, "Mr. Tackett, how are we doing today?"

Henry grinned. "We? Oh, Lord! I didn't know *we* was a thing. I don't know how *we're* doing, but I'm just tickled to death to be a part of something here with you. But you better not let my wife hear you talking like that and flirting so much, honey. She's a mean woman. Tell her, Chris, how mean your mommy is."

Chris waited on the nurse to respond.

She rolled her eyes in a playful fashion. Chris smiled. She said, "Well, it sounds like you're doing fine. I'm sure your wife is a very nice woman. Didn't she want to sit with you this morning? Or does she got something better to do, maybe fold socks?" She pulled a pillow off of his legs and laid it on the rolling table holding his clothes. She pushed it toward the wall with her back to Henry as she spoke.

Henry said, "No, she's just crazy jealous. Won't leave me be. I had to run away to lose her. Violent woman. She hits me. Beats up on me night and day."

The nurse trilled a little laugh. "Well, now, you might deserve it. Now, I just have a couple a questions. When was the last time you ate?"

"Why? You asking me out to lunch?"

She said, "No. I'm too scared a your wife to ask. But when did you last eat?"

Henry said, "She won't feed me. Tries to starve me to death. But I did have me a cold bologna sandwich last night."

Chris caught the nurse's eyes. He nodded his head to let her know there had, indeed, been a bologna sandwich and nothing since.

She continued, "And it looks like you're on Metformin and Warfarin. Do you know when you last took the Warfarin?"

Henry dropped the ruse. "My wife makes up the pills. She gave them all to me this morning about 7:30, right before we left."

Chris interrupted, "Is that a blood thinner?"

The nurse said, "Yes, it is."

Chris said, "He stopped taking them Monday night."

The nurse smiled, added a quick note to the papers near Henry's feet, and left the room.

Chris looked at his phone. It was eight thirty in the morning.

Henry suddenly spoke: "You need to take your mommy up to stay with you for a week or two."

"Why's that? Is she *actually* driving you crazy?"

Henry sat up. "I ain't ever seen her like this. She's got to where she's just stressed out over ever little thing. She's too old to take care a them kids like she does, too. She just needs a break, I reckon. Just a little time to breathe."

Chris put his phone back in his pocket. "Yeah, well . . . you're just trying to get rid of her long enough to get that nurse to come back with you."

Henry chuckled. "She is a pretty little thing. But I'm a old man. I just admire em these days."

A hiss invaded the air, and the blood pressure cuff on Henry's arm began to expand. The men sat in silence as if they might interrupt its counting of his pulse. It hummed and tightened as machines beeped slowly but with predictable rhythm. The cuff exhaled without warning, and Henry rested his arm, which he had unknowingly tensed.

The big-armed man in scrubs reappeared.

"Alrighty, Mr. Tackett. I'm just here to get you prepped for surgery."

Henry gestured around him. "Hell, buddy, y'all got so many pipes and tubes hanging off a me you might as well install plumbing and charge somebody rent. How much readier can I get?"

The man in scrubs grabbed the stack of papers at the foot of Henry's bed and slid them into a folder. "Well, you're still talking to me, ain't you? I figure if you're still talking, you ain't ready for surgery."

Henry nodded. "Well, now, you might just be a educated feller after all. Y'all at least gonna give me the good stuff?"

The man in scrubs tapped the bag suspended from the pole, kicked a brake release on the bed wheels, and pulled the bed toward him in an impressively fluid motion. He said, "Same shit that killed Michael Jackson."

Henry laughed. "Well, damn. I'm getting the celebrity VIP treatment."

The man in scrubs wheeled Henry out of the space, handing Chris a slip of paper with a number on it. "Just look at the screen," he said, pointing back at the door Chris walked in. "This number'll let you know where they are in the procedure. Shouldn't be an hour, tops."

Katie had already chosen a chair in front of the monitor. She sipped coffee from a white Styrofoam cup. Chris handed her the piece of paper and chose a seat near her so they both faced the display.

The screen read *pre-op* next to the number from the paper.

She turned to Chris. Her eyes looked heavy. "That was fast."

"Yeah."

"Well, what they say?"

"Said if the surgery didn't kill him the nurses might have to."

Katie nodded. "I reckon."

Chris said, "Yeah."

A gray line collapsed down the screen, refreshing the information behind it. Henry's number was unchanged.

Katie said, "Did you tell em about the blood thinners?"

"Yeah. I even wrote and sang a song about it. Called it the Warfarin Blues. They're probably gonna send me down to Nashville."

Katie creased her lips into a damp curve. "But you did tell em? Be serious."

The gray line fell again. The display shifted from *pre-op* to *in progress.* The nurse's phone vibrated against her laminate desktop. Katie sat her coffee down and placed her hands on her purse.

"Yeah. I told em. Said he took it Monday night."

She nodded and said, "That's good."

"And he didn't even know when he took em the last time."

"I know."

They waited together.

The clinic insisted on pushing Henry out to Chris's car in a wheelchair, so Katie had a few minute's head start home on her husband and son. She unlocked the front door to the trailer and left it cracked.

It sometimes got so stuck that Henry just didn't have the strength to open it by himself anymore, and she didn't want Henry to have Chris see him unable to open a door. Just one more thing to deal with.

The grandkids were in school, but a person could sense their presence in any room. Phone cords by the sink, shoes dispensed with in the middle of the floor, half-drunk pop cans left where each of them had felt their fill. None of them ever stopped to ask themselves if what they did would affect another person, ask themselves who might someday pick up that can. Though God knows she had told them over and over again. Life could be so different if she had any help. But they were kids. Kids were assholes like that, and that's what made them loveable. Cause at least they didn't *know how* to know to think about other people.

She'd choose assholes by accident over assholes by choice any day.

Katie's own mother had made sure that she had known to see herself only through the eyes of others. She was a sober woman. A perfect woman. But that was a different time, a different world. A world long dead. As a child, Katie knew that every wrinkle in her dresses had to be accounted for, every chore done before there was a chance for her mom to remember the chore existed, every light left on lectured over and apologized for until she burned with shame. She was reminded daily of the cost her existence brought and her potential to bring shame to herself or her family. It was a childhood in which every move she made or didn't make shoved her into the headlights of someone else's car, somebody going where everybody else was going, a constant threat to ensure that Katie showed up there, too. There was no making your own path back then, just one road. And folks were too hard off to imagine a new one.

So yeah, maybe her grandbabies didn't have shame—but, given her experience with the emotion, she was proud of the fact. Katie's own mother had died of thyroid cancer two decades ago. Katie would drive to her house daily and make her breakfast in those final months, even after she stopped eating. When her mother became bedridden, Katie changed bedpans and washed her body. Katie was the one to call the coroner when she died. She was the one to organize the service and to write the check for the funeral. She made sure her mother's hair and simple makeup were perfect, her clothes starched and ironed, exactly as she had wanted, before the long days of preaching at the funeral home. Katie, however, did not iron her own dress before the funeral service.

Katie emptied the pop into the sink, threw the cans in the garbage, and dropped the shoes in the box by the door she had long ago covered in Wildcat stickers, hoping it would make them pay attention to it. It had not.

She finished up the dishes she had collected, glasses in floors and bowls in the middle of unmade beds. She wiped the kitchen counter and rinsed the sink rim with the wet dishrag the way she'd been taught as a child. She swept the living room dirt out the back door and sat down at the kitchen table to make out her grocery list.

Henry was the first to come in. He squeaked the door open and kicked off his boots with difficulty. Chris followed, shoes on.

"What, no breakfast?" Henry's voice was dry and pitiful, but he sauntered into the living room with a lively little step.

"Well, no. It's three in the afternoon. And Dr. Yadav said no solid foods."

"I didn't hear her say that."

"That don't shock me none. But it don't change the fact that she did."

Henry went to his recliner and turned on a daytime judge show. Chris sat on the couch beside him. It was a new episode but an old story: some woman was telling the judge that she had made an arrangement with her now ex-boyfriend to keep the house clean in exchange for her half of the rent. Her name was on the lease separately because they wanted to make sure she and her kids had a right to the apartment, but her boyfriend had made it clear to her that she wouldn't have to pay anything. And no sir, she didn't put anything in writing because he was her boyfriend and people in relationships don't go writing out agreements with each other. And yes sir, she understands that checks show she paid half the rent the first three months, but that was just because her boyfriend was in between jobs and she was helping him out, but that was never supposed to be the plan.

Katie was frustrated with the woman. She was either lying or stupid. Maybe both. Cleaning a house for rent. Nobody makes a deal like that. And if a woman already has kids with some other man, then she oughtta know men by now—even a man who takes in another man's kids. Judge Esposito would see right through her. Katie felt her anger rising to her throat. She swallowed. She softened. She couldn't blame the woman for trying.

Believing in a man was a woman's curse.

Not believing in any man as a result, well, that was the curse that followed.

Katie handed Chris the aftercare instructions with the hospital's phone number in case there was an emergency and made sure he'd be able to stay until she got back. He said he'd wait on her. She grabbed the keys and headed to town.

The store had changed names five or six times since Katie had married and moved to Big Branch, near Mosely, from the next town over some forty years ago—once a Save-Some-More, once a Pick-and-Pay, and other names she couldn't quite recall—but the layout never changed: vegetables to the left, mostly onions and potatoes and a few green things from local farmers, premade salad kits with wilting lettuce, an aisle that housed cheap toys marked up two or three times what they were worth, and the deli in the back that still made the same spaghetti salad, soup beans, and fried bologna sandwiches that the unmarried miners used to buy daily back before the mines shut down.

This was not a week for the extravagances of the deli. Not the year, either. One child in rehab. One in prison. Chris, all the way out in Lexington. Five grandchildren living with her. Insurance didn't cover the use of the outpatient facility, even though they couldn't get it done at the VA without having to stay three nights in West Virginia, so money would be tight for a while.

She filled her buggy with potatoes, cabbage, oatmeal, ramen, eggs, milk, pork, checking off the list as she trekked down the aisles. She stopped at the pop. She wouldn't spend any more money on cans of pop—it would only go to waste, but the kids were too spoiled for the powdered drinks, even the more expensive ones, so she compromised and grabbed a few two-liters of the store brand instead. This would have to do till the first. She eyed a 12-pack of diet ginger ale, which only came in the name brand. Henry wouldn't be able to hold those two-liters steady. She studied her list carefully until she found something else she could mark off in its place, scratching a line across the paper towels. She could just use rags, after all. Weren't no real need. She added the box of ginger ale to her buggy.

Katie finished her shopping. Made small talk with the young cashier about who'd been arrested and who should've been but wasn't, and then wrote out a check for the amount of the total.

"Oh—you don't have to fill it out, honey. The machine does that now."

"I already wrote part of it."

"That don't matter. It don't even look at your handwriting." The cashier pushed the half-written, unsigned check into a black plastic machine that sucked it in, made some dry clicks, then shot it back out. She pressed some buttons on the screen in front of her and then handed the check back to Katie. "You can just throw it away when you get home. It got what it needed. I wouldn't do it here, though. Snoopers."

The machine had printed over her own handwriting in clean black type, completely ignoring the ink she had just left on the page.

Chris was in the kitchen, opening the fridge for the tenth time, more as a reflex than for want of food. His mom had been gone almost an hour and a half when she finally reappeared with four plastic grocery bags dangling from her fists.

"You need help with the groceries?"

"There's a couple a bags and some pop out there, still. Put that 12-pack in our bedroom." She stopped, dropping the bags to the floor. "What's this?"

"What's what?"

"This?" She pointed to some plates and a pan in the sink.

"Oh, I'll wash it. We just had some egg sandwiches."

"I told you he can't eat nothing yet. He could mess up his throat. That's the whole point a this stent."

"Well, you know how he is. You can't tell him nothing."

Katie dropped the bags on the floor. "You can try."

Henry could hear them from his recliner in the living room. He said, "Well, if the Viet Cong couldn't take me out, I don't reckon an egg and some bread is gonna take me down."

Katie yelled back, "The Viet Cong wadn't fighting a half cripple past seventy with a new goddam stent!" She grabbed her head with her hands, her thumbs driving into her chin on either side and fingertips pressed against her forehead like she might hold herself back from saying more.

Henry kicked the footrest of the recliner down to sit up straighter. "I am a man, goddamnit. I do whatever the hell I want to do. You hear me?"

Katie didn't flinch and her fast words exploded past her restraint. "Oh, you think you're telling me something I don't already know? Big man! Big strong man! Does what he wants. Let's just bring in every whore in Mosely. I know they all wanna see just how big a man you are. See if they clean up after your sorry ass." Heat rushed angry blood up her neck, which reddened more with each word.

"What the hell is wrong with you? Why don't you go take one a your pills?"

"Ain't nothing wrong with me a pill's gonna fix." She flung her arm out and pointed toward Henry, kicking one of the bags in a thud against the sink as she did. "Not unless it knocks you the hell out."

Chris looked at the bags on the floor. A cabbage had rolled out in front of the sink and gotten lodged under the counter. He wanted to busy himself, to empty the bags, to put the food away, to do something. He moved to help his mother. "I can get the—"

"Don't you fucking bother. You don't listen, neither. And you don't say nothing. I just asked you to tell him. *Just once.* I'm sick a being the only one who says shit around here." Chris started to respond, and Katie cut him off. "No. I'll get the rest myself."

The slamming door sounded like punctuation. The fall air cooled her skin in a soothing undulation of breeze as she walked toward the car. Her angry arms trembled, but her breathing was calm, almost peaceful.

She opened the car door, looked at the two plastic bags and the 12-pack of diet ginger ale in the passenger seat. She got in, slamming the door shut, leaving both of those assholes on the other side—of the vehicle, of the porch, of her mind.

She put the keys in the ignition, and her eyes traced the road as it stretched along the creek and disappeared into a curve along the hill. She started the car. Sat still as the engine grumbled. Music was playing, barely audible. She turned it up. The station had on an old Stevie Nicks song she hadn't thought about in a long time. She raised the volume until she couldn't hear her thoughts. Let it wash over her. Remembered. Her first job at the nursing home. Her first paychecks. Buying cheeseburgers with the girls at Jerry's Restaurant. The sticky floors at the bar and the pink neon sign above the liquor bottles. Her old powder blue Oldsmobile, purchased brand-new, with the automatic windows and how the smell of its leather seats in the summer made her want to drive faster and smoke more.

A tapping on the window stopped her reverie.

The car was still parked and vibrating. A school bus was bending around the curve down the holler just beyond her driveway. One of her grandbabies was on the other side of the driver's side window. He was clutching a giant Pokémon backpack against his left shoulder. His right hand was a closed fist he had used to knock on the window.

"You okay, Mamaw?"

She turned down the music. Her words were now slow to come. And soft. "Yeah, baby. Just getting groceries outta the car."

"You need help?"

"No, I got it. You go on in the house." She watched him in the side mirror. He skipped toward the steps, dropping his backpack on the porch and leaving the front door wide open.

She pulled the keys out of the ignition, placed them into her purse near a used check no one would ever need her to sign, cradled the remaining groceries, and followed him back inside.

Chris had put away the shopping and was now sitting beside Henry and looking through his phone. They both pretended to watch television. She closed the door after her grandchild, hung his backpack on a hook by the door, placed the rest of the food on the counter, and stood at the sink. Henry turned the television down.

He spoke up. "Hey, Katie, why don't you let me do them dishes?"

Katie turned the water to scalding hot, then used a rag to scrub the inside of the basin with dishwashing liquid. She shoved the rag into the drain, and steam began to rise up, pulling soapy water behind it. "Nah, that's alright. I got it. Doctor said you should take it easy."

"You sure?"

Her hands turned red in the water, which made her blood feel cooler. "Yeah, I'm sure. You and Chris keep on visiting while you can. I got this."

Henry turned to Chris. "You see how she is, Chris? Over there doing them dishes out a pure spite. When you get yourself a man, you better make sure you pick better than I did. I been cursed with a cruel woman."

Chris looked to his mother to see how he should react. Her eyes narrowed, but a simmering smirk managed to lift the borders of her lips into a wry smile. She declared to Henry, "If you find a better woman than me, let me know, buddy. Either you marry her or I will. Either way, we'll both be better off." Chris laughed and eased back in his chair, Henry restored the television's volume, and Katie began to wash the dirty dishes left behind from the egg sandwiches. She scrubbed the plates, rinsed them with hot water, and stacked them in the drainer. She scrubbed the pan, rinsed it, saw a stain, then scrubbed it again. She pulled it from the soapy water and then noticed that it wasn't a stain at all, just a dry dent in the metal made from years of use. She rinsed it a second time and then leaned it carefully against the plates so that it would be sure to dry before dinner.

SOMETIMES I MISS THESE HILLS

when we all lived with my aunt—
just too many young'uns
and not enough doors
in that tiny white home
propped up on the hillside,
so the adults would force us
out of the house
into the creeks
into the hills
into the sky
and anywhere else
that kept us away
and kept us
from talking over TV.

Me and my cousin Jenny
were the soft ones of that lot—
just old mountain talk
to keep from
calling us fat.

We determined to ride bikes
to the head of Cow Creek,
rusted chains squeaking out
the promise of freedom
as we chased each other
close by the grown-up
chattering of the creek,
tires bucking off the blacktop
and running their thick rubber hands
in the churchless mud eating at the road.

We got halfway up the hill
when the once cool sunlight
felt dry, dense, thirsty.
Our lungs complained
and our legs turned to weeds,
so we set to pushing the bikes
toward the head of Cow Creek,
imagining the ride back down,
the free wind sweeping our faces
like invisible sheets pulled fast
by the hands of Jesus himself.

A little ginger girl stood barefoot
in front of a trailer painted
bright green on one side
and rusting over on the other.
She stared at us
from under heavy strokes of eyebrow
that hated us from across the length
of her emptying bottle of pop.

She watched us
as she licked the final drops.
She threw the bottle to the ground
fast, fluid, perfunctory
like it was a hot-boxed work-break cigarette
like she was a divorced mother of two,
though she couldn't have been
older than ten.

Them bikes work better, she said,
when you sit on em.

The ginger girl smiled teeth toward us,
her hands slapping at her hip.
She put out her discarded
pop bottle cigarette
with her bare feet.

I looked ahead.
Jenny did not.

We climbed the hill.
We rode back down.
Eventually they turned the TV off
and we were allowed to come in,
eat our supper, take our baths, go to bed.

Next morning, my cousin Jenny woke me up
so we could climb Cow Creek once again.

The ginger girl was no longer in her yard.
Neither was that pop bottle.
One of the windows
on the part of the trailer
that was painted green
had been busted clean out
and pink curtains shuddered
in the dewy truth of the early morning breeze.
I pointed to the window.

I looked at Jenny,
who only looked ahead
and said,
Hey. Let's ride em down the creek this time.

TORE ALL TO PIECES

Cow Creek. Fall 2023.

"Shew. What, Mommy? I been awake." It wadn't a question. More accusation and defense, really, as a shoe thumped against her face. Technically, she'd been awake for hours. A single thread of thirsty sunlight sewing itself across the sky had woke Keesha up at daybreak. Then its friend, a second thread. She'd been watching them threads of light grow as she fell in and out of sleep on the living room couch.

"You mommy ain't here."

Wadn't a shoe he threw. Not really. Was her mommy's little purple velvet house slipper with the hard bottoms she'd wear like they was dressy shoes, sometimes to the church down the holler, especially if they had potluck nights or barbecues outside where you wouldn't have to hear no preaching. Sometimes out with men like Big Jason, Mud Jenkins, or even Uncle Jamie.

Keesha pushed the slipper to the floor, where it landed on top of the homework she'd been finishing up the night before.

Just yesterday, her and Jamie'd been making a comic book for her social studies class. They was supposed to pick somebody from Kentucky history and tell their story in a comic book so the teacher could make a classroom library. Like they didn't already have a million books on this stuff. School was pointless like that. Keesha was the last one who hadn't turned one in, and Ms. Martin was acting huffy, so Keesha swore she'd do it before Monday. She already had to do kindergarten twice. She didn't want fourth grade to be the same.

Ms. Martin had said that all that was left as options from the preapproved list was Henry Clay and some dead racehorse from all the way over in Louisville.

So after school yesterday, Jamie had drove her to the new Dollar Store to get some crayons and paper. His truck had real seats in the back just like a car, and it was so big she had to pull herself up to get in.

Jamie never tried to lift her in, neither, like Mud Jenkins woulda done. Mud didn't even have a working car, noway. Never would. But Keesha knew he woulda tried to lift her up just the same.

He was like that.

Jamie played old country women songs and sang along the whole way back, looking at hisself in the mirror like he was the one on the radio too while he took the curves of the holler like they was part of the music. His hair was dyed blond at the ends and he was wearing a pink shirt with Dolly Parton on it. She watched him acting like he was the one singing, but even if she squinted, Keesha didn't see nothing but Jamie acting a fool.

Her mommy didn't have a kitchen table, so Jamie emptied out the bag on the cleanest part of the living room carpet between the couch and the TV. A box a crayons, a pad a paper, Christmas present tape, and some glitter sticks. The glitter was his idea.

"All right, Keesha-Bug. What we gonna write about?"

"I ain't writing about some sissy horse."

Jamie scratched his elbow. "Well, ain't nothing sissy about a horse. Even them fancy ones. And even if he was a sissy, that ain't nothing bad."

"You're only saying that cause you're a sissy."

Jamie eased a cigarette from behind his ear, flashing a tattoo of a pink rose on a pink vine climbing up his wrist. He lit the cigarette, relaxing in a slow draw. He released his first word in a tunnel of blue smoke. "Well." The metal string of a overhead fan clinged against an exposed lightbulb. "And here I am helping you with fourth grade homework. You know I'm a grown-up. Ain't got no homework at all. I coulda been doing something a lot funner than this."

"I know. That's why you're a sissy."

Jamie laughed so hard that cigarette smoke jumped across the room, widening out flat like a gray blanket getting spread across an invisible horizon, waving in the light coming in through the window.

"Damn, Keesha! You might just be harder on life than it is on you." He sat up straighter, pulling his right foot under his left thigh. "People better watch out for you, honey. No sissy horses, then. Alright. What else you got?"

"Henry Clay."

"Shit no. I seen his house in Ashland. Tacky." He picked up a beer can laying on its side on the floor, ashed into it. "And he's a loser. Tried to be president two or three times. You know that? Failed every one of em."

Keesha puffed her cheeks in frustration. "I can't stand Ms. Martin."

"Well, how bout Loretta Lynn?"

"She's alright, I guess."

"Young'un, you better watch your tongue. She's a helluva lot better'n alright." Jamie looked up, like Loretta might be listening. Keesha looked up, too, but only saw the shaking bulb of the ceiling fan. Jamie kept a talking. "But we ain't critiquing her singing. I meant how about doing your project on her?"

"She ain't history."

"How the hell not? She's dead, ain't she?"

She took the condescending tone favored by girls in grade school: "And she ain't even on the list, noway."

Jamie blew the smoke intentionally this time, pursing his lips together and exhaling toward the door, away from Keesha. "Fuck her list. And there ain't nothing sissy about Loretta. She was a workhorse, not a racehorse. Cussed out grown men and hauled coal. And we'll have a good reason to use all this glitter, too."

It was now already early afternoon the next day, and the house slipper Mud Jenkins had threw at her landed right on top of the purple gown that her and Jamie had drew and glittered in the night before.

Mud was standing where the hallway met the living room, in front of the space where the wall heater was before it got stole, traded, or sold. His wild, black hair was shorter to the sides but stretched out in all directions, landing in some parts as far down as his shoulders. It was the same color as the darkest parts of the paneling. He wadn't wearing a shirt.

Keesha sat up on the couch, scratched the back of her head. "Where's Mommy?"

"Gone. Down the holler. I ain't feeling good, so she went to get me some medicine. Why don't you haul your ginger ass outta bed and go fix me something to eat?"

"It ain't a bed. It's a couch."

"Don't be a smart-ass. I don't feel good."

"What is there?"

He turned his back to her, trudging into the darkness of the trailer and scratching under his pants. "Figure it out."

Dishes was stacked in the kitchen sink, and the big skillet wadn't just dirty; it was plumb at the bottom of the whole pile. Keisha didn't risk getting it cause she didn't want to make the dishes clank and risk pissing off Mud.

She looked through cabinets. Dusty cans a corn, soup, and sauerkraut that her third grade teacher sent home with her after the food drive. One a them giant bags a cheap brand cereal.

She opened the fridge. Milk jug but no milk in it. Cereal was out. There was a yellow Styrofoam carton of eggs hiding behind the milk jug. She took it out and placed it by the sink.

Four eggs. She cracked em in a coffee cup, added some salt and pepper, and then put it in the microwave. Stacks of paper on top of it kept spilling over in front of the door, keeping her from closing it, so she lifted em up to hold em in place and then slammed the door, fast.

"What the hell's the racket? You trying to piss me off?" Mud was always a asshole but not usually this mad.

"I didn't mean it. It was a accident."

04, 03, 02. Keesha opened the door before it finished to keep the microwave from fussing.

She plopped the heap of eggs on a paper plate. She didn't know how to make coffee, except with the machine that took them little plastic cups, the one her mamaw give her mommy last Christmas, but they never had any little cups to put in it.

She didn't know if he was pill sick or drinking sick, but good thing was neither Mud nor her mommy ever wanted coffee when it was either one.

Mud was laying on a bare mattress in her mommy's room, wrapped in the military blanket her papaw left before she was born and before he died. The air in the back bedroom was thick and rusty, like old sweat. The floor was covered in junk but not like the living room. This was junk, not garbage. The only spot at all that wadn't covered with something of her mommy's—makeup, T-shirts with country and rock bands on em, romance novels she had read a hundred times—was a cleared-off spot on a side table by Mud.

"Here. It's eggs. There ain't nothing to drink."

Mud didn't answer. She was glad.

Keesha went back to the living room and flipped through the comic book they'd made the night before. Her favorite picture was Loretta punching her boyfriend. She couldn't draw people too good and didn't know how to draw a closed fist. So instead she drew a giant hand to show smacking and colored his face all red to show how bad it musta hurt. Uncle Jamie had wanted for her to call it *An Appalachian Graphic Novel of Serious Literary Import About East Kentucky's Recently Departed Musical Queen* on the cover. It was still wrote down on a piece a paper on the floor beside a buncha other titles they thought up and scratched out. But that was embarrassing sounding, so they compromised and called it *Loretta Lynn: Kentucky's Dead Diva.* Plus, the title was so short they had room to cover it in glitter, too.

She put the paper booklet on top of the TV and laid back down on the couch. It was getting fall and it was a touch chilly in the living room, so the light coming in past the pink curtains felt good on the side of her face not laying against the arm of the couch. The passing clouds made it flicker in lazy bursts on her closed eyelids. She let it make red and black scenes in her mind: trees whispering to each other, a cat fight, minnows swimming away from rocks tossed into the creek. She drifted into a light sleep.

Laughter and metal clinking woke her up. She turned to face the door and window. She heard her mommy talking and making them little bubble giggles she does when she's in too good a mood, little laughs that pile right up on top a one another in squeaks and float across the room. The door was wide open, but her mommy was outside, her voice dripping in.

A man was talking.

"Mommy?" Keesha's stomach felt funny, nervous and hungry at the same time, like how it feels right before you have to go to the doctor. Tight but untied.

"I'll be right in, Keesha-Bug. My friend's just dropping me off."

Keesha looked outside. It wadn't Big Jason. A man she didn't recognize was standing just outside a gray car, its door swung open.

He was wearing brown pants like teachers wear and had on a thick, shining watch. His hands was holding on to the car door handle like he couldn't decide if he was coming or going, but he was leaning toward her mommy, who was standing at the bottom of the cinder block steps.

He musta asked her a question. Keesha couldn't hear him, but she knew what men was like. He got real big for a second and smiled at her, the kind a smile that if he didn't like the answer, he could turn that smile into laughing at her on purpose.

He musta liked what she said. He didn't holler or laugh. Just nodded, got back in the gray car, and pulled away while her mommy stayed and waved until after the car was completely gone.

Her mommy come up the steps. She'd left with her pocket book but didn't come back with nothing. She was moving her head back and forth like she was listening to a slow song.

She walked into the kitchen with her back turned to Keesha as she took off a red Dairy Queen jacket. The voice scared the both of em because neither one was expecting it.

"Who the fuck was that?" Mud Jenkins was standing behind Keesha's couch, again in the hallway entrance, but she hadn't seen him because she was eyeing her mommy's every move, looking for some inkling as to which version of her she might be seeing.

"Baby," she said to Mud, her eyes cemented to the floor. "You half scared me to death. I thought you'uns both was still asleep."

Keesha pushed herself down between the couch cushions and said, "But you done been talking to me." She knew she might be making things worse, but something inside her was feeling mean.

"I mean I thought you both was before, then just Mud. Anyway, but now I know you ain't asleep and Mud ain't neither." She laid her jacket across the kitchen counter as Keesha's eyes fell on its upside-down logo.

"It's three in the afternoon, Mandi. Who the fuck was that?"

"Nobody. That was just Misty's cousin from Pikeville, one that works welding them big trucks. You met him. Up at Big Branch. At Jimmy's thing."

Mud kept on looking at her, the wide rise and fall of his chest demanding she keep talking.

"Anyway, Misty made him drive me back cause a the fog down the holler. She got all worried I'd get hit walking around the culvert."

Mud brought his hand to his forehead like he was thinking. Keesha pulled the blanket back so Mandi might come sit down at her feet.

She didn't. She just started right back up again with her bubble laughing. "And Misty. She was supposed to grab me some milk. I walked in this morning, said, 'You get me that milk?' She said, 'What milk?' I said, 'What I texted you about last night, when you was on the way to Walmart.' She said, 'Was that you?' I said, 'Well, it damn sure wadn't Moses, was it?' and she said, 'Well, for some reason I thought it was Sissy sent that message. I drove plumb up Ice Plant Holler and give her that gallon a milk and she just said, 'Thanks.'' Can you believe that? Bitch didn't say a word and just took our milk. *Who does that*?"

Keesha felt sweat on her forehead.

Mandi kept on giggling. Mud kept on standing.

"Well? She give you any"—he flicked his wild-haired head down in a jerk toward Keesha without looking at her—"medicine?"

Keesha thought it was funny how they thought she didn't know about pills. Pills and sex. That's what grown-ups do and think kids don't know, even though it's all they ever seem to really want.

Mandi started stacking the dirty dishes to the left of the sink so she could pour a glass a water. "Nothing. And you know, it pisses me off cause you know I told her last week that she owed us." The faucet began to hiss. "She knew since last Saturday. And she's *had*, too."

Mud moved toward the cramped kitchen, his steps anxious like a horse used to a barn, not yet trusting the yard. His voice was calm. "Well, you seem to be in a good enough mood. I'm guessing that man that dropped you off wadn't holding out."

Mandi made the mistake of looking up at him. "I told you. That's Misty's little cousin. He don't deal. Got a good job and don't even know nobody."

Mud broke the fragile calm in a fit of cussing. It reminded Keesha of when you're walking and a dog you didn't know was around starts barking like it's crazy—feeling like school fire alarms in your chest. Even when you know it's gonna happen, even if the teacher tells you to get ready, it's always scary when it starts.

He kicked at the trash on the floor and punched his own stomach like he was mad at it. "God damn it. You went and took something off some random-ass guy when you *knew* how bad off I am. You goddamn whore! You fucking whore!"

Mandi said, "Mud, baby, I swear to God I ain't done nothing. You can ask Misty. Here. Call her right now. Take my phone. My hand to God"—she held her hand high in the air like she was testifying in church, extending the phone out like a hymnal—"he don't do nothing."

Mud looked like he was gonna cry. He bent over and leaned against the TV, which creaked against the particleboard stand that held it. "You know I can't help it! You know it ain't my fault. You know how bad I hurt. You know I can't do without. *You know*!"

Mandi stepped toward him. "I know that, baby. I know." She rubbed her hand up and down the length of his back. "That's why I walked all the way down to Misty's this morning, fog be damned. I was trying to help you."

Quiet.

Keesha could hear the sink running.

"Then why the fuck you go a whoring around when I'm in pain?" Mud's holler cut through the air. He grabbed Mandi at her shoulders, began to shake her, then shoved her back against the wall. He grabbed a stack of papers from the TV and began to rip em to pieces.

"Stop!" Keesha spoke with enough energy to be heard, but she didn't dare stand up. "That's the homework me and Uncle Jamie was working on."

Mud threw the papers to the ground. "He ain't your fucking uncle. He's just some ole faggot you mommy went to school with before she dropped out."

Mud stormed back to the bedroom, with Mandi following him like a dog after her lost pup. Keesha walked to the kitchen, turned off the water that was still spraying out at full force, and went outside.

Cow Creek was divided into three parts. Down near the mouth was the best part, cause there was always something to do. There was a couple churches, a food pantry where churchpeople kept crackers, peanut butter, and stuff in cans, the new Dollar Store, and a big gravel lot where people sold vegetables, honey, or sometimes even had yard sales for the traffic that drove by out on the big road. And sometimes, people just parked in the gravel lot and would sit around waiting to see who all'd show up that day.

The middle part was the houses. Real houses. They was all huddled together, sometimes two or three rows deep between the creek and the hill. There was even a project not too far from the mouth. It had a playground that they cut into the mountain for, just to make room. That part was full a kids who ran to it as soon as the bus stopped to let them out after school.

Then was the third part, the longest part, the part that went on forever and ever, and the farther up you went, the less houses there was, so by the time you got up near the head, uphill the whole way, the stretch a road between the houses and the trailers was so long that neighbors wouldn't even be able to see each other. That part of the holler was the skinniest, too, up near the head, so nobody had a whole lot a space for yards or even a big house, which is why it was mostly trailers and even a few campers.

That's the part where Keesha lived.

The closest house with kids was five lots up the holler. It was as far as Keesha was allowed to walk by herself. She got in a fight with the middle girl, Laney Carroll, in second grade when Laney took Keesha's seat on the school bus, so now their mommy drove em to the park at the mouth of the holler instead of just letting em loose outside. Keesha was not allowed to play with em.

The last time she tried, she walked up the hill and saw their mommy laying out suntanning on a bedspread while all three young'un's was playing freeze tag, which is a dumb game anyway cause the fastest person always wins, and even dumber if you don't have a whole lot a people. So she figured four would be better than three and they might just let her play, even if she had fought Laney Carroll in the second grade.

But their mommy saw her red hair rising up the hill and hollered for them all to go inside and get ready for supper. Like there's some kind of preparing somebody has to do for supper. She just stood there after they went in and stared at the empty space in the backyard where they'd been a playing just a few minutes before.

Keesha didn't really care if they liked her or not, not really, but that kinda stinging ain't something you want twice, so Keesha kept to herself in the summers and on weekends like this'n. She'd walk over to the creek and stack up the flat rocks. Sometimes, she'd just put in whatever she could find—pop bottles, paper, even leaves if she was desperate—and just watch em float down the creek.

There was a couple grown-ups she could visit, though. Ed and Della Hall lived just down the holler on the right. They had a big porch with a chair that'd swing if you kicked your feet. They didn't work anymore on account of being old and sick all the time, but Della always had extra food. She'd give Keesha a little snack cake and would let her watch her do jigsaw puzzles or tend to the flower garden outside. Ed was sick and couldn't get outta bed, which was actually a hospital bed set up right in the front living room, but she would sometimes watch westerns with him. It was boring, but it was something. Every now and then, he'd wave Keesha over and give her candy, and once, even a five-dollar bill.

That day, they didn't answer the door.

It was late in the afternoon, and the air was warm, and the ground soft under her bare feet, so Keesha decided she'd stay outside and away from the trailer, since her mommy and Mud would be in moods the rest of the day. She spent the next few hours keeping herself occupied. She poked at some bugs under rocks until she had killed em or they'd got away. Then she scratched pictures into the rocks with some gravel—a tomcat, which she could draw good cause the art teacher made em practice drawing em last year, and beside him a big tree. She added a little bird's nest to the tree. She messed up trying to draw the baby birds, got mad, and then scratched out the whole scene. Next, she gathered some empty bottles, climbed up the hill a bit and picked some ferns, some weeds, and the last chigger flowers huddling around in little clumps near the pile of cement bricks left over from when Mud said he was gonna build a hothouse. Some of the bricks was still flecked with paint from when Mud said he was gonna paint the trailer green, Keesha's favorite color. He run out halfway and never bought more. The chiggers was already starting to fold in and turn brown, but they was still flowers. She stuck the ends of the plants into the bottles until she had little bouquets, then she lined em against the cement blocks.

She figured they needed water and ran down to the creek. There was a slim wall of cattails on the far side, and she decided to pick some to add to the bouquets. She jumped across the narrow water and pulled at the first one she reached. It leaned forward like a dying man falling face-first into the creek. She laughed at the image, and pulled another, then another, one at a time, watching them bow over and fall dead. Soon she forgot all about the bouquets waiting for her behind the trailer and was now making a game of bringing down the army of cattails one at a time. She had just gotten behind em and kicked one over triumphantly toward the side of the creek facing the trailer when she seen Jamie's big truck pull up in the driveway.

She stood on the far bank of the creek, just looking.

"Hey, Keesha-Bug. What you doing down there?"

Keesha didn't respond.

"You mommy inside?"

"Yeah. Her and Mud's mad."

"Well, baby, that's what they do. She called me over. What you doing?"

"Just playing."

"Well, com'ere." He waved in a big gesture, and she crossed the road. He kept on talking from inside the truck as he leaned over the driver's seat to face her. "Here. Take it. It's a peach Nehi. Almost the same color as that mop on your head."

He pulled out a bottle of neon orange pop, wiping water from a cooler off it with the inside of his shirt. "Come from over at the Mosely Fast-n-Fill. This is a old-fashioned glass bottle like they used to make. Got it special for you when I seen it. So here, listen. I'm gonna go talk to your mommy and Mud and help em calm down, okay? You stay out here. You got me?"

Keesha didn't respond. She was looking to the sky. The clouds was big and rolling so fast she could almost hear em. Like a roar. Jamie waved his hands in front of her, his fingers spread out and moving so quick left and right that it was like he had thirty of em. The slim tattoo on his wrist become an electric bouquet of pink roses flashing in and out of existence, falling to the left and then to the right at the same time. "Earth to Keesha-Bug! This is the Vulcans. You hear me, child?"

"Yeah. I've been staying outside anyway." Her voice was a sad croak.

"Good girl. Just finish up that pop and then come on in. Drink it slow, now. Don't go and get yourself sick."

Jamie slid outta his truck, into the trailer, and Keesha stood, alone, holding the bottle of pop.

She was looking into the sky, trying to hear the clouds again, which now withheld their noise, when she heard the sound of talking. Kids talking.

It was two fat kids from down near the mouth of the holler, coming up the hill. A boy and a girl. Clean clothes. Boy with a new haircut. Rich kids. Probably kids who didn't have to stay outside while their not-uncle gave their mommy and Mud whatever he gave em that she wadn't supposed to know about but knew about anyway. Probably kids who got to go to the park, kids who Laney Carroll was allowed to play with.

They had bicycles. But they wadn't even riding up. They was just pushing em. Pushing damn bicycles when they was on the road and coulda been flying fast. Pushing bicycles cause they knew they would always have the chance, like it was part of the rules written into their lives that there'd always be a bicycle, always be a road. Rich asses.

That's how the world was.

Keesha wanted real bad to hate em and their bicycles. But they *were* kids, and they looked like they was about the same age as her, so she didn't want to miss a opportunity to play.

She took a quick sip of peach Nehi and gave a holler to em.

"Hey! Them bikes work better when you sit on em."

Keesha laughed hard at her own joke, grabbing at her hips to stop shaking. She hadn't spoken much the whole day, so the sound of her own voice coming outta her mouth surprised her. It didn't seem to surprise them, though. Them other two kids just stared. No response at all. Like she was invisible, a nothing. Like she didn't even say nothing, let alone a good joke.

She got mad, swigged the bottle fast, eyeing them both while the pop gushed down her throat. Carefully licked the extravagant stickiness off the mouth of a Peach Nehi from all the way over in Mosely while they watched, pop they didn't even have, them too awnry to even ride their own bikes, and then she threw it to her feet with the last sweet swill still puddled at the bottom like there was ten more where that'n come from.

She became just eyes.

The little girl with the bicycle stared back, probably mad that she didn't have a pop. She had long black hair and a ribbon in it. A white ribbon tied up so high and neat that somebody else had to a put it in for her. Her eyes was dark, too, like her hair, and from across the road Keesha thought her face almost looked like some kind of ugly bug.

The boy didn't even bother to turn his head. Just kept looking toward whatever was taking them up the road.

But the girl, she stared right past everything. Through the pop bottle. Through Keesha. Through the trailer. Maybe even all the way past the hill itself.

The boy Keesha could stand. A little boy that don't bother to see her is one thing. But the girl saw her and eyed her out of existence with some kind of meanness.

Still, Keesha didn't look away, neither. She wadn't no sissy. They just stared until the brown-haired fat girl had her fill. Then she turned and started pushing her bicycle up the holler. The boy followed beside her. And just as soon as they arrived, they was gone. Once again, it was just Keesha, the creek, the cattails, the gravel, and the clouds, like it had been all afternoon. She looked back up at the silent clouds. Swaths of vanilla and a deeper carnation yellow seeped across the backs of trees on the furthest hill, heralding a sunset.

She didn't give a shit what Mommy said, how Mud acted, what Jamie did or didn't do. She stormed into the trailer, slamming the door behind her.

Jamie was holding a garbage bag, scooping in cans, plates, and plastic wrappers from the living room floor. "Here, help me a little bit, Keesha." He opened the bag like a goal, and she tossed what remained on the floor like they was playing a game.

"Take this to the kitchen for me." He dropped the bag at her feet. "And here, take this shit, too." He handed her a box full a dirty paper towels. "Hey—Mud's asleep and your mommy's in the shower. You know he's sick. He don't mean it. I give him some medicine. He'll be good as new tomorrow morning."

Keesha didn't give two flying shits if Mud felt better, ever, and she knew Jamie knew that, but him pretending made her feel better about herself somehow. She walked the bag and box to the kitchen and plopped em both by the front door. The dishes was done, stacked up and drying on a clean towel. The trailer felt calm, the kind a calm you feel when stuff is so normal you might be able to guess what comes next.

Jamie waved her over to the couch where she'd been sitting earlier. The blanket was folded up across the arm, and the curtains was pulled back. The sunset was now a solid pink wrapped in yellow and orange, the same colors as the dreamsicle cake Ms. Martin had let the class share when one of the boys had a birthday the first few days of school.

"It tastes just like dreamsicle," Ms. Martin had said in that exaggerated way that teachers talk when she took her bite.

Keesha agreed, though she didn't know what a dreamsicle was. She thought maybe it was imaginary. Ms. Martin read a lot a stories about things that wadn't real like that.

Jamie pulled out a paddle brush from his purse. "Honey, now that's a rat's nest. Come over here. You've got such pretty red hair. I know a queen over in Battersburg who'd kill for them waves and that color."

She let him pull the knots out and—even when it snagged and hurt—didn't complain. He brushed her hair out while they both watched an infomercial where two fancy women in a fancy bright white kitchen acted surprised when a man showed em how a blender worked.

Jamie patted her head and put away the brush. "Hey, and look here." He pulled some papers from the windowsill. It was their comic book. He had taped the pages back together. "Mud mighta been tore all to pieces, but our comic book ain't. I think it looks better, now."

A few pages had ribbons of tape folding the pictures together. The pictures was all there, just pushed back together with rough lines cutting across em.

"I think it kinda looks cool," Keesha said. "All ripped up."

"Yeah. Miss Loretta would like it. It ain't no sissy story."

Jamie placed their Loretta comic in her bookbag, washed out the glass he was drinking water from, and left.

Mandi came into the living room. She wadn't giggling no more. Her hair was pulled through a pink bath towel wrapped around her head.

"You hungry, baby?"

"Yeah."

Mandi microwaved two individual chicken pot pies and put em on paper plates. She didn't mention Mud. Or all the tidying they'd done. Or where the pot pies come from.

They finished the infomercial, enjoying in silence the clean room and letting the easily pleased women's excitement over the blender they was helping sell wash their surroundings of the morning's fight. They placed their emptied plates on the floor and then changed the channel to *Law & Order*. Keesha put her head in Mandi's lap, and her mommy slipped her hands through her newly brushed hair until both of em started to doze off.

Keesha pretended to sleep as Mandi eased off the couch, replaced her lap with a throw pillow, and pulled the blanket up around her daughter. She turned off the lights. Went to bed.

Keesha soon slept, but the moon was chatty that night. It whispered in through the windowpanes and past the pink curtains, waking her slightly and softly from time to time, scooting shadows across her face. When she opened her eyes and caught a glimpse of the moon, she'd seen that it was shining the color of milk against a holler of stars, a winking swipe of silver glitterstick across the dark sky.

She turned her back to the light coming in, leaned herself against the firmness of the couch, and fell into a deep sleep.

She thought she dreamt the first sound—a kind of knocking—followed by a shattering, a dull thud, and immediate wetness. Now awake, and confused, Keesha didn't make a noise in response. Something had hit her in the face. It didn't hurt. She wrestled her tucked hands from under her chest and touched the skin on her forehead and around her lips. Her cheek was wet with something. Something sticky. She wiped her face with the back of her hand and then licked it. A familiar electric peach taste buzzed against her tongue. In the darkness, she slid her hands down the crevice between her body and the couch, found the dull roundness and hollow curve of the bottom half of a bottle, its edges sharp and cleaved clean in two. Her Nehi. She felt around. Three glass pieces. She could feel the shapes in her mind, could see the glass bottle that they formed when, in a different time and place, they was together and whole.

She did not cry. She did not call for Mandi. She did not call for Mud. She placed the fragments into what was left of the base of the bottle that'd hit the wall, broken, and bounced down to hit her in the head. Glass was sparkling in spiky shards scattered across the floor. The trailer's living room window was shattered.

She didn't bother getting up. She laid the bottle and its remaining pieces on the floor by the paper plates that once held warm chicken pot pies. Resigned, she wiped the remaining pop off her skin with her blanket and, turning to face the wall once more, simply went back to her dreams.

She slept in late the next day. When she finally did wake up, she saw that somebody had replaced the windowpane with cardboard. The morning was already over, the light unable to reach her.

BUTTERED TOAST

Care-A-Mark Incorporated reminds staff that every food transaction must be accounted for. Failure to document in the system may result in termination.

The poster reminded staff what they knew
but Wanda didn't have time to read cause
the buses start pushing the kids in at 7:30
and ringing bells pull them out at 8:05
then wipe, sweep, mop, soap, trash, smoke,
and do it all over once again for lunch.

And that day the door creaked open late
cold air percolation of leaves and diesel
cutting in floor cleaner and empty cafeteria
and a chubby boy made his way to the line
but Wanda's supervisor was already quoting
rulebook scripture in a lunchroom sermon:
Too late for breakfast. Get to class. Amen!
Can't serve after 8:10. System won't let me.
Praise Jesus!

His eyes swept across the room for authority
and found only the laminated poster hovering
above still warm real food and not real people
so he surrendered his empty tray and just left
as Wanda watched while gathering up the trash.

A tray of buttered toast dared her to choose
and so bare-armed and aproned she moved
along the morning outside brick of the school
until she found the boy on his way to class

and met him with a tray of toast so warm
he shoved one piece in his mouth and three in a bag
and Wanda fled to her car where she slid
her body and the tray each into a seat
and fingers numb with cold and slick
with margarine and laminated commandments
she began to eat the rest of the tray of bread.

McDONALD'S THANKSGIVING

Mosely. Big Branch. Battersburg. Fall 2023.

A collapsing hiss behind her pulled Wanda Spurlock away from the pan of frying eggs. Her only light, the weary bulb in the hood range, flickered a half-hearted yellow veil against the morning's grayness.

After living there forty years, she knew the layout and feel of her home well enough to deposit her glasses by the front door at night, leaving her often without clear sight until she walked out the door to work, so she had to back up toward the sink and squint to find the source of the noise. Of course. *Of course.* She pulled the eggs off the red eye, centered the pan on the stovetop, and grabbed a kitchen towel from a metal basket on the shelf between the stove and sink. Only, it wasn't actually a kitchen towel but rather an old bathroom towel that had long ago become too threadbare to dry off bodies, so she'd cut it into strips for moments such as these.

A button on the machine was stuck, preventing coffee from dripping into the glass pot below the filter. Brown sludge sloshed over it and onto the countertop. She wiped the spill with the saved remains of the exhausted cloth, poured the mess into a bowl, replaced the filter, repositioned the carafe, and then poured the bowl of dregs and hot water back onto the new filter. A slow but assured trickle promised some form of coffee. It would do.

It was Thursday. It was 4:45 am. Wanda had only a couple of weeks earlier hoped to be asleep at this very moment. But she could hope in one hand and shit in another. That's life. She worked weekdays at the grade school cafeteria, weekends at the McDonald's the next town over. The school had what was called summer and winter feeding programs, on account of the poorer families that can't always make ends meet, so there was no real vacation for the ladies of the lunchroom.

Today was Thanksgiving, a day that had become more and more important to Wanda, and in recent years, her favorite day, though her kids were grown and her husband now dead over a decade. She and her coworker Crissy had discussed her love of the holiday only last week when they took a cigarette break behind the dumpster at the far end of the elementary school parking lot.

Crissy was a young, plump single mom with chewed-off nails always painted in hopeful colors. Today they were a shiny fuchsia. She treated her hair in the same way, always carefully dyed and then never brushed. This month it was blond. She smoked skinny 120's that she kept in a purple leather pouch with a lighter holder sewn onto the outside. She offered one to Wanda by raising the pack her way.

"Lord, no. I'd rather quit than do them menthols." Wanda retrieved a cigarette from the folded part of her apron.

Crissy spoke as her menthol, long and white with a green strip around the base, dangled from her mouth, flapping up and down like a white flag. "Yeah." She lit it. "What you gonna do next week?"

"Hoping to have the boys up. Keith'll come. And Mark and his young'uns, I reckon. But maybe not. His wife's cooking, and she don't wanna travel. She calls the shots since he's been outta work."

As they spoke, Wanda stood perfectly still, her back to both school and dumpster, facing the cut-through. It sliced the distant mountains neatly. Years before, they had filled in the bottom with some of the dirt and even made flat land to build a Dollar Store and housing project on either side of where the mountain used to be.

Crissy was fidgety, always trying to find a comfortable spot. First she'd stand like Wanda, but she couldn't last a full minute before she'd find something to lean against, crouch up beside, or sit on. She'd move three times in the span of a smoke break. Finally, she tested some folded Care-A-Mark boxes for her weight, seemed confident they could support her, then took a seat. "Shit. I'd just go to your boy's if his woman's cooking."

"Well, I'd cook even if it's just me. It's my thing. I always done it."

"Not me. All I do is cook. Last thing I want is to stand over a stove on a day off."

"Well, it's my thing, you know."

Neither said more. It wasn't a real break, just taking out the trash. Officially, they weren't allowed to smoke at all, but the principal was fair, and he said as long as the lunchroom ladies stayed behind the dumpster so that he could reasonably say he didn't know, well then he wouldn't hand down commandments one way or the other. Still, their time was limited, and neither would waste what little of it they had with more words. So they fell into their usual rhythm of drawing smoke into their lungs, then exhaling it in unison so that it joined into a cloud hanging above the rusting green bin behind them.

Wanda, now standing in her kitchen, remembered her cigarettes and grabbed a pack from the pullout drawer beside the fridge and tossed them in her purse. Today was Thanksgiving Day, and she was pulling two fried eggs off the burner, her oven cold.

Usually, she only worked at the Battersburg McDonald's on the weekend. It paid. At five years, she had been there longer than any other employee, unless you counted the owners, which Wanda did not. They initially put her up working the register, like they did all women, but when she lost a bottom front tooth and showed no indication that she planned to do anything about it, they decided her decades of experience as a lunch lady would best serve the establishment in the back, on the grill.

The grill suited her fine. At lunch, it was easy enough work, so she never clocked out tired. Her favorite part, though, was breakfast. Breakfast was a little more complicated. There was sausage, ham, regular and Canadian bacon, two different types of eggs, gravy, and even biscuits to maintain. The teenagers she worked with had a hard time keeping up with everything, always forgetting one item or the other, resulting inevitably in chaos and frustrated managers, so they kept Wanda at the grill every weekend, fifty-two Saturdays and fifty-two Sundays a year, giving reprieve to the other adults who worked the weekday morning shifts. Wanda liked the feeling of being able to do what the young people couldn't. She imagined herself a visiting pastor at a pastorless church—a stand-in who becomes more important than the real thing because of the intensity of the need.

Wanda didn't go to church.

And today, she wouldn't make Thanksgiving dinner. She was going to McDonald's.

The old shift manager had quit suddenly two weeks prior after a spat with the new store manager, and the new store manager seemed wholly unaware that the schedule didn't make itself, so by the time Friday rolled around, he realized he had no idea who was supposed to be working the next week. Unable to get into the computer program they normally used, he wrote up a schedule on paper, stuck it to the back wall, and announced it to everyone. The problem, however, was that the whole store seemed to have Thanksgiving plans and couldn't come in. The manager roped in those he knew wouldn't say no, namely teenagers, who he could lure with the promise of the now open shift manager position, and Wanda, who wouldn't be at her regular job on account of school being closed and who said yes to everything.

The store manager asked her to work Thanksgiving Day at the end of her shift on Sunday.

The moment she found out, she immediately called her married son, Mark, to let him know she'd be working and wouldn't make it to his house. No answer. She left a voicemail.

She then called her single son, Keith.

"Yeah."

"Keith. You busy?"

"You know I ain't busy. What would I be doing?"

"I gotta work on Thanksgiving."

"At the school?"

"No. McDonald's. They ain't got nobody for the morning."

"Probably better anyway. You ain't gotta cook now."

"Well, I like cooking." She paused like she wanted a response. When she realized Keith wasn't going to say anything further, she said, "Well, what about you? You want me to drive you up Mark's?"

"Nah. I ain't going up there without a escape plan. Them kids'll drive me crazy."

"Yeah. Well, what you gonna eat?"

"Mom, there's food. I eat every day. I reckon I'll eat on Thursday, too."

"You're gonna stay home?"

"Where else would I go?"

"Well, I'll come by day of and keep you company."

"Alright."

"Alright. I'll see you Thanksgiving after work. I open, so I'll get there half past one."

Wanda hadn't talked to him since. He stayed at a government apartment over by Mosely. He had moved in with a woman and her kids who was getting it for free, some Slone from over on Fox Creek, but she left him and went back to her ex-husband down in Canard County and now Keith just stayed on in her apartment and nobody at the Housing Authority seemed to notice or care. Money's money, even when it's the government. Keith didn't work, didn't drive, didn't go to school.

Wanda finished her eggs, took a sip of her coffee, winced at the bitterness, and then swallowed the rest in coursing gulps to avoid the taste. She texted Mark, "Happy Thanksgiving," and texted Keith, "See you in a little bit." She grabbed her glasses and name tag by the door and headed to work.

She parked in the far end of a parking lot, mandatory for employees, who weren't supposed to take the good spots reserved for paying customers. The McDonald's in Battersburg sat beside a Walmart and a few other outlet chains on top of a hill that had been blown up and paved over to create space for commerce. The parking lot backed against some thin woods at the base of the rest of the mountain, which towered upward in a vertical cliff of exposed rocks and a few stubby trees trying to grow where they didn't know they couldn't. The cold air pushed back the noises of the hills and the down-mountain traffic, making every sound—the creaking car door, the crunch of leaves under her black anti-slip shoes, the soft pulse of her purse rubbing against her coat as she walked—exaggerated and crisply intonated.

Ordinarily, the smells from inside the fast-food kitchen, trapped by the mountain on one side, hovered thick across the entire development and spilled down the hill, even reaching the cars on the highway, but in the early mornings there was only a vague hint of rancid oil from the day before. The moment held liminal magic for Wanda, who liked the idea of being the only person privy to this space-time, before the world turned on, when the stars and frost accompanied her in a dream state, a beforeness when restaurants and eating were still ideas and not yet reality. She imagined herself turning on the smell of bacon and sausage like a kind of radio for noses and actually waking up the entire world.

The doors were kept locked before the store opened, so she tapped on the drive-thru window to be let in. The new store manager was in the back office doing something on a clipboard. He signaled with his finger in the air, continued writing for another thirty seconds, and then let Wanda in the back door.

He was younger than she was, maybe late forties or early fifties. It was hard to tell because he was heavyset with a baby face that he kept shaved. He wore a white shirt and a red tie, like they all did, but he chose a short sleeve button-up. Even though it was five in the morning, he looked worn out. The particular combination of exhausted youth, a tie paired with short sleeves, and a shiny name tag gave him the appearance of a Mormon missionary. The name tag didn't help, though. Wanda thought his name was Paul, but she didn't bother learning it, because, like with any missionary, Mormon or otherwise, who found his way up Big Branch holler and on her porch, she knew her presence would last longer than his. Equally, she had no need to use his name. Wanda held no animosity. She simply held no curiosity, as it would not have served her.

He unlocked the door but didn't open it. As she stepped in, her lenses fogged up in the warmth of the interior, making her thick, caterpillar eyebrows seem like they rested above two large, empty gray stones. The manager said, "It shouldn't be busy, I don't reckon. Most folks is gonna get coffee, maybe some getting breakfast. I'll do the front and we got a couple a kids for the drive-thru. I'll put one back to helping you if it gets too busy. But, I'd say only make half a what you usually make."

As he spoke, she stepped to the wall and grabbed an apron. She had already turned on the grill before he finished talking. "Alright."

Wanda set the oven to preheat and pulled a tray from the fridge. A few years earlier, someone would have mixed a powder mix with milk and rolled new biscuits. A few years before that, someone may have actually mixed shortening or butter with the flour—Wanda hadn't worked there long enough to know the stories of now-dead people who might have made real biscuits from scratch at McDonald's. But now, they came preformed on trays that Wanda would simply slide into the oven.

She cracked eggs and she made sausage. Greasy scents roused upward, then outward, and clung to the fabric of her uniform.

After half an hour or so, a kid who looked to be at best twenty years old appeared. He was a tall but skinny little thing with soft hair that fell down over his ears; under his nose, a thin mustache toiled to grow. He was swimming in his crew trainer work shirt, which couldn't have been larger than a medium. He joined her from the other side of the assembly line where they put together the food. His shirt looked ironed.

"I ain't ever worked with you. Morning." He wiped the surface of the table, which was still clean and hadn't been used yet, with a white kitchen towel.

"Morning."

"You need any help?"

"No," she said, placing a large tray of scrambled eggs into a heated cabinet. "I got it."

"Are you the lunch lady that works on the weekends? I do evening shifts mostly, but I know about you."

"Yeah. That's me." The grill top opened automatically, and Wanda turned away from him to pull evenly spaced-out sausage patties off with a spatula.

"This must be boring for you, since you know how to cook real food."

Wanda shoved the tray of sausage into the heating cabinet. "I know how to. But it ain't like that no more at the schools. It's pretty much opening cans and bags and heating em up. All premade. Closest thing to real cooking we do now is making toast."

"That right?"

"Toast is Fridays. It's donuts in plastic and cereal boxes otherwise."

"Back when I was in elementary school, we had biscuits and gravy and bacon and all kinds a good breakfast at school. My mom wadn't much of a cook, so I looked forward to it."

Their conversation was interrupted by the manager, who might be named Paul. "Hey, Kevin," he hollered at the skinny boy talking to Wanda, "is there something special you gotta do to turn this register on? I got customers."

"No. It should kick on at five o'clock automatically."

"Well, it ain't coming on. Hey Wanda, can you make me two sausage and egg biscuits?"

Wanda began to assemble the sandwiches. Kevin went to the front, where Maybe-Paul was standing in front of an unlit monitor, on the other side of which stood a retired-aged-looking man and woman in matching holiday sweaters.

Maybe-Paul said, "Here. I'll get their coffees, you try to get this on."

He poured the coffees. Wanda slid the biscuits forward. Kevin looked under the machine and unplugged and replugged wires.

"Excuse me, y'all. We can't ring this up with the computers being stalled, so . . . Happy Thanksgiving!" Maybe-Paul handed the couple a bag of food and two coffees. They beamed as if winning the lottery.

"Are you serious?" the man in a sweater asked.

"Sure am. Can't make a sale without the computer."

Another customer came in, this time a man carrying a small child wrapped in a blanket. The drive-thru dinged, and Maybe-Paul's neck glowed the tomato red of his tie. "Here," he said to Kevin, handing him an audio-headset connected to the drive-thru, "take this, see if they can wait. I'll try and call IT."

Kevin began to speak over the headset to a customer in a car outside. The screens refused to come on. A few people were now gathered into the restaurant. The men called back orders to Wanda.

"Two biscuits and gravy."

"Three sausage biscuits."

"Bacon, egg, and cheese. Two biscuits and gravy."

"Just a plain biscuit, but break it open and butter it."

Wanda simply said "Okay" each time and quickly and efficiently prepared the items.

Maybe-Paul stood up front, clinching a cordless phone between his face and shoulder while writing down people's orders and calling them back. By the time he'd hung up, his shirt was damp with anxious sweat and there were six customers standing up front with no way to pay, eyeing their food, warm in paper bags left waiting in the landing zone.

He sighed some heavy noises into the receiver, then laid the phone on the counter, turned to give the boy in the drive-thru an exhausted look, then flipped back around to the dining room customers. "Hey, folks, I'm so sorry. Please, y'all take your meals on the house and enjoy a happy Thanksgiving on behalf of Battersburg McDonald's," he said with nervous theatrics as if this were somehow part of a larger corporate plan. He smiled at them all, walking into the lobby and then ushering out the customers as Kevin cleared the drive-thru. He locked the door behind the final customer.

"Kevin, go kill the drive-thru sign. Hurry."

"What's going on?"

"We ain't even supposed to be open. Damn it. All this food is wasted. The operating system won't come on cause the store's closed." He grabbed napkins from the drive-thru cart, wiped his forehead, said, "Shit."

Kevin ran to the office, turned off the lights, and then sprinted back, awaiting instructions as if something were on fire and he needed guidance before moving.

"When Lisa quit, you'd think she woulda had the sense or dang decency to tell me we ain't open today. I only been here a few weeks. How's I supposed to know? And she's done made y'all get out here today and us not even open. Shew, I swear."

Kevin nodded sternly in agreement. Maybe-Paul threw his sweaty napkins in the can for wasted food, which was currently empty.

Wanda wiped down the grill, waiting for them to tell her what to do. Maybe-Paul inspected the warming cabinets full of the breakfast items she had ready for the morning rush.

"You know what? Y'all just go ahead and bag all this up and take it home. It ain't like we coulda planned this. Shut her down." He threw his hands in the air in a sign of resignation, then retreated to the office. Kevin followed.

Wanda, indifferent, shut down the grill, took apart and cleaned the equipment as if this were the close of any other shift. It wouldn't do her any good to care one way or the other—like her daddy always said, teachers gonna frown, politicians gonna lie, and preachers gonna ask for money no matter what she felt about any of it. She would get paid for the time she was here, and she bagged up a sizable haul of a couple dozen biscuits and enough breakfast items to do a small family a week.

She knocked on the office door; Maybe-Paul gave her a thumbs-up to leave. Kevin was standing seriously, watching Maybe-Paul, who was seated in the only chair and frowning at a screen. She clocked out, grabbed her coat, and left. The sun pumped blue into the sky, the cobweb frost was melted, and the smell of breakfast fat was creamed into the air of the parking lot. She got into her car and laid the bags on her lap. The food felt warm and alive against the cold stiffness of her work jeans. She kept the bags there as she drove, feeling the heat from her morning's work sinking into her body.

By the time she got to Keith's apartment building, it was already pushing nine in the morning. There was a woman and a fat little boy putting up a Christmas tree in the window of the apartment between Keith's and the parking lot. The kid waved excitedly at Wanda, who gave him a clipped head nod, like he was a work colleague.

Wanda knocked on Keith's door. There were no lights. There was no answer.

She went around to the side windows and peeked inside through a torn window screen. She could see her old blue love seat that she gave to Keith and the girl, the mountable television she got for him last Christmas, still leaning against the wall, even make out a coffee cup sitting on the floor beside the couch. But no Keith.

Wanda tried calling him. No answer.

She got back in her car. Waited. It was cold in the car, but the bag was still warm, so she held it again in her lap. Maybe he had gone to a neighbor's to have coffee or bum a cigarette. Maybe he had gone to the store with somebody. She waited, and then she tried to call again. Still no answer. No text from him or Mark.

She had a cigarette. She watched a red cardinal scratching at the dirt. She watched him get joined by a second red cardinal. She watched them fight over the dirt, each pecking toward the other and throwing open his wings in fluid and prescient drama. Their conflict was graceful, almost beautiful, and they reminded her of fighting roosters, only nobody made or lost money and nobody prevented the loser from flying away. She had a second cigarette.

When the food was cold to the touch, she started her car and returned home.

She put her glasses and name tag by the door, then went to the fridge to put up her McDonald's bags. The turkey she had bought on Saturday was still there, fully defrosted, taking up half the shelf. It was still early enough, and it was a small bird. She could have it out of the oven and ready by the time her original work shift would have been over, and then she could take it over to Keith's apartment.

She had never bought the rest of her meal's ingredients because she thought she'd be working the whole day, but Wanda enjoyed the challenge of creative cooking. She rubbed the turkey down in oil, pepper, and salt and put him in the oven. She sliced thin some onions and a carrot and put them on the stove in some butter, then, once the carrots softened and the onions turned clear, she added chopped squares of the leftover sausage. She crumbled most of the McDonald's biscuits, tossed them with sage, salt, pepper, the sauteed onion and carrot, then poured in the first drippings from the turkey and made dressing. She had most of a head of cabbage left of what her friend Doug McCoy Jr. had given her last week, which she cut into chunks and tossed with some grease she kept in a coffee can, vinegar, sorghum, and the McDonald's bacon she brought home. She tore the folded breakfast sandwich eggs by hand into pieces and stirred them into some mayonnaise, minced onion, and various spices. By the time afternoon arrived, her leftovers were gone and a full spread of turkey, dressing, gravy, biscuits, egg salad, and fried cabbage was ready.

She carefully placed everything into transportable containers, which she covered and cushioned in the strips of bathroom towel she kept by the door, and placed them in her flat tub that read "property of United States Postal Service" across its side, which she used for carrying food that might spill. She hauled it out to her car and headed to Keith's apartment.

The cardinals were still there—or at least, some cardinals were, since Wanda wasn't a bird expert and couldn't be sure. They were hard to miss in the dull gray of late November, pops of red like Christmas ornaments against the listless light smothering the drab housing project. They were no longer fighting. One was surveying the project from atop a light pole at the edge of the parking lot. Another was flitting around the chain-link fence down the hill a bit at the edge of the apartment complex. Perhaps they had drawn their lines and divided up the space. The Christmas tree belonging to Keith's next-door neighbors was now fully decorated. But Keith was still nowhere to be found.

Wanda checked her phone. She went to Keith's porch to wait. She smoked another cigarette. She turned down the coffee that the woman with the tree and the chubby boy offered her when they noticed Wanda sitting on a folding chair by the locked door in the cold. The boy stood behind the woman while she talked to Wanda about what she'd just seen the governor saying on TV, though both stayed noncommittal because it was too cold to stand around and have a political conversation should they have to agree or disagree, and, after all, it was Thanksgiving. Wanda thanked them for the company. The woman smiled and the boy watched her with big eyes as she returned to her car.

Soon, the sky started to lose light.

She returned home.

The temperature would be close to freezing that night but not much below, so Wanda didn't even get the crate out of the car. It would keep till morning, and she had the day off tomorrow.

She went into the house. Started the coffee pot. Forgot about the stuck button. Sludge again. She wiped it down, but this time did not salvage the remains. She placed her empty coffee cup back in the cabinet. She turned on the television and flipped through channels. She landed on an old episode of a black-and-white western. The bad guy from out of town had stolen from the general store. Now the sheriff was after him, and it turns out he was trying to take care of a sick kid. She felt annoyed at the whole story and didn't want the happy ending she knew would come, where the sheriff and the town give them what they need and he learns to ask for help. Shit. He coulda got a job in that town. He coulda worked. Ain't no excuse for stealing. She got so annoyed that when it cut to the commercials and some woman acted like a new dishwashing liquid had saved her from depression, Wanda turned off the TV. Real life was better than stories. She flipped on her old police scanner and listened to officers talking about road blocks, traffic stops, drug busts, and domestic disputes, nodding off to the comfort of a world she knew.

At eight o'clock at night, her phone woke her up. It was a text from Keith.

"Got anything to eat? I ain't ate all day."

She didn't text back. She turned off the scanner, grabbed her coat, and drove over to Keith's apartment, the entire turkey dinner, though now cold, kept safe by the hostile late autumn temperatures.

She walked past the apartment with the tree and the fat kid, who this time nodded through the window like a familiar coworker instead of waving. Wanda nodded back, her small frame weighed down and pulled forward by the heaviness of the Thanksgiving dinner in the U.S. Post Office bin.

She sat the bin on the folding chair outside the door, dimly illuminated by the distant parking lot light, and knocked. This time Keith answered.

He was smoking a cigarette. He wore pajama bottom pants with some cartoon character on them that Wanda didn't know and a black long sleeve T-shirt. His hair needed to be cut, usually Wanda's work.

He looked down at the bin. The great weight of it caused the chair to buckle and sink.

"What's all that?"

"I made a whole dinner today and brought it over here. Didn't see hide nor hair a you. I waited."

"Yeah, I had some stuff to do." The black air felt thick despite being cold. Felt layered and somehow intentional. Wanda reached for his cigarette, which he handed to her without taking his eyes off the food. "Anyway, I'm starved."

She moved quickly but took a long, purposeful draw, pinching the tip between her thumb and index finger of her left hand. She repeated the action and then threw the lit butt to the ground, several draws worth of cigarette still remaining. "You'll have to heat it. It ain't been heated."

"Well, I wish you'd a told me. I ain't got no microwave. Ashley come took it."

A scant breeze struggled against the porch, making the light of the grounded cigarette grow more intense, like the universe itself had taken the final draw off it. The night's darkness intensified against the glow, and suddenly the fire of the discarded butt seemed to grow beyond the ground, beyond the porch, above the housing project and past the mountain cut-through that joined previously divided parts of the bottom.

Wanda fell forward toward the folding chair in a mad fit, like a woman possessed by something wild that had long been caged. She reached into the bin and grabbed the butter-slick turkey out of its aluminum tray with her bare hands and hurled it directly at Keith's head. It smacked him in the face head-on like it was flying at him in a form of attack, then slid down the front of his shirt and pants, landing on the bottom of the door frame in a hollow thud. She seized the bin with both hands, pulling it to herself and swinging it fast and outward like a slingshot that flung the rest of the meal away from her, the entire supper—biscuits, gravy, dressing, cabbage, and egg salad—careening in a turbulent explosion toward her startled son, her youngest child, aged thirty-seven, who was standing in the doorway of a government apartment that didn't belong to him, smoking a cigarette he didn't pay for, wearing cartoon pajamas she didn't understand. His face was shining with turkey fat and shock. Thick slugs of dressing and wet masses of cabbage clung to the brick, to Keith's pajama pants, to the door frame, and splashed into a pool of congealed gravy crawling its escape from the violent scene of the little patio porch.

He stood frozen.

Wanda's screaming voice traveled past her son and bounced off the walls of his sparse apartment, echoing back out across the whole housing complex and racing up the hill. "I bought you that microwave! *I did*!"

"Jesus fuck, Mom, what the hell is wrong with you?"

"Damn it, Keith. You could've . . ." She didn't want to say what he could have done. So many could haves that were so obvious that somehow her saying them out loud would only make her more embarrassed, more frustrated, more alone. The dressing was now a broken country of divided lands huddled in small islands on the cement, the gravy a clotting ooze slowly flowing over the edge of the porch and onto the ground. The turkey had landed right side up between them, but its skin had been ripped off in its fall, its meat exposed like a new wound taking in fresh air. Wanda thought it looked almost like a confused drunk, waking up and trying to figure out where he was and how he got there.

They both stood in silence, each unaware how they could move forward in such an unprecedented scenario. The turkey slipped, falling over headfirst from the doorway onto the concrete below. In the hushed stillness of the moment, it sounded like the taking of a step.

Wanda didn't say another word. She didn't put out the cigarette. She turned and walked back to her car. She didn't see or nod at the boy watching her from his window as she got in. When she backed out, Keith was still standing in the doorway, almost as if he was waiting on her to retrieve a towel from her car, or perhaps thought she might have a backup turkey with dressing prepared and waiting in the backseat.

She drove away in the direction of the cut-through and the elementary school. There was a Dollar Store and a 24-hour drive-thru cigarette place shoved against the side of the hill on the turn to get out of Mosely. The cigarette place was the kind of store that had twelve-packs of pop, milk, and the legal paraphernalia people use to smoke pot. In a different state, it would have had a couple of poker machines. In a bigger town, it might have had a tanning bed. She went through the drive-thru. Asked for a carton of what she smoked. While the cashier, a pretty girl with short brown hair and a man's hunting coat, was ringing her up, Wanda asked, "Y'all got coffee?"

The pretty girl said, "Yeah, but it's probably old."

"Honey, that's fine with me."

"Well, it's on the house then."

"Thanks."

She handed Wanda the cigarettes, then a Styrofoam cup of coffee with a plastic lid. Wanda took a sip. It was old, but it was still warm. It was old, but it was good enough.

BOYS SAVED FROM THIS

Not every southern boy with his back held hard by a preacher
slipping him under a mud-streaked creek
wishing those waters might just wash away
his still tight clinging daydreams
of buck naked men
flickering like distant flesh fires
holding beer cans in his mind's cold night
muffled preaching rushing in familiar ambling waves
against his face now flooding by icy baptismal wetness
and in the name of the Father, the Son, and the Holy Ghost
while his family flings singing voices at the wheeling clouds
makes it. But I did.

And now transparent Sunday mimosa flutes
flatten the fat of my bottom lip
a table garnish sprig of friends with degrees
dill-and-rosemary-sown brunch casseroles

and now everything hovers
like cellophane surfaces
over the grammarless echoes
of hushed boys who sanctified dance floors
twisting pulsing bodies into Madonna and Britney

but never danced to Gaga—
heard their truth on sabbaths
knew deconstruction or DEI

who never even had the chance
to cut out blond highlights
or finally quit smoking.

Boys who are no more.

In the early morning when time is still wet and wavering to and fro—
I can remember
the hope that glitter brings
the light a music
knocking down church walls
and I can see
them made new and washed clean
by sound waves that soften
on their way across the cosmos.

SHOOTING UP JESUS

Ice Plant. Mosely. Late Summer 2003.

My mamaw always used to say that murky water holds unseen things not fit for the Lord. Now she spent a lot of time quoting Eugene Mullins, her pastor, but she was always one to give credit, and I think this one was something she made up on account of water moccasins and snapping turtles or trying to scare us all outta mud puddles and dog day creeks. I was thinking about her when I started washing my hands cause the water made me want to puke—just perfect lukewarm, like the exact temperature of body fluids: the temperature of something with germs in it. I can't stand the feel of tepid water. Like the water you find in a bad jacuzzi in a cheap hotel. Or in a slimy puddle of water in the late spring. It makes me feel gross and dizzy, like my head is just floating off. So I turned up the hot tap clockwise. Steam rose to the mirror.

I didn't even bother looking at myself. I knew I looked pretty. I had just got my hair done: cut and got highlights that same day down at the Magic Clips up on the hill in Mosely—the one they'd just opened. New highlights. The woman that did them was trying to flirt up a storm, love her heart, just *Yeah, I might go out and party over at the Holiday Inn tonight* and *Can you believe my boyfriend, well, ex-boyfriend, tried to say I was fat? I told him, how you gonna call me fat when you ain't seen your own wiener in ten years?* I gave her what she wanted, told her, *Honey, how's any man gonna call you fat? You're sixty percent titties.* We both laughed and she didn't even charge me for the shampooing.

I also didn't look at myself cause I was instead looking down at my little rainbow-colored "What Would Jesus Do?" bracelet that the church got in a collection bag from a preacher who came up from Tennessee. I lathered it up in soap, shoved it back under the water, and wondered if I was the first person to wash another man's semen out of a rainbow WWJD bracelet . . . or any WWJD bracelet, for that matter. No, probably not. I know some a them Baptist girls over in Battersburg was pure heatherns. It was untelling what all they got up to while managing to stay virgins for Jesus. Well, good for them. But I know they were just as likely to have washed something unclean out of a cotton chastity bracelet as they were to have performed sign language routines during praise and worship songs at church camp—those kinds of girls were always hiding a wild freak. If not the first *person*, then I thought maybe I was the first *man* to have to wash out his WWJD bracelet. Excepting maybe some of the churchier boys who might have got too excited after seeing Amy Grant and her date ride that Ferris wheel in the "Baby, Baby" video. But *another man*? Yeah. I reckoned I was at least among a chosen few.

Patrick Case, one of the chosen few. The idea of being *chosen* appealed to me, so I made a mental note to write in my journal about the word *chosen* when I finally got out of the holler and got back to campus. But to do that, I first needed to get back to my car.

I was currently stuck at my parents' house up Ice Plant Holler. I was stuck there because I had spent the last few hours in the company of a very nice, but otherwise unknown to me, man. See, this very nice man was first just a phone number. He handed it to me when I rang him up his cigarettes at the Mosely Fast-n-Fill, where I run the register on the weekend. He wrote it on the back of his receipt. Plumb cute. Polite, handsome, khakis. Clean cut, thirties. Not the most Mosely man, to be honest, but we get traffic off the highway from Battersburg and even folks from up in Lexington coming in to see their country families, and he was so obviously married I knew better than to ask. He just handed his number to me and said, *In case you ever want to hang out.* Now I ain't sure how straight men indicate their interest in friendships with one another, but I doubt clandestine phone number exchanges or offers to *hang out* with some feller they don't know is part a the ritual.

So I called him. And he called me back the next day when I was at my friend Trina's house, which is so hard to find I offered to walk down the main road a bit and meet him. He liked that. So from there we drove around for a while before finally parking on the far end of a strip job, away from any four wheelers or drug users trying to find some solitude in the leveled remnants of a mountaintop.

It was a rushed evening ending in the backseat behind the line of trees separating the slate dump from the backroad to the mines, but we had a good time and spent a whole Outkast and half a Britney album together. I'll leave it at that. And he was kind enough to drive me home—well, to my mommy and daddy's house over on Ice Plant, because it was already dark and I didn't want to have to explain to him how to get up to Trina's house. I bummed a Marlboro Red, finished it before he dropped me off, and now was washing what remained of the evening down the sink from a rainbow WWJD bracelet given to me by the Big Branch of Beaver Creek Pentecostal Church.

Getting to my car, then, meant getting back to Trina's house. And that meant getting a ride.

Mom, Dad, and Mamaw Vicky had gone to a part–family reunion, part–porch building over at my aunt and uncle's down in South Carolina, so all I had left was Rayeanne.

My older sister, Rayeanne, was sitting on the couch in the living room. Well, sitting is a really strong word. Really, she was more sprawled out like some drunk and powerful queen from the days of Moses, some large royal woman in gray jogging pants and a yellow T-shirt advertising a local social security lawyer. She had positioned a network of blankets and throw pillows just so—so she could eat without turning her head, only instead of a pile of grapes like you might have seen in antiquity, it was canned cheese dip and tortilla chips. She was mid-episode in an endless parade of police detective TV shows she watched day in and day out. Her hair was pulled back from her face with a pair of sunglasses, but I'd bet a carton of cigarettes that she had not left the house, hell, maybe even the couch, that entire day.

"Hey," I shoved her feet so I could sit down, "drive me out to Trina Johnson's house to get my car." Rayeanne and her couch were in pure symbiosis. She repositioned herself after I moved her legs without even taking her eyes off the screen, like she was using some third eye to know what was happening beyond the scope of the screen.

"Fuck I will." A cop in a suit had just laid a book on a table from the other side of a woman in an interrogation room, raising his hands up dramatically while he yelled. The woman looked around anxiously for help. Rayeanne had lost a piece of chip in her dip, so she was using the sturdiest tortilla in the bag to scoop out the helpless piece drowning in its surrounding cheese. "Them Johnsons is crazier 'n tits on a turtle. Ain't no way I'm getting my ass shot driving up there at night. Hell no." She didn't even look at me as she lifted the vessel and its lifeless chip rescue to her mouth. The television woman put her face in her hands and cried desperately in front of a group of investigators who had entered the room to play collective good cop. Keeping her head right on the screen, Rayeanne's eyes moved slightly up and to the left and at an old fake pendulum wall clock our uncle Ed from over on Cow Creek had won in an auction. It was just after midnight.

"It ain't that late. Come on now. I've gotta get back to school tomorrow. I got class at eight a.m."

"You already call em?"

"Well, I tried. About a hundred times. But Trina ain't picked up and Little George goes to bed at like eight o'clock and probably don't even know how to answer his phone."

"Nope. Ain't no way. They're about to show whether or not this bitch killed her own babies. Just cause some man told her to. I swear to God, people's messed up."

I got up and stood in front of the TV. "Shew, come on, Ray. You know she killed em. If she didn't they wouldn't be showing her crying for pity this early in the episode. Plus, I'm gonna need my car before it's too late. I gotta drive back up early. I got a test in the morning I can't miss."

"It's already past midnight. You might as well give up. I ain't going up there around no crazy Johnsons who'd kill you as sure as look at you. Now, go on and get out from in front of the TV."

"Well . . . the least you can do is drive me to the railroad tracks. I'll walk the rest of the way. They're gonna have to get affidavits and search warrants and fight the magistrate and DA before they can even get close to finding out how she killed them babies. And we don't even know who the red herring is yet. You'll be back before they even get to the trial."

"Shit, then." She rocked herself off the couch in a wooden creaking, her quilt and blanket nest tumbling down onto the floor like a discarded robe. She put her chips down and let out a low burp. "Come on fore I change my mind."

I handed Rayeanne the keys to our mom's Oldsmobile from off the table behind where she was sitting, worried that her taking the time to look for them might draw her back toward the couch and ruin my chances of getting her out of the house. We stepped out into the muggy September night to retrieve my little gray Pontiac Sunbird from the Johnsons' house.

Now, in her defense, Rayeanne's hesitance wasn't exactly without warrant. Trina Johnson's family was wild, to put it mildly, was a little crazy, to put it plain. Her dad, Little George, was a sycamore trunk of a man weighing a good 400 pounds. He ran his own mines after a bad strike with the big guys. Her mommy died right after Trina was born, but Little George had a whole convoy of brothers and sisters to help raise her. They were the sort of family who had all kinds of secrets, some I knew and a lot I didn't, but what was not a secret was that they owned an arsenal of guns and would shoot on sight anybody they thought was trespassing on their land, which was a sprawling mass of woods, hills, and mud. Their solitude was so intense that there wasn't even a real road to their house, which was actually a family compound, a whole big old clump of four or five houses belonging to multiple family members taking up the hillside. To even get up there, you had to take first a service road that intersected a railroad track and then drive along the railroad track a good half a mile before you got to a dirt driveway hidden in a line of trees.

Rayeanne was not about to get as close as the driveway.

So she dropped me off at the edge of the tracks, as promised, and sped away before the passenger side door even fully shut. I bet she even made it home in time to see the woman from the witness stand break down when the evidence mounted. I bet she lit a cigarette when the woman started to cry and then laughed at her. Ray couldn't stand a crying woman. That was just one of her truths.

And one of my truths was that there I was, standing beside a railroad track on an unlit service road after midnight in the heat of September, and I was feeling chilly. It got so dark out here that you could see the Milky Way splashing around with stars, drawing your head to the sky, and somehow the extra stars made it feel even darker. I thought of my mamaw, who always said you could hear the stars. Dark like this made their hum even clearer. The air was thick and clinging to my shirt. Even my boxers felt damp from the heat, but there I was wishing I'd worn a jacket.

I started down the tracks.

The side of the railroad rose up sharp in a little hill made out of rocks, making it hard to walk a straight line on the road, so I climbed up to the railroad track itself and took big, exaggerated steps to catch the wooden planks. I worried that I might look goofy, like some kid playing, then it occurred to me there wasn't a soul to see it, so I let myself enjoy the giant stepping. *Thwomp, thwomp, thwomp.*

I realized I hadn't walked down a railroad track in a long time, not since I was a kid, maybe eleven or twelve, and me and Shawn used to hide under the railroad bridge that ran over the creek where Ice Plant Holler meets Mosely. We'd hide when the trains went over it. Shawn. Our families went to church together when we were little. I hadn't talked to him since high school started, really. Different crowds, and he started using hard. His cheeks were thin and skeletal now, and his facial hair looked tense and on edge, like the wires of some kind of brush. But his face used to be so soft and pretty. Boyish, but pretty. Such light brown eyes. And he was the one who showed me how to hide under the moving trains. Me and him would walk out on the railroad bridge from Mosely, then swing down under the tracks onto these wide wooden support beams and just lay down on our backs and watch the trains run over our heads. The first time he showed me, I didn't expect the train to scare me so much. I mean, I knew it would be loud. But this was something. It felt like thunder, like we were inside of the cloud during an electric storm, the wind whipping hard down the length of our whole bodies, shaking us from the inside out, lifting up our shirts, and the heat of the train melted the tar until it dripped down and smelled like another world. The first time, I tried to get up and Shawn grabbed my hand. Said it was dangerous to move and to lay down until it passed. It did, and he didn't let go of my hand right away. He held it until the train was gone, and then just half a second more. We never talked about it, never mentioned it outside of that world made by trains from far away needing to cross the waters of our creek on their way to places we didn't know. We spent that whole summer risking trains and for just a few supernatural minutes we'd hold hands while the passing engine and its cars shook the whole earth.

Shew. I don't know why I was thinking about Shawn. Maybe because the air was muggy, just choked with smells: woods, the autumnal threat of September, sweat, and little shushes of railroad tar floating on the dead air. And when you can't see, smells are always louder. Memories, too.

Me and Trina Johnson worked together at the Dairy Queen in downtown Mosely my sophomore year of high school. I worked because I was saving money for college. Trina worked because Little George forced her to—a prerequisite to him making her car payments for her. She didn't use the Dairy Queen money *for* anything, since it certainly wouldn't cover the payments on the new sports car her dad leased for her sixteenth birthday, but the job probably satisfied Little George that he was teaching her what work meant.

I wasn't a whole lot like Trina, but I loved that she just didn't give a shit.

I guess she liked me for my willingness to like that about her.

We were on our ten-minute break, smoking in her car at the far end of the parking lot. Employee parking butted up against the cliff that looked over the creek, which curved behind the businesses on the main street in Mosely like it couldn't make up its mind up where it wanted to go. I was just being kind of mindless, watching the water try to dislodge a white grocery bag from a tree limb to carry it away, when Trina rolled up the window on my side. It was so tinted that I couldn't see the creek anymore.

She was hunched over in the driver's seat like she was looking for something in the floorboard, but she was holding her driver's license. It had a thin line of powder. She pushed in her left nostril with her thumb and inhaled the line through the other side of her nose.

I guess I was staring.

"What?" She gave an extra sniff, wiped under her nose, and then slid her license into her jeans pocket. "I mean, everybody does it."

"Oh, it's fine. I just didn't know."

She winked. "Well, Sherlock, now you do. Hey, come with me to my house real fast. I gotta get something."

"Trina, we gotta get back to work."

She put the car smoothly into reverse without looking behind her, slid it to first before it came to a full stop, and started out of the parking lot. "Shit. It ain't like they're gonna have an ice cream emergency. Live a little. Come on, it'll be five minutes."

That was my first time up on the compound. We drove out of Mosely, took a service road up past the cut-through, and then turned right not *at* the railroad track but literally *onto* the railroad track. Her car was throwing rocks and juddering along.

"What are you doing!?"

"Jesus, calm down. Being gay ain't no excuse to be so gay." We pushed on a bit more, then took a left between some trees onto a long dirt driveway that petered off into a gravel lot with little patches of grass popping up. There was a mess of big houses and trailers. Nice trailers, too. They were just sitting up on the side of the hill like there had been a road. Like they were supposed to be there and it was not the least bit unusual for there to be five houses a good mile from the nearest hint of civilization.

We parked right in front of the biggest house closest to the hill, and Trina handed me half a cigarette, still lit.

"Stay here, Hoss. I'll be right back." She hopped out of her silver Camaro, left the door wide open, and ran into a house three times the size of my family's double-wide.

I looked around. There was no sign of Mosely, which would have been on the other side of the far hill behind the tracks. On the near side, where the houses were, there was a hill that had been burned clear and now housed a couple dozen roosters in little cylindrical chicken-wire enclosures. Some of the roosters were standing on upside-down buckets. Some not. And just above the roosters there was a family burial lot with five or six tombstones huddled at the feet of a life-size cement statue of Jesus.

First I thought I saw a bear, but no. Out from behind the statue came a shirtless man holding a post-hole digger in his left hand. He was older, maybe in his late fifties, fat, but solid fat, what my Mamaw Vicky called *hard fat*—the kind made from eating because you were hungry from hard work, as opposed to the kind I carried, the kind that jiggled. He was wearing mining boots and had the telltale dark bottom eyelashes of a coal miner. I always think it makes men look handsome—kind of like they're wearing eyeliner, like they're these manly blue-collar emo goths. So down the hill came this big old hulk of a mountain man carrying a five-foot tool in one hand, above his waist wearing only what looked like eyeliner and a brown fishnet cap.

He started toward the car, so I decided to get out. Something about being seated around a man that big seemed disrespectful. And, to be honest, I was kind of scared.

He stopped just shy of the car and leaned on the digger like it was a walking stick. And he was definitely big enough to use a post-hole digger as a walking stick. He scratched his left forearm with his right hand. "Who are you?" His voice was hoarse and scratchy. Not upset, just questioning. I figured that made sense, since there was nothing intimidating about me at all, and since this man was a literal giant. He wouldn't have had a reason to be upset.

"Patrick Case."

The giant narrowed his eyes. "You ain't Bimbo Case's boy?"

"Not me. But Bimbo's my second cousin on my dad's side."

The giant looked relieved. "His oldest boy's dead, ain't he?"

I said, "Reckon so. Got electrocuted working on the lines during a snowstorm last year. Was up in a cherry picker. Real sad. His first real job."

"Shew. Well, I hate that for Bimbo. Glad you ain't him, though. I ain't much for ghosts."

"Good thing I ain't dead yet."

He gave a laugh and shook against the post-hole digger. Something about making a man that big laugh made me feel all the bigger myself. He said, "So you from around here?" He gestured with his head toward the other side of the hill, toward the creek and town. He coughed and spit something green on the ground.

"Over just up past the mouth of Ice Plant Holler, out on the Mosely side. Just down the road from Mickey Tackett."

"Mickey's a good guy. Who's your people?" The giant coughed into his fist and then moved the digger closer to him, leaning on it like a crutch.

"Mom's a Hancock. My dad's Dan Case, goes by Danny. Some people call him Reverend, on account a him not going to church even though he lives across the road from one."

"I know your daddy. Union man."

"Yeah. That's him."

"Well, you tell him Little George Johnson said fuck the foreman but don't let him like it."

Little George smiled at his own reference, and I didn't ask what it meant. Trina interrupted us, appearing at the edge of the porch with a carton of cigarettes now in her hand. "Daddy," she said, hopping down and walking between me and the large man, "what the hell are you doing out here?" She emphasized *the hell* like she was hitting a xylophone in ascending notes.

"Nothing, baby. Just checking out the graveyard."

"Well, I see that." She took the cigarette I forgot I was holding and used it to light a new one. She tossed the old one to the ground. Left it lit. "But why are you outside? Doctor said to stay in bed. I was just coming to see if you needed something to eat."

"Well, Pumpkin, I got up and my lungs was hurting something awful. Worse than yesterday. Worse than I ever felt before. I thought I'd just get out here and clear the graveyard off, just in case. I wouldn't want y'all to have to deal with all that mud if something was to happen to me. I dug me a little ditch in over on the backside a the Jesus statue. Should clear up that standing water by the weekend, Lord willing."

Trina threw her hands up. "Jesus Christ, Daddy! You've got the flu. Shew, you ain't dying. You can't be dying—hell, there's people living can't even dig a ditch. This'n right here, probably." She paused, pointed to me with her thumb, then took a draw. Exhaled. "Jesus, Daddy! Why are you like this? Would you *please* just go get in the damn house?" Her tone did not suggest that he was three times bigger than her.

"Alright. Let me just go put this digger out in the shed."

"No, dammit. No shed. No working. Lay it down."

"Well now, baby, Bible says, '*The craving of a sluggard will be the death of him, because his hands refuse to work.*'"

She rolled her eyes. "You gonna preach your own funeral, too?"

"That there's the Book of Proverbs. Where Jesus hid all his fortune cookies." Little George laughed, triggering an angry cough that ended in angrier spit.

"Hell, Daddy," she said, playing along. "Jesus wasn't even born when Proverbs was wrote."

"Don't matter. Son a God's liable to do anything and turn up anywhere. Was your own mommy told me his'n mighta been the very body that jumped into the fiery furnace with them Shadrack fellers."

He nodded hard at me, like I had been there when his wife had said it.

I nodded back.

"Shit. Well, here, I mean it," Trina pointed up to the house with the burning end of her cigarette. "Go on in there and lay down."

"Alright, baby." He laid the post-hole digger across the steps, then grabbed a banister and heaved himself up as it creaked under his weight. "Y'all get on back to school, now. I'm fine."

"Daddy, it's June."

I watched Little George the Giant walk down the long porch toward the house, which I was finally truly taking in. It was absolutely enormous. A ten-foot-wide covered porch wrapped around the house on all sides.

Then a honk. Trina was already back in the car. "You coming, Hoss?"

I climbed in.

"How can he say he's fine," she shifted gears, "when he's out here digging his own death ditch?" She turned up the radio. Salt-N-Pepa. "None of Your Business." "I just can't deal with him. Besides, ain't no ditch big enough to keep the dead dry round here."

It was probably pushing one in the morning. I had class in seven hours and an hour drive to get to the college, and there I was now standing where the bottom of the Johnson's driveway met the railroad track. I could see the hillside at the end of the drive and just make out the outline of my little gray Sunbird, which was parked more or less exactly where me and Trina had parked the first day she brought me out to the compound a few years back, which meant close to her house.

I started to think strategy. My car was pushed up beside the large wraparound porch. There was no streetlights, but with the stars so bright I could see the house and just make out the shapes of the roosters and the family graveyard with its cement Jesus. The whole length of the driveway was otherwise clear. The fastest way to the car would be to walk directly up the road, but there was just enough light that somebody looking out a window would be able to see the shape of an unknown man approaching. Unknown means fair-for-shooting to most people, especially a Johnson, especially in the middle of the night. I could yell and announce myself as I walked up, but the noise might scare them so bad that they'd shoot before they knew who was yelling or what they were yelling for. Another possibility would be going up the side of the hill, hiding behind the trees at the edge of the woods, and getting to my car from the tree line, but on the off chance someone did see me, they would then *definitely* shoot, since only somebody with bad intentions would walk up the dark side of a hill at midnight.

Not that I had bad intentions. I just needed my car to get to class in the morning. That damn test.

I decided to take the tree line. Cover just seemed like a good idea.

So I darted toward the side of the house, and I put my arms out in front of me, feeling ahead in the dark just in case. I am not a graceful being, so I was careful not to trip or make any noise. I reached the first tree and slipped behind it. I took slow, light steps. I glided up past the caged roosters and dropped back behind the little toolshed. A noise stopped me. There was a sleeping hen nesting on top of it, feet away. She half opened the eye facing me and started a cluck, just the inhale part of it, a "don't you mess with me" warning. I stepped a little closer to the hill, giving her space, and held my breath as I continued. A couple of the roosters scratched a bit, but, luckily they knew me, so they weren't too invested in my current drama.

I reached the end, just uphill from the gravel lot, and stood a few feet from the Jesus statue. I had never climbed up here before. This Jesus was not playing. He was definitely life-sized, taller than me, and surrounded by the graves of Trina's dead family members and unfinished tombstones still waiting for more of them, looking out over the whole Johnson compound in his blue-and-white robe and sandals. I wanted to tell him that sandals were not a good choice in this mud, even though Little George's now three-year-old death ditch was still doing a pretty good job draining the water, but mostly I was just killing time with Jesus because I didn't want to make a definitive move. I was nervous and not a good runner. And I didn't dare speak.

But I would need to run.

I could see my car. I was close enough even to make out the pink fruit-shaped air freshener hanging by the rearview.

Me and Jesus surveyed the giant house, its all-encompassing porch, the roosters, their buckets, the double-wides. The curtains were closed. No movement. I took off running down the hill to my car. The door was unlocked, so I was able to fling myself into the driver's seat in one quick move. The sugary sweetness of strawberry air freshener wafted out the door as I very quickly, but softly, pulled it closed.

And then the squawking came. It was clapping off the side of the hill in rapid successions of noise. Every damn rooster on the hillside had turned on me. Once the first crowed, it was over. They sounded like somebody was trying to murder them—even with my doors closed all I could hear was a frightened chorus of startled chickens warning half of Appalachia of impending doom. I did not fumble the keys. I was alert, terrified, ready. My dad woulda been proud. I had that car in reverse in half a second. Then I lurched forward, a hillside full of fighting roosters continuing their defensive sirening while I pushed the stick up to first. Just as I touched the gas pedal, I heard the first hollering. Human hollering. Couldn't make out what they hollered, but it was loud and sure.

Then the unmistakable boom of a shotgun.

I ain't one to play around with guns. I put my foot down as hard as I could, and my little Sunbird spit gravel so hard and far I could hear it pecking on the tin siding of one of the trailers. The roosters were squalling. Boom! I held on to my steering wheel as tight as I had ever held anything and cut to the right as hard as I could to get down the driveway. A third gunshot sounded as I curved around, and I closed my eyes. When the final report rang out, I was leaning against the car and down to the left to keep it from flipping over and to avoid whatever was being aimed at me. For a split second, my driver's side of the car lifted off the ground, flat tearing through the thick of those trees and landing trackside.

The car was shaking so bad it was launching itself upward in little bursts, like a dolphin coming up for air. That's how I came to know I was now outta the driveway and finally pushing out along the side of the tracks, rumbling on the rocks. I was too far away to be hit unless they came after me.

Still, I didn't take any chances and just kept on as fast as I could go. The service road appeared, and I cut hard onto it without looking for traffic. I'd have rather got hit by a car than a bullet. But there wasn't no traffic, and soon enough I was down the hill, out of the cut-through, and coming upon Mosely.

I laughed the whole way home and desperately wanted a cigarette.

Rayeanne was asleep when I got there, stretched out on the couch, her arms flung off to the side, still holding the remote.

I went straight to my childhood room without taking off my clothes and went to sleep.

I got up early; a quick coffee, no shower, and out the door just before sunrise without much sleep. I reckoned Little George was a early bird given his bedtime, so I decided to run over to the Johnson compound and let him know what had happened before getting back to school.

He was on the porch when I got there, sitting in a wooden chair barefoot and peeling an apple. He was shirtless, and his fishnet ball cap was sitting on the chair beside of him. The bare feet and bare chest were one thing, but seeing him without his hat made me feel like I had walked in on him showering. I waved. He nodded.

"Trina's still sleeping."

"That's fine. I was just coming to say sorry about getting my car so late."

"I guess it was you that stole your car?" He laughed and edged a pocketknife under the apple's skin in round curls, revealing a string of wavy red skin and white apple flesh.

"Well, that's one way a putting it. I just didn't want to wake nobody up. I didn't mean for y'all to have to go shooting. But at least nobody got hurt."

"Well, I wouldn't say that."

Panic rose up in me. "Wait, what happened!? Was somebody hurt?"

"Yeah, son." He popped some of the apple string into his mouth and spoke through bits of apple and skin. "One of em's done killed Jesus."

"Wait, what?"

He offered me some of the apple string, motioning with his uncapped forehead toward the hillside. I turned and scanned. Roosters, buckets, trees. Then there it was. The Jesus statue, or what was left of it. His head had been blown completely off. Now, it was just a blue robe and a gaping wound opening up to the sky. Concrete chunks of painted Jesus head were strewn about the ground at the statue's sandaled feet.

"What the actual shit, George? Did you do that?"

"Why in the hell would I shoot my own Jesus? I know my time's a coming, but I ain't that far gone yit. You know how hard it was to pack'm up there? Jesus might carry you in the sand, son, but in the mud, you're carrying him the whole way uphill yourself."

"So what happened?"

"Well, I was sleeping in the living room, front of the TV, and them stupid-assed roosters went off something wild and brought me out on the porch. Then I saw somebody in your car, so I start a hollering.

Next thing I know, somebody took to shooting. Well, what happened was my sister Pauline just heard them roosters going wild and me a hollering and thought the world was ending, so she grabbed a gun. Saw the shape of a man up on the hill and just blew his head right off. Kept shooting when he didn't fall over. Can't blame her for not remembering it was Jesus. We ain't really had the occasion to bury nobody since I drug'm up there."

I hadn't taken any of the apple peeling, so George took the rest he was offering and placed it into his own mouth. There were two birds in the distance singing, each returning the other's call after small bouts of silence. I turned again to face the headless Christ.

"Well, damn. Better him than me."

He talked through bits of apple. "You got that right, honey. Jesus got nine lives anyway."

"That's cats, Little George."

He swallowed. "Well, I reckon if a cat has nine, then surely Jesus got at least that many."

"True. So what you gonna do now?"

"I'mma have to haul that'n down to the railroad bridge and throw'm in the creek. There's a place over to Hazard that sells em, so I'll go pick me up another'n. Might even go today. Trina's mommy always wanted a Jesus standing over her. I reckon she was worried what would Jesus do when the rapture comes and instead a being buried down on flat land she's laying under six feet a mud up on a hillside. Reckon she wanted to make good and sure he seen where she was."

"Sounds like Trina took some smarts off her mom, too." I put my hands in my pocket and rocked my knees. "I gotta get up to class. You need any help before I go?"

"Nah. Doctor says I need to move more." He had peeled the entire apple at this point and took a bite of its whiteness. Juice dripped down onto the stretch marks covering his tan belly.

"Alright, well, good luck with your statue. I reckon I'm gonna get back up to school. Y'all don't shoot at me this time. And for sure, don't shoot Jesus again."

Little George pointed to the chair that his hat was on. There was a shiny neon spool beside of his old brown fishnet cap. "Don't you worry. I got my reflective tape out of the basement. I'mma wrap some around his head. Ain't nobody gonna forget him again."

He winked when he said it, but I knew he would do it.

I gave him a nod and went back to my car that smelled like fake strawberries, started the engine, pulled her in reverse, then once again pushed forward down the hill, this time puttering along at a normal speed, this time not getting shot at. I looked out the rearview and took a final glance at the headless statue of Jesus stretching his neck up toward the morning sky. I drove the length of the railroad tracks, turning the radio on halfway. Dolly. "Here You Come Again." I drove through Mosely, along the little creek that cut through town. As I approached the railroad bridge, I slowed down. Thought about Shawn and the sound of the trains. I still had a few minutes. I pulled over, got out of the car, and walked over to the edge of the bridge.

The water was moving fast for this late in the summer. Jumbled gushes of brown water were threading together and pulling apart in a chaotic run as they spilled over rocks, old car frames, and railroad ties, just as, in due time, they would a headless statue of Jesus. Morning comes slow in the hills, so the sun had just risen over the east ridges and was flashing through the trees like it was taking pictures. Of the hills. Of the bridge. Of the water. Of me. I stood there and let the sunlight take its picture. I hadn't showered, and I had slept in my clothes, but I still felt pretty. I breathed in the railroad tar and old dirt smells that the breeze was praying into the daylight. I let the mossy air floating up off the restless creek water brush against my bare arms. I held them out in front of me, noticing how strong my hands were, thinking for the first time that they looked like the hands of a grown man as I stretched them out in the creamy light. These were arms that could dig a ditch if they needed. On my wrist, the silver letters stamped into the knitted rainbow of my "What Would Jesus Do?" bracelet flickered warmly under the sun.

Everybody loved Jesus, and yet despite that love he was standing just a few miles downstream of me surrounded by fighting roosters without even his own head, pieces of his shattered face sinking further into the mud. And here I was, just some young, queer hillbilly, looking pretty good with his new highlights, getting phone numbers, going to college, and decidedly not shot and decidedly in possession of a face, eyes, and a mouth. And strong forearms. I eased the tension of the strip of fabric, then pulled the rainbow colors through the little plastic buckle until the band was free. I took off the bracelet, stepped onto the bridge, just feet above where Shawn would hold my hand as passing trains remade the world, and flung it as far as I could and watched it get eat up by the wildness of the creek.

BLOWING DANDELIONS

Thirsty countryside trees
dropped crumbling leaves
like they were memories
like they were too tired
from years of working
midnights at the hospital
to hold on.

The slack creek slowed
and curved around
the hillside
dragging mud
and pushing garbage
toward what we knew
had to be the Mississippi.

I liked the way you looked
when you took off your shirt
and threw off your shoes—
you were all lines
and fine clean edges
what I could fall off of
what I could hide behind
and we would tiptoe
into the creek water
that got to touch your feet
and sometimes even run
its cursive hands
across the fresh muscle
of your tanned cream legs.

But the creek was warm,
thick fish sweat suspended.
So long as I didn't
tell the other boys,
you and I could blow
dandelions into the dead wind,
squatting under the trailer
where dogs had tore up the underpinning.
I said I couldn't do it like you
because I was missing my front teeth.
Your lungs were strong.
Your parachute-men-seed wisps spiraled
fast and reckless into the heat,
daring for the sky.
But mine arced dead
toward the gravel at our feet.

MATCHING TUXEDOS

Mosely. Fox Creek. Spring 2003.

"Wait a second, now. Am I going to the prom with you because you're gay, or are you going to prom with me cause I'm fat?" Melissa wobbled the corded computer mouse across a library desk that housed a half dozen computers in a row, trying to force the cursor to move. Her friend Jamie Conn, in a slim burgundy button-up and tight jeans, had arranged himself on the desk in front of the computer beside hers. His long and angular legs were stretched out and crossed, the heels of his feet tilting back the chair in front of him. Posters of teen celebrities from the eighties and nineties watched him from the walls, where they held books and were framed by pithy sayings about the importance of reading. Jamie looked like he was in the middle of a photo shoot. Melissa did not. Physically, she was his opposite: short and round, hidden in an oversized black Linkin Park T-shirt she'd worn at least once a week since her mom took her to a concert all the way down in Tennessee last year. Unlike him, she was firmly planted, sitting in the sort of metal-framed plastic chair found in public high school libraries. She was pulling her shoulders together, leaning forward toward a computer monitor.

Jamie waved his free top foot from side to side in a distracted little dance. "Honey, you ain't fat. You just curvy." He was looking upward, nearly reclined and inspecting his nails with outstretched hands, creating the odd effect of making him appear to be searching the sky for something, except that nothing was above them but fluorescent lights and the decaying industrial tiles of the dropped ceiling of the Mosely High School Library.

"Jamie, look at this. Curves ain't supposed to jiggle." Melissa took her hand off the mouse and shook her arm dramatically, waving the fat slipping out from under her shirt sleeve. She pulled her lip up and raised one eyebrow, challenging him to disagree. With her dark eyeshadow and short hair parted with snap clips, Jamie thought she already looked like she could be somebody's mom.

"Every girl's arms jiggles."

"And how would you know? It ain't like you been inviting no girls under them bleachers after basketball games."

Jamie used his sneaker to ease down the chair his feet were resting on, leaning in toward Melissa and whittling his voice down to a wide whisper. "Hush, now, before somebody hears. And sad thing is, he didn't even show up no how. I waited forever under them dirty old bleachers. Just me and the dust. And *he* was the one," Jamie flattened his upturned palm and extended it forward, pointing to an imaginary Jason Miller, "who invited *me.*" On the word *me*, he flung his hand toward himself in an eruptive gesture like he was indignantly reciting the pledge of allegiance, his open palm collapsing against the part of his chest exposed by the unbuttoned part of his shirt. His shush was pure drama—they were the only two at the computer station. In fact, the only other person in the entire library was a string-haired goth girl in black clothes hiding in the corner, headphones over her ears and a book in her hands. It was an old book with a solid cover, like the kind a teacher might make copies out of. The rest of the other students were at lunch, but Melissa had brought Jamie in to show him something on the computer.

"You really expect me to believe that Jason Miller asked you under the bleachers on Friday? Jason Miller!? And when was he even supposed to come? Ain't he on the team?" She was scrolling through her Yahoo email while she talked, being more playful than contradictory, but Jamie still felt a little sting. Melissa was his only confidant—without her, he'd be totally alone at school, in the holler, in life, really.

"Hell, don't go acting like I know anything about tournament basketball. But I do know he was supposed to come after the game, said they don't push the bleachers back up till Sunday. And you can believe what you wanna believe. He just chickened out."

As he spoke, Melissa opened an email and then clicked something. "Well, anyway, here. Look. The Bridal Shop puts up pictures of all their dresses on the internet now. You can look at em before you even go in. Alright, what do you think a this? Be honest. Is this one too much?" Jamie pivoted around to look with her. On the screen was a picture of a voluminous midnight blue chiffon ball gown with a violet-sequined sweetheart bodice. The sequins flowed down onto the chiffon, tapering off like stars sprinkled in the dark. Melissa clicked and a second image appeared, this time of a nondescript teenage girl standing in the dress against a white background. "Well?"

"Girl. It's beautiful. And listen, I mean, it's okay on her. Heck fire, it'd even look pretty on me. But, I ain't gonna lie. That dress is gonna be absolutely beautiful on you. That cut right there, it's perfect for you. That's the dress. And it looks like stars!"

"Shew, Libras like shiny things, Jamie, and you know I do love the stars. But, you don't think it's too much? I mean, I can get a little shawl or something to cover my arms."

Jamie turned from the screen to his friend. "Mel, you know I ain't gonna lie about chiffon gowns, Loretta Lynn, or what I do or don't do with Jason Miller. And I'm telling you, it's perfect. But promise me one thing."

"What?"

"You won't cover your arms unless you're just cold."

The doors to the library flung open and a tall clump of loud boys in jerseys plowed their way to the librarian's desk. One smacked another across the shoulder with a math book as the rest laughed in obnoxious little chokes. The string-haired goth girl looked up from her book. Jamie watched them, his head fixed in their direction, his caramel-colored eyes passing along the length of their bodies as they knocked and shoved each other across the room. Melissa closed the window on the screen. "You still didn't answer my question. Am I going to the prom with you because you're gay, or are you going to prom with me cause I'm fat?"

Jamie turned from the boys, who had now swelled around the return desk and were competing to see who could touch the ceiling. One of them pretended to hump the book return slot while another cheered him on. "We're going together," Jamie hopped down off the desk and smoothed his button-up in careful waves, "because everybody else is a idiot."

Jamie and Melissa had managed to finagle identical schedules from the time they were sophomores, but they didn't have class together the last block this year. Upperclassmen got their choice of four math classes.

Melissa was taking Life Math, which you only took if you didn't really plan on having one. Jamie had heard they spent the whole first month just learning how to write checks, and the next month how to balance those checks, which seemed to him another way to say practicing numbers followed by addition and subtraction. The smart kids took Calculus or Trigonometry, and Jamie didn't even know enough about what those were to make snarky cracks about them. But they did offer one class called College Prep Math, made for people who were not great with numbers but who had dreams of getting out. Of having a life. That was Jamie: not smart enough for the smart kids, but he had dreams. He had already applied and been accepted to the community college the next county over—a county big enough for a community college and a Walmart. He might save some money, maybe share an apartment with somebody, work a little, maybe eventually transfer to a four-year school like Morehead State or Eastern Kentucky. No big fancy place too far away. Not somewhere they'd snicker at his accent or not know what a holler was. Just somewhere with all the stuff like you see on TV: dorm rooms and sidewalks and places where you can sit outside and order a coffee.

But first, he'd have to get through his last month of high school.

The teacher was out for the day and they stuck a coach man in front of the classroom. That meant the noise of pregame interviews clunked out of his little radio across the classroom while the students did worksheets in groups—which meant that a total of four students were actually doing any work at all. Jamie distracted himself from the piercing sports fervor of the postseason tournament by making himself one of those who were working. He was humming a Tammy Wynette medley and staring at a sheet of polynomials while Mandi Gunnell, a junior sitting to his right, flirted with a dumb-looking boy with cutoff sleeves and a long, greasy mullet. She took breaks every few minutes to copy down Jamie's answers.

She picked her cheap blue ballpoint pen back up and made a sour face at him. "Jamie, this is so hard I don't even know how to copy off you." He lifted his hands off the paper so she could see it better. "What even is this? Where are you even getting them numbers from?"

"It's just like we done yesterday. FOIL: first, outer, inner, last. You just gotta times em in that order."

"Times what?"

"F. The first parts. That one starts with a x. And that one does, too. So that's two x, x times x. That's x squared."

"You actually understand this?"

"Not really." As soon as he answered, Jamie didn't know if he was being humble, funny, or truthful. He *did* know how to follow the steps like they were told to memorize them. He *didn't* know what to do if there was a single deviation from the order of things, a new exponent or some unknown element. He didn't know what any of it amounted to, what it stood for. But he hoped he'd sort that out in college someday.

"Well, I'm just gonna wait till you're done to copy it. This is a buncha bullshit. Shew, buddy. I'll be glad to get outta this place next year."

Mandi turned back to the mullet boy and grabbed his arm. Something caught Jamie's eye. A white something, bobbing up and down on the other side of the window above the door. It was a sheet of notebook paper. *JAMIE!* was written on it in massive block letters. Jamie looked around. Mandi was now drawing a tattoo on the mullet boy's bicep, her own name in thick, bubbly cursive. The rest of his classmates were otherwise occupied with the radio, with math, or with copying down someone else's math. He walked to the front of the room and asked to go to the bathroom.

"Take the pass." The coach man at the teacher's desk was one of many men hired in various positions around the district—assistant teacher, curriculum advisor, student behavior specialist—whose only real purpose was to coach. The school would bring them in under any pretense for the sake of sports; even the students could see this. Jamie didn't bother learning their names because he had no reason to interact with them and because his knowing their names increased the likelihood that they would know his. These guys were all the same, so he didn't want to take the risk of being noticed. The coach man gestured at a blue plastic card on a string. Jamie took it. "And no smoking."

He stepped outside the classroom to find Melissa holding her long pink lanyard, which ended with two keys and a dozen or so trinkets, one of which was a pewter cast of the scales of justice, her astrological sign, that she had her uncle solder into a keychain. She was swaying them like she was in a hurry.

Jamie looked around for teachers. "Is something wrong?"

"No. I told Mr. Spoon I had my period. He just turned purple and told me to leave. He won't ask questions. I'm gonna sneak out early. You still gonna order your tux today?"

"Yeah. I'm heading over after school."

"Listen, I gotta run with mommy over to Pikeville. I plumb forgot I was supposed to go pick up my little cousin Nathan and take him to order his. Order's gotta be in today."

"Who's your little cousin Nathan?"

"You know him—Nathan Hackworth. Didn't he used to live across the road from you?"

"Wait—that Nathan? How is he little? Last time I saw him he was like six feet tall."

"Well, I'm a year ahead a him, technically, cause he's a Scorpio, so he didn't start school when we did cause he wasn't old enough for kindergarten, even though I'm only a month older."

"Wait, what's he got to do with anything?"

"Shew, I talked him into taking Ashley Slone to prom, but his starter went out last week. He ain't got no sense neither, so I don't trust him to do it by hisself, so will you just run him up there and make sure he gets the exact same tux as you?"

"You want us to wear matching tuxes?"

"Ain't nobody gonna notice. They all pretty much look the same, but you know what looks good. It ain't like y'all gonna be taking a prom picture together, so it don't matter. Plus, Ashley's wearing a dark dress and when I showed her yours she said it was perfect."

Jamie looked at the round analog clock jutting out of the wall of the hallway. School let out in half an hour. "I'll run out and get him. His family still live out by Danny Mullins over on Fox Creek?"

"Yeah, that little yellow house down past the bus garage."

"He know I'm coming?"

"His school lets out early on Fridays. I'll call him and tell him as soon as I get home."

Jamie told people he drove a boat. Technically, it was a late '80s tan-colored Buick Regal that his mom helped him buy off a man at church for $500 when the man's mom died. But it was big and square, with carpeted insides that made it feel like you were stepping into a yacht. Nothing Jamie did could make it stop smelling like an old woman; decades of sunlight had baked a peony-based perfume into the carpet and interior as it washed away their colors. He was only eighteen, but this was already Jamie's third car. However, it was his first car that was built after the year of his birth.

He had just turned onto Fox Creek. Fox Creek eventually ran into Beaver Creek, which is where Jamie and most of his cousins lived, in the same bottom between the hills where his papaw and his papaw's papaw had lived. Precious flat land that had once been used for farming was now divided up among children and grandchildren and the half-dozen families who bought a lot when somebody sold out, so now trailers and little houses clung together in the dry space between the hills and creek.

Jamie hadn't really talked to Nathan Hackworth in years. When they were kids, maybe eight or nine or so, there was a large group of teenage boys—neighbors, cousins—who would drink beer, ride motorcycles, and otherwise swarp up and down the holler in a kind of gang. Jamie and Nathan idolized them, but they were both too young to be included in anything they did. There were some young kids, babies through five-year-olds, that would ride bicycles or play in the dirt, but neither Jamie nor Nathan could be caught dead playing with them, being self-respecting third and then fourth graders, so they kept each other company in the hours and months when school wasn't in session, going down to the creek, telling each other stories, or playing video games.

Jamie slowed down for a steep curve. A white dog standing in front of a duplex apartment came running toward his car like it had some kind of chance to catch him, barking wildly. Jamie couldn't see it as he drove by, his car being so big, so he slowed to a crawl, growing frustrated at the dog's willingness to take on an entire automobile as he drove past its yaps, the dog heard and not seen. He passed it by, finally seeing it appear, and then shrink, in the rearview. It stood in a fury of confrontation, aggressively gnashing its teeth by the curve, its snout spasming up and down, its head thrown back demanding he return and fight. Jamie accelerated around a curve. "Screw you, you little bitch. I don't owe you shit." He laughed at his own voice. He didn't know why he was so frustrated with it. It was just being a dog. And

Jamie liked dogs as much as the next person, even dogs like that one that pretty much hate you before they even know you.

Nathan had a dog when they were kids, an enormous, friendly collie mix named Finley that followed them everywhere. Finley liked to dash ahead of them and always seemed to know where they were going. Many mornings, he would walk straight up to the door to be let into Jamie's house minutes before Nathan arrived, like some kind of herald. Jamie learned to associate the dog with the coming arrival of his friend. Nathan always kept a hand near that collie, stroking his neck, scratching the base of his ear, or just resting his back on the dog's back as they sat together. In rare moments of excitement, or when Nathan seemed to forget that he and Jamie went to the same school and so therefore Jamie could talk about such things in front of other people, he would even drop to the ground and hug that dog around the neck.

Nathan did not hug Jamie. They were not exactly the most likely of friends. In fact, had either of them had options, they'd not have hung out together. Nathan was boyish, pure and simple. Jamie wanted to pretend the cattails by the creek were witches and listen to their spells and write them down. Nathan wanted to pretend they were pirates and attack them. Jamie wanted to make wishes on dandelions. Nathan wanted to make swords with them after they were blown bare. Jamie wanted to play *Zelda.* Nathan wanted to play *Street Fighter.* Jamie wanted to stack rocks and build towns and bridges with them. Nathan wanted to throw them and see if they could hit the boulder that jutted out of the hillside just above Jamie's mamaw's trailer.

Instead of taking turns with each other's wishes, they'd often do whatever Nathan wanted to do, since, even if it wasn't interesting to Jamie, there was a certain exhilaration and affirmation of worth for him to be included by someone who ordinarily would not have included him. And even in fourth grade, he was drawn to Nathan's boyishness. Sometimes, however, they'd expand their interests in whatever common pleasures they had, like drawing, kids' shows, or swimming in the creek. When middle school came, Nathan's family moved away. Jamie didn't even remember the moment it happened. There was no grand goodbye. No letters, calls, or promises to keep in touch. Nathan's family was there one day and just wasn't the next. Jamie went to Mosely Middle, and Nathan to what they called the Opportunity School, where they taught welding, mechanics, and other skills for boys whose minds were made for machines. But Mosely was a small town in a small county. They'd pass each other every now and then at Walmart or a gas station and give each other a nod. And now Jamie was driving to Nathan's house to take him to pick out a tuxedo rental.

Jamie pulled into the driveway. A tiny one-story clapboard house with peeling lemon-colored paint looked tired in front of a hillside. The grass was neatly cut, and a row of rose of Sharon bushes divided the road from the yard. They were just starting to bloom, the earliest peeks of pink and white buds blinking from inside the green. Summer was coming soon. Jamie cut the ignition, opened his door, but before he closed it back a brown-haired teenager shot out of a screen door and hopped off the porch, ignoring the steps. Jamie stood in between the open door and the vehicle, not in, not out.

He was no one's little Nathan. He was definitely over six feet tall, and his shoulders were now wide, sharp, and holding up a white tank top that hung loosely over a pair of jeans. What had been slightly angular features were now solidly square ones. The smooth waves of his neat, short hair brought out the blueness of his eyes and made his beard stubble look coarser and more pronounced. Nathan easily looked five years older than Jamie, even if they were effectively the same age. Jamie suddenly became aware of the soft, rarely shaven fluff on his own face.

"Hey." Jamie tried to control his voice a bit, to sound more like any other eighteen-year-old guy and less like himself, but his throat was drier than he knew, causing the word to slide downward in an awkward pitch and end in a sort of cough. Nathan didn't seem to notice.

"Man, I can't believe she made you come out here. It ain't that big a deal."

"Oh, it's fine. I was heading up there anyway."

"I mean, I have a truck. Just a no-good starter is all. My uncle's gonna gimme a free one'll fit it. That's why I ain't went out and bought one yet. He's supposed to be up here by the weekend." Nathan opened the passenger door while he was talking and slid into the car before Jamie had got back in.

Jamie followed him. Nathan kept on talking. He was speaking with a boyish glee, scanning the interior of the car, running his hand over the dashboard as he spoke. Jamie remembered this quality—this willingness for enthusiasm that Nathan held for the world. He felt something inside himself opening back up.

Nathan said, "Hey, man, this is a nice car."

Jamie started it. "Listen, no need to flatter me. I'm already taking you to order your tux. If I didn't, Mel and Ashley would both kill me."

Nathan swept a row of white teeth into a large smile. "No, these old Buicks are solid." He patted the console with his right hand, running his left hand along the smooth run of fabric that separated their bodies. Jamie thought of the surely now long-dead collie. "And don't worry about Mel or Ashley. I'll protect you."

Jamie backed out of the driveway, the softness of the seat a faint buzz against his thighs as the old car vibrated over the gravel drive. Nathan turned on the radio and changed the station, drumming with youthful excitement as a rock song pumped out of the speakers. "Hey! Do you like 3 Doors Down?"

Jamie nodded and put it in drive.

Most girls drove out to Battersburg, Pikeville, or even Lexington to get a prom dress, but boys could just go to Mosely to order a tux at Martin's. It was what was left of the many local clothing stores that once dotted the towns in eastern Kentucky. Jamie's grandmother said that when she was a girl, the owners would drive to Lexington or even to Huntington, West Virginia, and pick out clothes for certain families, buying them pants and hats and dresses before they even asked if the people wanted them. But folks would take them because there was no other option and because the clothes buyers knew their customers so well they'd almost always make the right choice.

Most local clothing stores shut their doors when the coal mines started shutting theirs. Big stores like Walmart and Kmart opened, but Martin's managed to stay downtown by figuring out exactly what those stores didn't sell and offering it on purpose. They had selections of real leather boots and hats, bridles, and saddles. They kept heavy-duty coats and pants for jobs that required them, even rubber knee pads and hard hats. There was a section for big and tall men by the dressing rooms, and in that section was a pair of dress pants so large that they hung on the wall from two separate clothes hangers. Jamie's cousin told him once—when they were waiting on their moms to buy all the men their boots for Christmas—that the man who ordered the pants had died before they finished making them, so now they just hung around waiting for another man in town to get that big.

Jamie and Nathan entered the storefront, a little bell ringing to announce them. Jamie looked immediately to the back wall for the pants on the two hangers. They were there, as always, but the row of dressing rooms had been replaced by tanning beds. A sturdy but tired-looking twenty-something woman in a maroon vest was folding neon safety shirts and stacking them on a display table.

"Can I help you boys?"

Jamie spoke. "Yeah, we're just here to order some prom tuxes."

"Lemme get the catalog."

She lugged a thick and glossy book onto the counter. Jamie reached for it, then she pulled it back. "Nope. Wait. That's the Summer Catalog. It's still May. Summer ain't till June 21st. Did you boys know that?" They both looked at her, and before Jamie could respond, she said, "Hold on, let me switch it out with the right one." Jamie nodded in silent agreement as she brought down a second catalog. She opened it to a bookmarked section and pushed it across the counter toward him. There were full-color images of teenage boys in formal wear. The woman said, "They tell you what color to get or if you need a cummerbund or vest?"

Jamie leaned across the table and flipped through the book confidently. Nathan stood near a rack of pearl-button cowboy shirts over by the boots, anxiously moving the same few shirts back and forth. Jamie stopped on a page and dropped his index finger onto a picture of the one he wanted, worn by a boy with frosted-tip highlights in a full-color spread. The boy in the picture wasn't shown with a date. Not even an environment. The photo was just him against a solid white background, his context fully removed. To his side was a box with sizes, descriptions, and prices. Jamie pointed to the well-dressed boy against the white background. "This one here, with the ivory shirt, but no vest."

"Do you know your sizes, honey, or do you need to be measured?"

Jamie rattled off his jacket, pants, and shirt sizes, even his neck and arm lengths, then handed her his bank card for the down payment. Most places around Mosely only took cash, so he always became excited when he had the chance to use it, feeling very much like an adult. He motioned for Nathan. "Hey, it's your turn."

Nathan stepped over to the counter. A thin line of sweat was forming on the top of his forehead. Jamie showed him the picture of the tux he had just ordered. "Ashley said for you to get this'n, here."

Nathan swiped his forehead with the back of his hand. "Okay."

The woman in the maroon vest copied some numbers on a piece of paper, then said, "Do you know your sizes, son?"

"My pants is a 34. I usually wear a large shirt just cause they're more comfortable." He rocked himself as he spoke, rolling his foot onto his tiptoes, causing his calves to tighten against his pant leg. The rocking was Nathan's nervous tick, one that Jamie had forgotten and now remembered, something Nathan did if a situation was testing his comfort. Jamie had found it just a part of who Nathan was when they were boys, but now seeing a nearly grown man intimidated by clothes, he found it oddly charming.

"Well, this is a tux, so we want to make sure it fits good. You want me to measure you?"

Nathan looked to Jamie like there was a right answer that he didn't know. His eyes were wide and the sweat had already returned to the top of his forehead. Jamie answered for him. "Yeah, that's probably easiest, don't you think, Nathan? That way, Ashley'll be happy."

"Good point."

The woman pulled a folded measuring tape from the back of the catalog they had been looking through and held it between her two hands. She grabbed Nathan's arm like he was a mannequin and pulled it tight without a word, employing an assertive indifference that told Jamie she probably did this with men twice her age and size. Holding his wrist like she was about to lead him in some old-fashioned dance, she ran the length of tape past his forearms and along the curve of his upper arm, landing her hand on his shoulder. She said a number. She pulled the tape tight along the ridge of his shoulders. Another number. She measured around his neck. Across his chest. Down the length of his back. Along the outside of his leg. A number, a number, a number.

She wrote them all down at once while they quietly waited. Nathan's eyes caught Jamie's, and Jamie realized he'd quite obviously been staring at Nathan's thigh where the woman in a maroon vest had last touched him. Jamie jerked his eyes away quickly, pretending to look at other things, as if his eye had only passed by that very part of Nathan's body by accident. He was now looking at the white-button cowboy shirts. In the silence, he could hear his own pulse, feel it traveling in a tense and powerful rhythm through his arms and up his throat. He brought his gaze back from the shirts to the counter, intentionally passing by the same point he had earlier been staring at as a way to show that it just happened to be where his eyes fell as he turned. That it wasn't intentional. That it meant nothing. But when his eyes found the same place, Nathan's were still watching, waiting for him to return his gaze. For a very brief moment, they looked directly at each other.

A voice divided the silence. "Are you paying just the deposit or the whole thing, son?"

Nathan swung around to the counter, rocking his foot back down to a flat state. The woman was stapling two pieces of paper together. Nathan said, "Uh, the deposit. I've got the cash." He paid, and she told them both to be sure to come back in two weeks, to ask for Tammy, and to arrive early in case they needed alterations.

As soon as they got outside, Nathan turned to Jamie. "Hey, you hungry? Wanna eat something? I'll get it, since you drove."

"Sure."

They got value meals at the Dairy Queen, which was technically the only restaurant in Mosely, unless you counted the two benches in the back of the Pack-n-Save or the gas station snacks and sandwiches at the Fast-n-Fill. When they sat down, it started to rain, so they just stayed there and talked. The ice in their drinks melted as their chitchat turned to reminiscing. Jamie pointed out that they hadn't eaten together in nearly a decade, not since back in third or fourth grade, when Nathan's mom would make huge breakfasts on Sunday mornings: fried bologna, gravy, drop biscuits, eggs, and fried potatoes. Nathan said that saying it like that, using the word *decade*, made it seem like they were already old or something. They laughed. They talked about the games they used to play and people and moments they remembered from when they were small. In a strange way, their time apart was not a hindrance for Jamie but was instead an unexpected advantage. He felt an intense nostalgia, an emotion that, being a high school senior, was new to him. It warmed the surface of whatever friendship they had had, sewing meaning throughout events and stories he hadn't given thought to before. They talked about what they had been doing since grade school. Nathan had been doing the automotive track. He was good at it. He wanted to open a garage someday, save some money, maybe move somewhere a little bigger than this, somewhere closer to a city. They spent hours refilling time gaps and emptied drinks, remembering what was and imagining what could be.

A worker came over to tell them that they closed the dining room at 9:30. They thanked her and left. The rain had stopped, and the air now felt cool and new.

As they got back in the car, Nathan said, "See man? Right there. It's 9:30, and there ain't a place in Mosely to go and do nothing, not even eat a cheeseburger."

Jamie pulled onto Main Street. "Yeah, it's part a why I gotta get outta here, too."

"Shew. Remember all them older guys we used to be afraid to talk to?"

"Remember em? Hell, half of em is my cousins."

"Well, then tell the truth. How many of em is on drugs?"

Jamie pulled them all up in his head and sorted them into categories. User. Maybe a user. Churchgoer. He turned onto Fox Creek. "It's funny. You know, I don't even smoke cigarettes. But heck . . . those guys? I bet at least half I know is, for sure."

"And let me ask you another one, then. Can you blame em?"

Jamie didn't answer immediately. He was always frustrated with the drug users, because he saw the chaos they created in his family: old women raising their own grandkids, worried parents, broken lives. He knew the right answer they were taught in health class—that drug abuse was a disease, that people had challenging circumstances, that most people who used actually wanted to quit. He knew about drug companies selling drugs to people. But that's not what Nathan was talking about. Jamie understood the point of the question—there really wasn't a whole lot to do around here.

He didn't get time to answer. The silence was interrupted by the barking of that same dog from earlier, which was just ahead of them, but not yet visible, on the right. It was dark now, and Jamie was driving much slower. "Shew, here we go. That stupid little bitch is back," he said, scanning the darkness for the oncoming source of the noise. Before Nathan could respond to him, a flash of white appeared feet in front of the car. The dog was standing directly in the road, its entire body daring the old Buick in an angry confrontation. Jamie slammed the brakes and the car began to spin out of control, sliding off the road and toward the creek. He lifted his hands off the wheel, throwing his right arm back in front of the passenger seat in an instinctive and protective manner, securing Nathan across the chest. Nathan leaned over and knocked the transmission up to neutral, grabbing the wheel and pushing it deftly into the direction of the skid. The wheels shrieked and the right side of the Buick slid into the guardrail, bringing the car to a stop with a concentrated jerk.

Both boys stared ahead, the ripple of their hurried breathing suspended above the sound of the motor in the otherwise silent car. The inky darkness of the holler waved in the heat fanning up from the hood and into the post-rain humidity.

"Nathan, you okay?"

"Yeah. I'm good. You okay?"

"Yeah." Emotion split Jamie's words into wet fragments that fell back against themselves in his throat. "I'm so sorry."

"Hey. No, you did good. You didn't hit that dog. And throwing your hands up, that's what everybody does. And you even took your foot off the brake when we started sliding. Not everybody thinks to do that." Nathan's voice was calm, even. Jamie just wanted him to keep speaking. "And you drive a solid old car. I mean, that's good. That's all good. You did good."

The car had come to a stop on the shoulder of the curve, and the white dog was now standing in its own yard, barking triumphantly from directly in front of two wild shrubs that looked like they were ready to back him up in a fight.

Jamie was shaking, staring directly ahead at the porchlight of a house on the other side of the creek, feeling outside of himself. Like he was remembering this instead of experiencing it. A clasp of warmth brought him back. He realized that his right hand was still pressed tightly against Nathan's chest and tangled in the fabric strips of his tank top. Nathan had brought his own hand to Jamie's.

"Oh, I'm sorry. I wasn't trying to be weird. I'm just used to driving my little brother to school. It was just instinct." Nathan did not remove Jamie's hand. Instead, he wrapped his own over it, covering Jamie's clenched fist with his warm palm. He pressed toward his body in a curved motion with the base of his thumb, opening Jamie's fist until it slid under the shirt and was stretched out like a reclining body across the surface of his chest and the top of his abdomen.

"It's okay. You can keep it there."

They sat, silent, listening to the sound of each other's increasingly calm breaths while the hum of the engine flooded over them. Jamie could feel the heat of Nathan's chest against his palm, feel the rise and fall of his breath, feel the electricity jump as each breath in brought the edge of Nathan's stomach to meet the fingertips of his outstretched hand. The fresh spice of excited perspiration flickered in the space between them.

The barks grew suddenly louder and more accusatory. Jamie looked over his shoulder, and a man had appeared on the doorstep of the duplex, where the white dog joined him. He was large and shirtless and the door behind him stood open to a dark interior. He hollered out, "Y'all okay?"

Jamie rolled down the window with his left hand, unwilling to remove his right from Nathan's skin. He yelled back. "Yeah. We're fine."

The man waved back in response and then cussed at the dog to get on in the house. The dog barked at him just once, like it was cussing back, then it ran into the unlit space behind the opening. The man followed behind it and closed the door.

Jamie imagined the man and the dog continuing their argument, and the absurdity and tension of the entire night spilled over onto his face, across his skin, down his arms. He began to laugh, first a diluted chuckle, but as Nathan began to laugh, too, the chuckle grew to such forceful laughter growing from his belly that he had to bring both hands to hold on to the steering wheel and catch his breath. Their bodies vibrated in childish giggling that fluttered out the open window and freed itself into the damp air of the holler.

Eventually, the laughter slowed. Jamie checked for traffic, then pulled forward onto the road, driving another couple of minutes and then turning left into Nathan's yard. This late at night, he couldn't see the yellow of the house or the roses of Sharon along the edge of the road, but his mind was actively mapping their presence and superimposing their echoes onto the blackness of the yard.

He cut off the engine. Neither boy had spoken since they pulled away.

Nathan opened his door, sat without moving for a second, then turned. "Hey."

"Yeah."

"You wanna come in?"

"Sure."

Jamie spent the next two weeks with a boy he had spent years of his childhood with, but this unexpected time had brought a newness that life had never given him, a reason that he had never before given himself the license to imagine. He and Nathan shared every possible minute together; he hadn't seen Melissa outside of school at all. They played the same video games at Nathan's house as they used to. They told each other the same stories. Jamie even stayed over and had breakfast at Nathan's house on Sunday morning. Same mom. Same fried bologna. Same drop biscuits. Same fried potatoes. Same gravy.

But nothing was the same.

They took long drives up and down the hollers and through town. In the familiar warmth of the car, Nathan would reach for Jamie's hand and hold it against his chest as they barreled alongside the creeks and in the shade cast by the hills. Jamie would do the same for Nathan, and it quickly became their ritual, their tenderness, their affirmation that something had always been and that something new had happened.

And there was other stuff, too. It was slow, even awkward. But no matter how awkward, there was no way to compare it to anything that may have happened under any bleacher. They would lay together in Nathan's bed, first just letting their feet touch as they played video games. Then, slowly, their legs. Then their entire bodies, bringing together as much skin as they could, sinking into each other and melting into something. Every action was built of constraint, question, and meaning. They lacked a script. They lacked words. Every gesture was a step into a space that had never existed before, and every returned gesture a response, a willingness to create a world and to say to the other, *I want you to be in it with me.*

They hadn't even kissed. But it was good. So good that it gnawed at Jamie while he listened to Melissa talk about prom, it ate at him while his teachers talked about dividing polynomials, and it covered him like a quilt when Jason Miller, who only a week before Jamie had waited on for hours under a dirty set of bleachers, caught Jamie in the parking lot of the Fast-n-Fill and asked if he wanted to do something later. Jamie just thought of the feeling of his palm on the chest of the same boy he used to fight cattails beside, the memory of the skin of Nathan's chest warming his own as they lay together without words, unspeaking, unmoving, unbeing in his bed, and he was able to tell even Jason Miller that no, he had other plans.

Juniors and seniors got to leave school at noon the day of prom since the girls needed time to do their hair. Jamie drove straight home and put on his tux. He even shaved just so he could use aftershave. He put gel in his hair, tried to style it, decided it was too much gel, took the suit off, washed and dried his hair, put the suit back on, then did his hair again, this time adding miniscule amounts of product at a time to make sure it was perfect.

It was perfect.

It was Friday. Nathan's school would already be out. Jamie called him.

"Hey, you home already?"

"Well, I hope so. If not, who answered the phone?"

"Good point. Hey, do me a favor."

"Sure. What you need?"

"Put on your tux now."

"Alright. Will do, but listen. You're gonna have to do me a favor."

"What?"

"Come help me. Cause . . . I can't figure out how to put this thing on. I mean, there's buttons and holes I ain't never seen before. I am not the man for this."

Jamie was at Nathan's door in under ten minutes. He knocked.

Nathan called out from his bedroom, but the house was small and his voice boomed. "Come on in! I'm in my room."

Jamie usually took his shoes off at people's houses, but he had shined up some boots he borrowed off his dad and didn't want Nathan to see him without the full effect—or the added two inches of height, which would bring him almost to Nathan's barefoot stature. He stepped in to see Nathan standing in his bedroom wearing only black socks and boxer shorts. He had seen him in his underwear before, of course. Just the day before, they had lain in bed with neither of them wearing more, but something about the fact that Jamie was dressed so formally made Nathan, standing only in his underwear, seem all the more nude, made the moment feel all the more intense. A different form of intimate. It was obvious they could both feel the energy.

Nathan turned away, then rocked forward off of his bare heel. He was holding a pair of pants in his left hand. "Hey, sorry. Wow. You look great in that suit. Let me put on some pants. I didn't know if I was supposed to do the shirt first or . . ."

Seeing him feel vulnerable caused Jamie to turn away, too. He felt suddenly anxious, like maybe he was pushing too fast. Like asking him to put on the suit meant something. He turned his face away. "Take your time. I'll show you the shirt. The buttons ain't as hard as they look."

"I'm good now."

Nathan was now wearing the pants and holding the shirt in one hand and a small plastic bag filled with accessories in the other.

"You've got to pull the pants up higher, up toward your belly button, not low like jeans." Jamie reached forward as if to pull them up onto Nathan's waist, then pulled his hands back. Nathan had already leaned his bare torso toward Jamie as if he was inviting the help. The horizontal tan line separating the olive skin of his back from the cream skin near his boxers hung in the air at an angle.

Nathan spoke calmly. "You okay?"

"Yeah. Just thinking about prom and stuff."

"Okay." Nathan grabbed the belt loops of his pants and jumped, lifting the waistline and landing in a solid masculine gesture. He held out the plastic bag he had been holding. "It came with these things."

"Here, let me show you." Nathan slid into his shirt, pulling his sleeves downward. Jamie straightened them, holding onto Nathan's upper arms and feeling their tautness, taking in the moment, pushing it all across and deep down into his memory like a net, trying to disperse his anxious happiness into all parts of himself. He brought the cuffs together and added the cuff links. Nathan watched him quietly assemble the sleeves. Jamie said, "Alright, now let me get the front buttons."

"It's good. I think I got this part."

Jamie froze. He worried he was being pushy, offering unwanted help, that he was shoving himself into a place he didn't belong, into spaces that weren't his. Nathan grabbed hold of the bottom of his shirt as if he was going to button it. Jamie stepped back. Nathan looked at Jamie, searching his face for something. Nathan's forehead smoothed and he stepped forward, releasing the bottom part of his shirt. He pulled Jamie into him, and his hands on Jamie's back directed Jamie's face against his chest in an embrace. Nathan brought Jamie softly and solidly against his skin. The two sides of Nathan's unbuttoned white shirt closed over Jamie like curtains shutting out the old world, creating a boundary that laid claim to something as yet unnamed. He dissolved into Nathan's chest. Clean skin. Deodorant. Body. A faint and familiar hint of black pepper. Nathan spoke, his tone soft but firm. "Stop stressing about stuff. Now what's the favor you wanted?"

Jamie pulled himself from Nathan. "Put on your jacket."

Nathan finished getting dressed, and Jamie motioned to the door. "I thought we could get a picture. Before the girls and all. You know. Just a boys picture."

"Okay."

They stepped outside in their tuxes. Jamie had a digital camera. He placed it on the hood of the Buick, set a timer, and then he and Nathan stood in front of the row of roses of Sharon lining the edge of the yard. They still were far from fully in bloom, but the buds might show up as a glittering hint of pink in the picture, and even if they didn't, the clean swath of greenery would make for a nice background. They stood close, their hands in their pockets, the outsides of their arms just touching, looking straight ahead. The camera snapped three times.

Jamie retrieved the camera from the hood and brought it back to Nathan. "Look."

Nathan smiled, "Hey! We're wearing twin tuxes."

Jamie smiled back. "We are." He put the camera in his pocket and walked to the car, standing tall and feeling confident in the height of the boots. "We'll see y'all at dinner? I've gotta run home and let my mom see me dressed up before everybody else or she'll beat me. Me and Mel'll find y'all."

"Sounds good to me."

Jamie drove away, a childhood dream left lingering above a row of bushes heavy with petals desperate to finally unfold and breathe in some light.

The before-prom activities were typical. Melissa and her mom stopped by Jamie's parents' house. It was agreed that her gown was beautiful and that she was beautiful in it. Her mother took awkward pictures, as did Jamie's parents; one involved him fashioning onto her wrist a corsage that she had picked out herself and brought with her. Neighbor children gawked and picked their noses. Neighbor women told them they made such a lovely couple. Neighbor men winked at him in some sort of knowing way, playing out the scene like they would with any other boy, though not a one of them believed that he and Melissa had any sexual chemistry. Any Pentecostal widow and her house cat could see that Jamie would never kiss a woman.

There weren't enough sit-down restaurants between Mosely and its surrounding towns to fit every student going to prom, so people got creative. Some just had fun with it and went to the Dairy Queen in their prom attire for the laughs. Some unlucky teens had dinner with their families at home. Others attended the formal banquets hosted by local churches. Jamie and Melissa wanted to feel fancy for the night, and neither one of them had any interest in going to church, so they had made reservations at the Holiday Inn restaurant in Battersburg early in the spring. Ashley and Nathan came, too. Jamie understood that their prom coupling was simply an arrangement that Melissa had made and that Nathan and Ashley had no feelings for each other. Besides, Ashley was no one's type, at least not yet. She had the emotional range of a lapdog and anyone looking at her would guess that she was the kind of girl who not only decorated her bedroom with ceramic unicorns but who still talked to them for comfort. The kind of girl who used fuzzy pencils and watched the television network for kids. She was sweet, but it was clear enough that she still saw boys as foreign creatures.

Jamie even understood, technically, why Nathan was paying so much attention to her, pulling back her chair and reminding her how beautiful she was. Asking her if she needed anything and if her food was good. Because that's what you do. Those are the lines of dialogue you are handed to say—and prom matters to girls, so it's important to try to make them feel special, especially if their date isn't their boyfriend. Especially if this was probably the first time a boy had ever taken her anywhere. On some level, it even made Jamie want Nathan more, seeing the breadth of his kindness for an awkward girl he barely knew. But he couldn't help feeling jealous every time Ashley laughed at something Nathan said or when Nathan told her how pretty her hair looked.

But he didn't want to risk ruining anything.

So he smiled. He made people laugh. He ate overpriced pasta.

And after dessert, the young men paid what was owed, and they went to prom.

On television, high school proms were filled with actors in their thirties, and those proms necessarily fell along two possibilities: either the gym looked like some dreamlike fantasy land and everyone marveled at how it could be so magically transformed, or the gym still looked like a gym, and everyone complained. Jamie decided that this was somewhere between the two, except that the teens were indeed actual teens, and so it was therefore neither. The Mosely High School gym prom looked nice. It was a gym, nobody would say otherwise, but it was nice. There was a dance floor, there was music, there were streamers and glittery decorations and evidently a smoke machine. They were playing soft music while people filtered in and took pictures under the balloon arch. Jamie and Melissa staked out a table, and Ashley and Nathan soon followed. They commented on the decorations and how nice everyone looked.

The soft music tapered off, followed by a scratching noise, and after only three notes Jamie bolted up. "Well, come on y'all. It's Britney. It's now or never. Let's dance."

Melissa was holding on to her purse. "Jamie, I don't know. My arms'll be everywhere. People'll stare at me."

Jamie cocked his head to the side. "Can I be blunt?"

"Of course. You're a Capricorn. When have you ever had to ask?"

"Ain't nobody gonna look at your arms, Mel. Honestly, they're gonna be too busy looking at your boobies."

The whole table laughed, and Melissa pulled her eyebrows up just slightly. "Okay. But you gotta make me look good."

"You already look good. And remember, everybody else is idiots anyway."

They took to the floor and started dancing. The music pumped through the air and the air lifted with static. A few others were there already, moving under a string of lights that reflected off of decorations wrapped along the walls. Jamie noticed Melissa holding her arms to her side. He took her hand. "May I twirl you, my lady?"

"You're going to anyway."

"But may I?"

"Please, sir."

He spun her under his arm and back. A few people clapped and whistled. She started to truly dance. Ashley and Nathan soon joined, and the four of them gave in to the moment. They were turning together and swaying as a group, facing each other like the four corners of some temporary space set into motion, coming alive. They leaned in toward each other to sing the more dramatic lyrics. They held each other's shoulders and swayed. The group cheered itself on until the rest of the people in the crowded gymnasium formed a colorful background, sequins against tuxes twinkling like stars in the evening sky of some distant planet. It was a dream. Jamie understood the limits of the evening, but when they locked eyes, brushed arms, or would momentarily face one another and sway in the same directions, Jamie would get caught up and feel like he was actually dancing with Nathan. Like he was moving to music on the surface of an impossible world with a multicolor sky where two boys could look at and touch each other in a crowded sea of strangers and let the beats wash them away until they, too, were part of the sky like everyone else, stars in constellations with names. Life opened up as a bigger thing than Jamie thought it could be. His mind became a map with roads appearing from nowhere, with new bridges, with passes and cut-throughs clearing away mountains. He let the music flow through his body and was nowhere and no time and also grateful to be here, right now.

Eventually, they had to take a break. Another slow song started, so they joined the crowd of decked-out high schoolers in dispersing toward the scattered tables, leaving the dance floor for the actual couples who just wanted to lean against each other in public.

Jamie spoke loudly across the noise of the room. "I'm gonna go get a drink. Y'all need anything?"

Ashley grabbed her purse. "Me and Mel's gonna go to the bathroom."

Nathan leaned back in his chair, one arm folded behind his head. "I'm good, man. They left bottles of water. But thanks."

It was strange to see everybody in such a new context. There were teachers in dresses and coach men in jackets, actually smiling. People he hadn't spoken to in years smiled at him and said, "Hey, Jamie!" or "Nice moves!" He waved at Mandi Gunnell, who had somehow managed to get that mullet boy in a button-up shirt. Jamie finally made his way over to the bleachers, where they had set up a long row of drinks on a folding table.

Jason Miller was standing beside the punch bowl, drinking from a clear plastic cup and eyeing a tray of assorted chocolates. He wore an expensive gray suit that had been tailored to fit him exactly, made with clean piping that accentuated his athletic build down to the last detail. He had clearly not ordered his tux from a catalog in Mosely.

Jamie grabbed a cup from a stack and smiled at him. "Hey, Jason. Nice suit. Having a good night?"

Jason finished the drink and nodded. "Yeah. It's alright. You?"

"Yeah. Music's good." Jamie gulped down the punch, then refilled the glass. The dancing had made him thirsty.

Jason watched him for a second, then stood closer. He lowered his voice, as if he were asking for a cigarette in a school bathroom. "Hey. You wanna go check out the library with me? There ain't nobody there."

Jamie took a step in so he wouldn't have to yell over the music. "Hey, you know what, I gotta get back to my friends. We're just having some fun. But have a good night, man."

"I see how it is. You brought your little dick-sucking boyfriend to prom and now you think you're hot shit."

The music suddenly blurred into a discordant noise and Jamie felt icy pins holding him in space. He took a breath. Stepped back. "He ain't my boyfriend. This ain't about you. I'm just trying to enjoy tonight, is all."

Jason's voice now raised. "You know what, fuck you, you little faggot."

The ice pins were gone. Jamie lunged toward Jason, who was much faster than him, and he fell directly into the punchbowl. The bowl and table tumbled toward the bleachers as Jamie crashed into them both, razing the table to the floor in a husky blow that smacked and echoed across the gym. Red punch splashed across his white shirt and jacket, then ran along the length of the floor in front of the bleachers. A small crowd started to gather, and a coach man came running.

Jamie was lying on his side against the folding table, which was flat on the floor, covered in red punch.

The coach man started roaring. "What the hell is going on?"

Jason had calmly stepped to the side. He spoke up. "Jamie here was bragging about bringing his boyfriend to prom." Some nervous laughter emerged from the people standing around him. Most people just looked confused.

The coach man looked at Jamie like he was diseased. "Are you hurt?"

Jamie turned over, felt the sticky cold of the punch on his shirt press against the skin of his ribs, like wet paper. "I'm fine." He was sprawled out on the collapsed folding table, his gaze tightly attached to the borrowed cowboy boots now reflecting the colored lights of prom in the wetness clinging to them.

The coach man eyed Jason. "So you knocked him over?"

Jason was by this point smirking. "No. He tried to lean up against me and tell me how pretty I was in my suit." At this point, people started laughing hysterically. The coach man snapped his fingers at them as he looked back to Jason, who continued. "Man, I just moved out of his way. Sorry, but I ain't *like that*." More laughter. "And then he just fell over. He's probably on something. You might wanna check him for drugs. Check his boyfriend over there, too." Jason Miller pointed directly at Nathan, who was standing with Melissa and Ashley at the edge of the crowd, now watching the scene.

Jamie sat up on the folding table on the floor. The flung chocolates, wet with punch, looked like muddy gravel.

He stood and faced the coach man, feeling the cold drink drip down his legs. "I'm fine."

The coach man looked above the heads behind Jamie like he was searching for someone with a degree adequate to deal with the situation. "Well, what's your name, son?"

Jamie looked him dead in the eyes. "I've been here for four years. You should know by now."

Somebody in the crowd hollered "faggot" and another roar of laughter waved across the students. Jamie turned, stone-faced, his back to Jason and the coach man, and walked away. The crowd parted, watching him as he crossed the gym. As he neared the edge of the crowd closest to the door, he saw Nathan, standing with Ashley and Melissa, all looking anxious and confused.

The sight of friends reminded Jamie's body that he was human. A tide of something lifted to his chest, constricting his breathing. Waves of humiliation crossed his skin. Tears stung the sides of his eyes. Ashley was crying. Melissa already had napkins pulled from her purse, reaching them out toward him. Nathan's eyes were wide. Jamie reached out for his arm. It jerked back so quickly that Jamie thought he had somehow aimed his grasp wrong and missed it.

"Dude, what the fuck? Are you on something? Don't touch me like that." It was Nathan who had said it.

Suddenly everything froze and the sting of clarity pulled Jamie back into the room. He looked up. Nathan's hands were in the air as if he was proving to the crowd that he wasn't touching Jamie, like Pontius Pilate before the throng. Ashley was still crying. Melissa was still holding napkins. He looked behind him, and the crowd was still staring.

Jamie walked past them all, making a straight line for the exit. He looked back at his high school classmates, at his teachers, at the stage, at the decorations, at the coach man. He yelled, "You're all fucking idiots!"

Jamie walked out the side entrance to the gym, where a rush of warm air and the smell of weeds and woods encircled him as he cut down the sidewalk along the parking lot. A group of smokers huddled under the awning where teachers did bus duty. At least not everyone had seen him at his lowest. The boy with the greasy mullet was mid-story with a guy with wild, unbrushed brown hair wearing blue jeans and a pearl-button cowboy shirt. He recognized the string-haired goth girl from the library, who was wearing a simple black dress and heavy boots. "Got a cigarette?"

She handed him a white cigarette with a yellow filter. He looked at it.

"Sorry. I ain't never actually smoked. Got a light?"

She didn't ask questions. She retrieved the cigarette from his hand, put it in her mouth, then used the fire from her own to light it, the tobacco cracking as she inhaled. She handed it back to him. The tip was now the same dark purple of her lipstick. Jamie put the cigarette between his lips and attempted a draw. The goth girl said, without any judgment in her voice, "Pull it through with your lungs. Not your cheeks."

Jamie coughed the first couple of times. None of them laughed. None of them asked or seemed to notice that his shirt was covered in red liquid. The guy with the greasy-haired mullet even offered a friendly pat on the back when he was coughing. He finished his first cigarette while they all made jokes about how terrible everyone and everything was. Jamie followed their lead, throwing the last of his cigarette on the ground and putting it out under his boot. "Thanks, y'all. I'm gonna head out."

The goth girl smiled at him and handed him another cigarette. "Hey. People are assholes."

"Yeah. They are." Jamie took it and walked away. He tried to slide it into his front jacket pocket, then realized it wasn't real. It was just a sewn flap, for show. He slid it behind his ear. He walked the length of the parking lot back to his Buick. He'd expected to speak to no one else for the rest of the night, but Nathan was standing by the passenger door.

Jamie stopped at the opposite side of the car from him, waiting for Nathan to speak.

"Where did you go, man? We were worried."

Jamie looked at Nathan's face. He was telling the truth. With the setting sun behind him, spilling orange paint across the lavender sky, he was achingly beautiful in his dark tuxedo. He felt like home. He felt like something new. He now also felt like something unknown.

"Was that what you were showing? Worry?" Jamie had never before used a sharp tone with Nathan. He felt each word stab itself into the air across the top of the Buick.

"Hey. Can we get in the car? People might hear."

"Where are the girls?"

"They're pissed at me. Mel said she was gonna take Ashley home in my truck and that I could walk. I didn't fight it. I figured I'd come see if you had left, but your car was still here."

"They still at prom?"

"Yeah. Mel said she wasn't gonna let me ruin Ashley's prom, too."

"Good."

"Can we get in the car?"

"It's not locked." Jamie opened his door. Nathan slid in and shut the opposing one before Jamie was even seated.

"Listen, I'm sorry. I just . . . I didn't know what to do." Nathan sat motionless, his head turned away and facing the school parking lot like he was waiting for the crowd to reappear.

Jamie pulled forward and cut away from the school. "Well, what you did was what not to do."

"I think—I think I just panicked. You know? It's just . . . I don't even go to this school and those people don't even know me."

Jamie's heavy laugh fell out in a single note of incredulous and aware breath. "Yeah? You think it's easier having them assholes know you?"

The car passed through the entire town, which didn't take long, before Nathan answered. "No. I guess not."

Jamie tried to let the quiet absorb his tension. He turned onto Fox Creek. He said out loud, not necessarily to Nathan but to the universe stretching out in front of him, "Who am I kidding? None of them know me, either."

They rode without speaking the rest of the drive to Nathan's. They pulled into the driveway, away from the road, past the flowering bushes, and stopped in front of the yellow house. Jamie put the car in park, leaving the engine running, and looked straight ahead.

"Jamie, listen." Nathan touched Jamie's hand and pulled it closer to him. "I just . . ." Jamie felt something soft brush against his fingers. He turned. A rose. A pink rose on a short stem. A boutonniere with little white plastic beads glued to the base of the petals. "I was gonna give this to you to put in your suit pocket. It ain't fancy. I seen it at the Fast-n-Fill after you left today. But I didn't know how to give it to you."

"It's a fake pocket."

"Oh." He pressed the flower against Jamie's palm, letting his fingertips brush against Jamie's hand in a soft sweep of tenderness. "I want you to have it anyway. I, uh, I just don't know what's happening. I don't know what any of this means. But I do want you to have it."

"Thanks."

They sat for a few moments without words.

"Hey. If you want, you can come in. I got all kinds a t-shirts."

Jamie moved the flower into his lap. "Nah. I'm good. Thanks, though."

"You sure?"

Jamie wasn't sure. Even in the wake of the betrayal and humiliation, his skin wanted the comfort of Nathan, wanted to hide under his warmth until he dissolved into something safe and unseen, something desired, if only in secret. He was still angry, but his anger was being replaced by something. He could feel it taking on form, something with lines all around it, something with definition and truth pulsing through it. Jamie turned to face Nathan, who was looking at the floor. "Yeah, I'm sure."

Nathan opened the door, then evenly, calmly, and with disappointment weighing down the word, said, "Okay." He stood up outside the door, bent his tall frame over to look back inside the car at Jamie, and added, before closing it, "I'll see you around, man."

Nathan stepped up to the porch, then leapt past the steps in one quick and easy jump, looking impossibly dashing doing so in a tuxedo. He disappeared behind the screen door.

Jamie pulled away from the yellow house and started out of the holler with a pink gas station boutonniere in his lap. He rolled down his window and put his arm out the side of the door, letting it dangle in the breeze as his car sped down the holler. Air rolled up his prom punch–covered sleeves and breathed warmth against his back and chest. It felt like the holler itself was holding him, a living caress coming from all directions. Jamie sunk into the warmth of the embrace until a familiar noise broke the moment. Barking. The white dog from the other side of the curve was at the edge of the road shouting into the street with all its previous aggression and canine piety. Jamie wasn't even to the curve yet, but he could sense it running up the shoulder, ready to fight his old Buick.

He slowed as he turned and there it was, its tail in the air pointed straight at the few stars already bright enough to be seen, its teeth glaring, running back and forth in excited sharp turns at the edge of the blacktop. Jamie pulled off the road onto the shoulder, forcing the white dog to back up onto the grass, though it never turned its face from the car. Jamie put his head out the window, the dog not stopping his yipping for a moment.

"Now hush. Just stop, God damn it!" The dog blinked and fell silent. He cocked his head to the left and stared directly into Jamie's eyes. For a brief moment, Jamie felt like they were about to have an intense experience together, that the dog might impart to him, in his hour of need, some important lesson right there on the side of the road near the mouth of Fox Creek. Instead, after a mere split second of silence, the dog recommenced barking at the car even louder and faster, like he was speaking in tongues.

Then, something new. The barks started to wash something away. He felt lighter. The dog was still yipping with all its might, the coolness of the oncoming night sharpening the ferocity of its incessant supplications. Jamie smiled at the damn thing. "You know what? Here, baby." Jamie tossed the pink rose boutonniere out the window toward the canine like he was making some kind of offering to it. "Keep on barking. Give em hell. All of em. Chase every car you see right outta this ole holler. Bark till your teeth fall out. At least ain't nobody can ever say you was anything other than what you are, a bitch of a little dog. Good for you."

REQUIEM FOR A DOLLAR STORE CHRISTMAS BEAR

They cut off the lights to the Christmas tree
when they cut off the lights to the house.

The discouraged winds cried through the December wood
paneled walls of our single-wide trailer, held just back
enough by the melted butter morning sunlight
for us to open the one gift my mom
had scratched out of money
meant for flour and eggs.

Me and sissy each opened a plush white polar bear
who wore a thick red scarf that felt soft like
rabbit ears lying in green spring clover
and if you held real tight to his paw
like you were afraid he'd leave
he'd sing "Silent Night"
in twinkling tones.

He was alive.

At night, I took hold of his offered hand
pressed my face into his soft bear chest
and let his carols bury me below the river
of frozen walls weeping old dirges
I was still too little to understand.

We moved to my aunt's house
when the water was scared stiff
and it wouldn't leave its pipes.

My breathing and my body were both too soft
for her husband to share air or blood with,
so Mom said, "Just try not to let him see you
and when we get money we can go home."

I built blood ties, breathed air, and kept warm
with the kinship of my white polar bear,
our scattered blankets rising snow,
our fire-swept igloo nestled in the tundra
of the soft light space-time that let us in
between the box spring and the floor.

One night it rained in the winter,
and the crying ghosts found us
came flooding down the walls
begging for us to remember
how they used to be alive.

I closed my eyes
squeezed his paw
and held my breath.

Before the bear even got
to the part that says
all is calm, all is bright
the door cannoned open
and the winds of my uncle
lashed us across imagined borders.

Bear and boy thud against the bed.

"I told you not to play that shit at night cause I need to sleep and you just live to irk me."

He mauled his shirtless path to the front door
lightning raging against itself in the sky
the bear dangling in terror and shock,

his last dull notes still spraying out.
The screen door screamed open
and rain punched the ground
even though the ground
was already dead.

He threw the bear into the thundering darkness of angry rain.

The walls were wailing.
My drumming breath kept time with them.
The world melted back into motion.
I crawled alone into our igloo.

My mom stood at the event horizon.

I spoke first.
"Do we have money yet?"

SHORTCHANGED

Mosely. Almost Winter 2023.

Tammy's nearly fifty-year-old feet ached. She pulled the push broom backward, scraping it along the curb as she did, watching the bristles grab the cigarette butts like they were rescuing fallen soldiers strewn over a battlefield. She had tried to teach the new purple-haired kid this technique, using the slant cut of the bristles and pulling the broom toward you, lifting the handle high so you could catch them angled against crevices and not have to move with the broom, but he was apparently too dumb to learn. Years of standing on her feet had taught her tricks like this one to dull her near-constant heel and arch pain. The kid clearly felt no such urgency. When he tried, he pulled too hard, and the broom bounced up and along the cement, completely missing the cigarette butts. Worse, he didn't seem to notice. Now he stood beside her holding a regular broom and pail, waiting to sweep up the pile she made. Too dumb even to sweep. An assistant to the sweeper, at best.

Tammy tried conversation. "You know, my ex-boyfriend's mamaw always said men can't sweep but women can't make good dumplings."

The purple-haired boy scratched the back of his head. "Shit. I cain't do neither one. Seriously. I cain't cook nothing but cereal."

"Well, it takes all kinds. I hope that little boyfriend of yours does all the cooking."

The boy grabbed a pack of cigarettes from his pocket, a reflex, then put them back. "Kevin? He's real good at cooking. Wants to be a chef. He's managing over at the McDonald's in Battersburg, but he wants to work in a big restaurant someday."

"Why do you smoke? I thought all you kids vaped nowadays."

"I don't know. It's untelling. But I used to light my mommy's menthols for her off the stove. I guess I just take after her."

"Well. I know your mommy. You don't totally take after her. I reckon you got better taste in men."

The boy chuffed a noise of agreement and looked back down at his phone.

At the edge of the parking lot, a twenty-something blond woman in a long blue denim coat appeared. She was walking toward them quickly, one hand pulling the unzipped coat closed, the other holding a purse. It was a cold day.

"I got this." Tammy handed the push broom to the purple-haired boy and went back inside to the register. She watched as the woman stepped inside and hurried to the back of the store. She recognized her, like she did nearly every customer who came in—the woman with two kids who lived in the brown trailer across the road behind the billboard with the giant picture of a sausage biscuit. The Dollar Store sat on the main road between Mosely and Battersburg, but out-of-towners rarely have need of a Dollar Store in early December. They'd come in near Memorial Day or July Fourth to get charcoal and lighter fluid or maybe some material comfort the family members they were visiting didn't possess. Sometimes they came in on Christmas Eve and picked up the $5 and $10 pre-packaged Christmas gifts for family members they had forgotten about during the holiday season. But that was always the last days before Christmas. This early in December, she saw locals.

She couldn't see the woman at the moment; she was hidden in the aisles. But Tammy couldn't leave the store with a customer alone inside, so she started unboxing some chewing gum she'd brought up that morning and then stocked the shelves near the register. She watched the boy outside light a cigarette and look through his phone. As annoying and stupid as these kids were, she appreciated this one's thoughtfulness. She'd been smothering to death with her asthma for going on three months now, so she had asked him not to smoke around her, and he was obliging, always waiting until she went into the store. She emptied the cardboard box of its contents: four containers of spearmint gum and two containers of peppermint gum. She arranged the magazines and pulled the candy bars, mints, and chewing gum forward to make the area neat, then folded the cardboard box and tucked it into the recycling bin behind the counter.

The woman in the denim coat moved toward the register with a half-gallon of milk and two white plush bears. Tammy said, "Cold enough out there for you?"

The woman set the items on the counter as Tammy spoke, then ran her hands together for warmth. "Lord, children. You're telling me. I cain't wait for winter to be over."

Tammy scanned the milk. "You want a bag for this?"

"No thank you. I can carry it."

"Well, sad part is," she scanned the first bear and plopped him into a bag, "it ain't even technically started. It's only the 6th. Winter don't technically come till the 22nd. So, it's actually still the fall. Can you believe that shit?" She scanned the second bear and laid him in the bag with the first.

The woman in the denim coat said, "Well."

Tammy smiled back at her. "But if winter weather can come early, maybe spring can, too. Alright. That's $14.39."

The woman looked startled. Tammy looked down to see if she had made a mistake, then looked outside at the purple-haired boy, who was pretending to sweep and still smoking. He had to be on a second cigarette by this point. "Everything okay?"

The woman shoved some items around inside her purse. "I'm so sorry. I didn't bring no more cash on me. I just got a ten. I musta did my math wrong. How much was them bears?"

Tammy looked down at the machine. "They're $5.99 each."

The woman shuffled around inside of her purse, then directed a watery smile just below Tammy's face. "I thought it said $3.99. I'm sorry. I got the money. I'll come back with it. I just only had this ten with me. I'll just get the milk for now."

Tammy put in her manager's code, voided the bears, and said, "That's $1.69."

The woman handed over her ten-dollar bill. "Sorry about that. Here, I can put them bears back for you."

Tammy handed her the change and counted it carefully. "Don't you worry about that. I needed something to do anyway. I've been bored outta my mind." The woman grabbed her milk and stepped back outside the store. Tammy followed her, pushed open the doors, and yelled toward the boy. "Hey! I'm gonna go to the back. Get back in." He swept the last of the butts and parking lot detritus into the long-handled pail, took a final draw off his cigarette, then tossed it to the ground and made his way back into the store.

Tammy left him to the register and grabbed the two white plush bears. She found the rest of them huddled together on a rack in the toy aisle above a sticker that read $3.99. That boy. It was her fault for thinking a kid too dumb to sweep could price a toy. And that poor woman thinking she had enough to get her kids one each. She pulled the sticker off, scanned the bear with her pricing gun, then printed a new one. *Christmas Bear $5.99*. She placed the sticker below the bears and placed them both back with their bear kin on the shelf.

She was getting too old for this shit.

Tammy was a dedicated employee, but she had worked her fair share of jobs. Straight out of high school, she had a dream job over at Martin's Department Store. Worked her way to management and did good work. When the big stores opened up, Martin's cut more and more people, and the more they cut, the harder she worked. By the end of things, she did it all: ordered merchandise, stocked the shelves, unloaded the trucks, took care of the cleaning. She even ran the catalogs for work clothes and formal orders. But then they built the cut-through and Battersburg, once an hour away, became a fifteen-minute drive. The store closed.

She worked odd jobs but nothing close to the freedom she had felt in management. With Martin's closed, the Dollar Store soon opened. She applied. Now she'd been there nearly ten years, working for much less doing the same work she had always done.

She was only months away from her ten-year anniversary.

She hoped not to be here for it.

She'd been taking online classes at the community college, now that they were free, and she would complete her associate's degree in business management in just a couple of weeks after finals. She only had time to take a couple of classes a semester, but she did well in them.

There had been breaks in the schooling, of course. Tammy was what they called a "non-traditional student"—even though only half of her classmates were young kids who transferred their free community-college coursework to bigger universities. Most of the other half were women similar to Tammy in age, size, and temperament, women holding down full-time jobs and pushing forward at whatever speed life would allow them.

The first time she stopped taking classes, she had to stop a whole year. Her sister Jackie and her wife, Nicole, had moved in with her. They both left their jobs at the same nursing home—where they had met—when a patient's daughter found out they were two women who were married. The patient, a ninety-year-old woman named Trussie Carroll who was friends with their mamaw, was not the problem. In fact, Trussie was so happy for them she demanded a copy of the wedding picture and proudly displayed it alongside the rest of her family photos. When you're in a nursing home long enough, the nurses, nurse aids, custodians, and other patients become your family—which was good, since Trussie's only daughter had moved to Lexington years before and only came in, to hear Jackie and Nicole tell it, twice a year, on Easter and Christmas, and then only to take pictures to put on social media so everyone could see what a great and dedicated daughter she was. So when Trussie's fancy Lexington daughter heard about Jackie and Nicole, she got so outraged that she told local churches to call, complain, and threaten to move their family members to other facilities on account of two women married together working there. The nursing home didn't fire them, but it made their lives awful—canceling shifts, writing them up for any and every thing, making sure they never worked the same hours. So they quit, moved in with Tammy, and stayed long enough to get jobs down in Florida.

Jackie said the hills were backward and she'd never step back into them.

Tammy didn't blame her. Jackie had a right to dream just like she did. So Tammy took care of them both, even letting them take over the payments on her car when they moved down, since she knew their old clunker wouldn't make the trip to Orlando. That was ten years ago, and the last she spoke to them, Jackie declared Florida was getting worse than Kentucky and they were thinking of coming back. Tammy hoped to have her degree by then.

She would have had it already, but she had to withdraw from her classes when her boyfriend left her last January. That piece of shit. After two years together, they'd planned on using their tax refunds as a down payment for a new car, but all of a sudden he started talking about moving back to Canard County, where he grew up. Said he could't make it in Mosely because he didn't know nobody. Tammy knew it was over the first time she heard him say it. Men don't yield their wants or needs to women. A woman's lucky if she finds a man whose needs don't fight hers. She told him she wouldn't move to Canard County for the same reason, so he left.

It had been trials and troubles, but that's life. She used the summer to get over him—she planted some of them big boy beefsteak tomatoes the week he left, and by the time she got to salting big slices of them and eating them on the front porch, she was already making fun of her ex and what musta been the only woman in Canard County that would take him, since they all had the misfortune of knowing him already. Tammy then reenrolled in school last August, her final semester. She was finishing her associate's. She didn't make a big deal of it—there wouldn't be a party or anything—but she would be the first in her family with any kind of college degree, and she was proud of herself.

Today was her first actual shot at an easier life. She had an interview later that afternoon at the district office of the school board for a high school secretary job. They invited her to call and make an appointment "for any time after two on Wednesday the sixth." She listened excitedly to the message five times in a row on her lunch break before calling them back. This was a job with a desk. A job with a pension. A job with vacation days. A job with a chair.

She had been thinking about the job nonstop since she got the call last week, though she tried to prevent herself from feeling too excited. She tried to focus on the tasks at hand, especially since she certainly didn't have any good help at doing them.

She checked the prices on all the products she had asked the purple-haired kid to label the day before. Most of them were misplaced or misprinted, but luckily, she could do in ten minutes what had taken him hours, so she repriced all the new holiday toys and softline while leaving him at the register, though he was equally likely to mess that up. Once she retagged the T-shirts, she joined him up front.

"Hey kid, I've gotta run to the bank. It might be a couple of hours. I'll be back before closing. Just stay at the register. Anybody wants propane or ice, just tell them we're out. You good alone for a bit?"

"Yeah. How do I get my final ten-minute break?"

"I'll make you a deal. If you don't mind waiting until I get back, I'll bring you something to eat. What's your favorite meal from Dairy Queen?"

"You sure? Instead of a meal, mind getting me two small peanut butter milkshakes?"

"Sure. Why not a large?"

"Well, I done eat. But that's one for me and one for Kevin. If that's okay. It's his favorite."

"Shit. That's sweet. Not a one of my exes was that sweet."

The kid blushed a bit and didn't respond to the compliment. The heat buzzed on and vibrated the tin of the ceiling. He said, "While you're gone, can I listen to music at the register? My headphones is dead."

"Sure. Have fun."

Before Tammy got into her car, she could hear something high-pitched with an electric beat pulse against the dusty glass doors of the Dollar Store.

The district office was only a few minutes away, up on the hill behind the high school, but Tammy gave herself enough time to stop over and change her blouse in the Pack-n-Save bathroom. She had paid to have it professionally pressed a week before, but she didn't bother taking it into her house. Between her sisters, daughters, and neighbors, there was a better chance than not that somebody would borrow it without asking and wear it off before her interview.

Only the locked doors of her car provided enough safety to keep it presentable.

Just a few years before, Tammy would have changed her top in the car. She figured anybody desperate enough to look at her titties, held up by their two-dollar brassiere, was welcome to the sight. But she was days away from having a college degree and would need to be a more careful and dignified version of herself if she was going to get the sort of work that paid people by the year instead of by the hour rounded down to the minute. She told herself she'd celebrate, in the unlikely chance she got the job, by buying a couple of new bras.

A woman in a white blouse with a headset greeted her at the district office. Tammy recognized her—Paula Conley, a former classmate.

"Hey, Paula! I didn't know you worked here. It's good to see you."

"Been here four years this January. You doing okay?"

"Finer than frog hair. You?"

"Cain't complain . . . but I might anyway." They both laughed—it was the next step in the dance.

"How's your sister?" Tammy didn't mention Paula's brother, who had been arrested for arson the year before. There were two types of arson, generally speaking—collecting insurance, which was basically a tradition around their part of the state, and the bad kind, the violent kind. Paula's brother had not collected insurance.

"She's good. Living up Hippo. The baby just started middle school."

They chatted some more and Paula, satisfied that Tammy had given due deference to her family history, said, "Well, I'm excited about your interview. Here"—she handed Tammy a stack of papers—"you fill these out beforehand. Just in case. Superintendent Miller will come out and talk to you for the first interview. He'll be out in a second." She motioned toward a small table and chair, the kind you might find in a classroom, pushed against a wall.

Tammy lined up the forms evenly and opened her purse. She had purchased a new pen for this and hadn't yet taken it from its packaging. Not wanting to seem unprepared in front of Paula, she opened it quietly inside her purse, coughing while she ripped the plastic to hide the noise. Paula grinned pearly teeth at her and returned to the computer.

The paperwork was usual—printed versions of information she had already given online: name, Social Security number, address. This being an interview to be the secretary at a school, there were other forms she had never filled out before—health insurance forms, optional death insurance forms, and even a form for a background check. They did not do those at the Dollar Store. While she was slightly annoyed at how long it took to fill everything out, Tammy's studies in business had already taught her that this was their way of having you do the onboarding without getting paid, whether or not you got the job.

Form by form, she flipped through the paperwork with her most careful handwriting. Finally, at the end of the stack, she got to something called "Moral Attestations." They certainly didn't do those at the Dollar Store. She was asked to initial, line by line, agreeing to specific moral codes of conduct. She would not steal time or materials. She would not speak to any news outlet as a representative of the school or about school occurrences. She would uphold the dignity of the education profession in her behavior outside of work. She initialed, initialed, initialed. Then, the final line. Revised June of that year. She would not reference, acknowledge, or endorse alternative gender or sexual identities while serving in any role with the Mosely Independent School District.

She froze. It was a strange line. An addition to the other rote declarations that seemed totally out of place. She had seen people fighting on social media and had heard news stories about LGBTQ stuff, stories that she hadn't paid much attention to, but here was something against gay people in writing on a school form. She thought of her sister Jackie and her wife, Nicole, down in Florida, a state they left Kentucky to be in and were now fleeing from to try to get back to Kentucky. She thought of her cousin AJ, who shortened their name to just their initials and asked people to use "they" when referring to them. She thought about that dumbass kid who wanted two small peanut butter milkshakes, one for his boyfriend, and who was probably miscounting change and listening to God-awful music at the Dollar Store while she was here having her interview for a better job.

"Hey, Paula." Tammy stood up, careful not to wrinkle her blouse, and stepped back to Paula's desk. Paula's hair seemed suddenly bigger, blonder, wider. Tammy pointed to the one un-initialed line on the document. "What does this line even mean?"

"Oh, you know. They added that this summer. People pushing all that gender nonsense and now we gotta change our forms. It don't mean nothing. Just gotta sign it. One more hoop to jump through."

Tammy returned to her seat and read the line. She would not reference. She would not acknowledge. She would not endorse. These words meant something. She clicked her pen closed and put it in her pocket. She put the papers together neatly in a stack. She returned to the seat meant for children to learn in. She waited.

Paula called her back and walked Tammy down a short hallway crowded with open doors. Behind them, women typed on laptops, made copies, or spoke on the phone. No one standing on her feet for no reason. No one opening or tearing down boxes. No one waiting for a teenager to spend half an hour sweeping a four-hundred-square-foot parking lot so she could use the bathroom.

The superintendent's office was at the other end of the hall, the only room with closed doors. It was also the only room with a solid wooden entrance—large polished double doors with a faux arch enveloping the hall above them. Paula knocked, waited for a signal to enter, and then announced Tammy to the superintendent.

The entire room was ornate and stately; clearly any piece of furniture here cost more than her car. Soft lighting hummed out of silver lamps shaped into letters representing the district initials, and giant planks of hardwood stretched the length of the room. A large man, younger than her by a decade, wore a tailored gray suit and stood up to greet her. He shook her hand, then sat down in a leather chair behind a heavy wood desk with a nameplate that read Dr. Jason Miller, Superintendent. He pointed to a chair and motioned for Tammy to have a seat.

"You like those floors? They're great, huh? Remember the old Mosely High School from before they consolidated? "

"Yeah, sure do. I went there."

"Oh, I see you did. Me too! Go Cougars! I had them pull up the gym floor and do this office with it. That shelf over there"—he pointed to a blue shelf behind her lined with diplomas and awards framed in metal—"is actually made out of the old bleachers. I played forward all four years. Graduated in '03. Wanted to bring the gym with me."

"That's real nice." Tammy tried not to slouch. She put her purse on the floor, then wondered if that was gauche. She picked it back up quickly and held it in her lap alongside her stack of papers. She made sure her posture was straight.

"Now, if you can hand over those." The superintendent reached for her paperwork. "Oh, yes. I remember your application. Not a whole lot of office experience."

"No, but I am finishing my associate's in business management in two weeks." She thought about saying sir after no, but couldn't bring herself to say it. Even if this man was educated and rich, he was from these parts. He might find it as offensive a word as she did. He was also a good ten years younger than her. She chose to speak slowly and look him in the eye to show her respect.

"No worries. We can teach any hire what they need to know, and you've got the credentials. But what impresses me is your work history. Nearly twenty years at Martin's. Man, I used to love that place! My mom got me a pair of new boots and a Carhartt coat every year when they were opened."

Tammy softened. He was human. She placed her purse back down to the floor. "Yeah. It was a special place. Hated seeing it closed. Good people."

The superintendent nodded. "It was a shame. But you picked right back up. At your current place of employment now for almost ten years."

"Yes, sir." It slipped out before she could stop herself. He didn't wince. He kept talking.

"Now, that's what we like to see. Dedication. I don't know if you have noticed, but the schools"—he dropped his voice, like he was about to say something scandalous or share a family secret—"they've got high turnaround these days. Pure politics. And this is a good place, Tammy. Good pay and benefits. You can ask around the office if you'd like."

"Thank you."

"Now, I don't like to use the word interview. That's a formality. I just like to get to know a person. And them us. You got any questions for me?"

"I don't think so. I graduated from these schools, and me and Paula go way back. I'm just excited for the chance to work here. I'm a hard worker."

"Your reputation precedes you. You don't have to convince me." As he spoke, he lifted a piece of chocolate from a bowl, popped it in his mouth, chewing and talking at the same time, balling the aluminum wrapper with his fingers and flicking it onto his desk. He tilted the bowl toward Tammy, who shook her head no, then continued. "Listen, you impressed me more than any other applicant. No need to sell yourself. I just wanted to meet you. File paperwork. You know. All that stuff. Stuff we hope you'll be doing for us soon."

Tammy tried to push down the excitement growing under her skin. She didn't know if she had the job yet. But the conversation seemed promising.

"I mean, heck, I'll be honest. If you're ready, we can just start processing things. I don't like games. I like straightforward people."

The excitement grew a faint pulse. "Well, I'd sure like that."

"Sounds great." The superintendent flipped through the papers she had given him without truly looking, then handed them back across the desk to her. He leaned back, smiled big at her, then put his hands behind his head. "Did you get your paperwork finished?"

Tammy suddenly remembered the last line on the form. "Yeah. I had one question. I just didn't know what it meant. This line here about alternative genders. What's it about?"

"Nothing to be concerned with. You shouldn't need to know what it means. Good, decent folk don't. That's just something we added when the state made some changes. Nothing that will affect you. Like I said, turnover is awful. It's all this crazy politics, the last thing we need more of. I'm here to put an end to it. We got all these people out here trying to push all this LGBTQ ABCDEFG stuff. And not just on each other—onto the kids! You'd be surprised, but even some of the teachers try to talk about this garbage. Now everybody's just fighting back and forth. So we just made it fair for everybody. Cut it out. It's not appropriate inside the schools, anyway."

Tammy was trying to take in what she was hearing him say. She knew she wasn't the most educated person—even with a degree just a week away. She knew she wasn't trained in how she was supposed to act in certain situations—she never had a use for it. But she also knew for damn sure she wasn't stupid. She didn't respond.

The superintendent kept talking. "It won't affect a secretary, anyhow. You just don't talk about it, and they don't either. If some teacher or student tries to talk about any kind of gender mumbo jumbo, just shut it down. That's not for inside the school."

Tammy's silence assured the superintendent that she had no more questions. "Well, it was nice to meet you, Tammy. You just finish this and hand the paperwork over to Paula on the way out and we'll get things rolling." Tammy nodded and stood. She reached out to shake his hand, but he had already taken another foil-wrapped chocolate and turned toward his computer. She pulled her hand back to her side and walked out of his office.

She walked down the short hallway, past the women making copies, making phone calls, and using computers while seated at desks, women waiting on their next paid vacation. She walked past Paula Conley, who was talking on the phone, her hair a giant yellow balloon. Paula called out, "See you, Tammy!"

Tammy left the school building.

She went to the Dairy Queen and ordered three peanut butter milkshakes.

She changed back into her work shirt in the bathroom.

She threw the paperwork in the trash can at the exit.

Tammy walked two empty buggies left stranded in the lot back to the storefront after she parked. Once inside, she gave the two milkshakes to the dumb kid with purple hair so that he could share one with his boyfriend who worked at the McDonald's the next town over. She said, "Hey, get on out of here. Take that on over to your boyfriend while it's cold."

"I still got another three hours to go."

Tammy approached the register, and he stepped aside to let her take it. "Listen, you ain't gonna get many chances in life to just be free, kid. Get out while the sun's shining."

The kid looked to the door, his hands full of peanut butter milkshake. "I can't afford to miss my hours, though."

Tammy took a sip off her own milkshake, peanut butter like his, and let the creamy soft serve melt under her tongue before swallowing. "You know what. I'll clock you out later. You'll have a full shift. Go on now, before I change my mind."

The purple-haired kid scratched the side of his head with the back part of his hand, lifting the milkshake into the air while he did it, looking confused, like he was in the wrong store. "You feeling alright? Why you being so nice?"

Tammy almost made a joke about just wanting him out of her hair, or maybe about how she wanted to be alone, or maybe about how she was so tired she didn't want to add babysitting to the list. But she didn't say any of those things. She just said, "Somebody's gotta be. Go on, and don't tell nobody I let you leave. And don't get used to it."

The purple-haired kid walked straight out the door. She watched from the counter as he struggled to figure out how to get two milkshakes and himself into his car. He made the ordeal ten times more complicated than it needed to be but eventually successfully managed to leave the parking lot without spilling his milkshakes.

She spent the next few hours doing whatever was left to do. When nothing remained, she just stood at the register and looked outside. Despite the cold, the fading sun was shining brightly, so Tammy stepped out into the parking lot and let the last remnants of light fall onto her skin. At two minutes before closing, the woman in the long denim coat walked down the hill from the little brown trailer that stood behind the billboard with the sausage biscuit on it. She crossed the road, then the parking lot, then smiled at Tammy, who followed her into the store.

She came to the register. She held a single white Christmas bear in a red scarf.

Tammy scanned the bear and placed him in a bag. "Did I remember you wanted two of these? Are we out already?"

The woman looked toward the bag. "No. I'm just gonna get the one today in case you run out. My little boy's been eyeing it and won't stop talking about it. I'll come back later for the other one or for something else if you're out."

Tammy would not return to the Board of Education. For the moment, this was where she was. It might be a long moment. It might be a short moment. But it was the moment she chose to be in. "Shew. I plumb forgot to tell you. I'm so sorry—I could have told you this morning and saved you a trip. Those go on sale tomorrow, buy-one-get-one. But since it's technically after closing time, it's tomorrow on the computer now, so the second one is free. Let me run grab that for you. I apologize."

Tammy walked to the back of the store, grabbed a second bear, scanned him, then put him in the bag with the first. "That's $6.35 after tax." The woman in the denim coat gave her seven ones, and Tammy gave her exact change. She thanked Tammy, took the bag, and left the store.

Tammy locked the door behind her. The till would be a little over six dollars short tonight, but she could just blame it on the dumb kid. Anyone would believe it, and no one would care.

SUNDAY SCHOOL MOVIE

People know by now that I run
my mouth, a vent, a hose, a window
lest the memories mutate and divide
into cancer.

It ain't healthy when a queer
still smells small church laying-on-of-hands
when we ain't being held no more—
first sign of a stroke.

So I found and shared online that film,
the one my aunt made us watch
when she taught Sunday School—
long-haired '70s women who could
have been smiling in tampon commercials
were holding their bleached split ends
through the rusty sides of a guillotine
because they wouldn't renounce
their Christ.

As a reward for not looking away
from the blood-darkened rapture skies
she took us all to Dairy Queen.

Rapid bites of my ice cream cone,
soft serve numbing my naked teeth
then shanks of pain lobbing
from tooth to eye to brain.
I wanted to taste it all
before the rapture came.

My memory teeth buzzed.
So did my phone.

In my inbox a stranger
who knew the movie from my post
who also saw the guillotined heads
who had dreaded the shadowy skies
who didn't get ice cream
after the credits rolled.
Instead she had strange men carry
her through the July Georgia woods
in a church camp simulation proof of faith.

They covered her face with a sack
and shot guns into the madness
of the muted-pine-tree forest
demanding she renounce the Lord.

Her undying love for Jesus
collapsed from her mouth
while piss ran down
her legs.

She said she was only thirteen.

I begin a response.
I abandon it.
I get in the car.
I drive to Dairy Queen.
I order an ice cream cone.
I eat it slowly.

THE RIGHTEOUS

Mosely. Ice Plant. Summer 2023.

Joyce slipped the cotton skirt down her thighs, carefully arching her foot forward and lifting it up so as not to further wrinkle the skirt or get it snagged on her white nylons. She had kept them for over a year after buying them on discount at an Easter sale, and now she felt pride at their persistence every time she slipped them over her feet and pulled them carefully up her legs. She was not a wasteful woman, a trait for which her husband, the pastor of a small church, was quick to compliment her when Sunday's leftover chicken became Monday's soup or the children's outgrown school clothes became a new quilt for the youngest girl-child.

Not that she could be wasteful even if she wanted. Since her husband was called the year before by the Lord to take over the Old Time Mountain Pentecostal Church up near the mouth of Ice Plant Holler, she had left her job at the Pack-n-Save deli over in Mosely to devote herself fully to the church. Joyce knew her husband had never liked her working, but he put up with it since she was only cooking, which was, in fact, woman's work, whether she got paid for it or not. And they had needed the money. But since she left, the Lord had already blessed them beyond what they had before. Her husband was a solid enough electrician, but as his reputation for old-fashioned preaching spread through the hills like the gospel itself, folks were soon enough calling on him to change out their breakers and switches, hang new light fixtures, even rewire their lamps just on account of how he could move a whole congregation to tears and bring down the Holy Spirit with his preaching.

God was good to the righteous.

She stood in her bedroom, the early morning light rolling across the double wedding ring quilt her mamaw had given her right before dying, when Joyce was only eighteen. Now thirty-five, Joyce still proudly slept under it alongside her husband. Joyce had eight brothers and sisters, but she alone had been chosen by her mamaw to preserve and keep the quilt. Joyce thought it was a judicious decision on the part of her mamaw. Most of Joyce's siblings were churchgoers, it's true, but only a good half of them were serious about the Lord, and she was the only one who had never backslid. Not even once. They were surely lucky to have her to hold the family together, to try to keep the circle unbroken. But the world was wicked, and Joyce knew her work was—and would always be—hard.

Somehow, the skirt had a wrinkled crease in the back. Joyce, now the Sunday School teacher, couldn't show up with some distraction like that. Now, the good Lord doesn't care how you dress for church. It ain't the clothes that matter if your heart is good. But some of the people who wandered in on Sundays were clearly only there for the food afterward—they'd show up just a few minutes before the end of the service in jogging pants, T-shirts, even grown men in shorts. It just lacked respect. Well, at least church was good for people like that, though, whatever their reason for coming. Man shall not live by bread alone but by every word that proceedeth out of the mouth of God. And how can a man hear the word of God without a preacher? That first part was Jesus Christ. The second part was her husband, David Sizemore. That's what good preachers do—they let plain folks who ain't filled with the Spirit know what the Lord meant. The Holy Word of the Lord! And the Lord would want them to know, even men in shorts or women in jogging pants.

Joyce did not own jogging pants. Women did not wear pants. Standing in her cream-colored slip, she laid the skirt back on the ironing board, passing the iron quickly, first over the bottom of the garment, just like her mamaw had taught her, then moving the skirt around the board and keeping the iron stationary, flattening her way toward the top and lifting the bottom to maintain the work already done. Steam rose up from the board and dissipated as it joined the sunlight. Joyce inspected all sides of the skirt, then, satisfied it was sufficient for the preacher's wife, pulled it carefully back over her calves and to her waist.

She caught sight of herself in the mirror. She did not look like the mother of four children. Her curves looked womanly, not sloppy like some of her sisters' were. Her hair was still mostly dark, and it shined like a teenager's. She wasn't just respectfully and modestly attired; she was pleasant to look at. This, too, was a gift from the Lord, who rewarded those who kept his Word. For the LORD taketh pleasure in his people: he will beautify the meek with salvation. That was Bible truth—and God keeps His promises. She thanked the Lord in her mind and then stepped out onto her front porch to wait for her brother-in-law to pick her up in the church van.

Seven children hopped off the van first, running down toward the creek to play. There was a grapevine on the church side that they liked to try to push across the creek. Above them, clouds stumbled over the hills, muting the sun so that it looked like a warm yolk wandering across the tops of egg whites. Joyce moved slowly out of the van so she wouldn't need to lean over. The van could have held three more—ten seats in the back, two up front—but the Reeds didn't answer the door when she knocked. Disrespectful, given the trouble they went through to try and pick up their kids. The church held strict rules, the keeping of which meant difficulties and sacrifice. Her husband couldn't have her driving the bus on account of her being a woman, but her brother-in-law, Jimmy, couldn't pick up the kids by himself on account of him not being saved. Watching kids being a woman's work, the church resolved that Jimmy, who didn't have his own car, could drive the church bus on Sunday mornings and then walk from Ice Plant over to Mosely to get his groceries for the week. He'd have to leave the van in the church parking lot for the shopping, of course, since his groceries weren't church business, but the arrangement worked out for everybody.

"Come on, young'uns! Time for Sunday School!"

The children were a scraggly bunch, but they were beautiful in the sight of the Lord. They wouldn't make it to church if not for her, since the bus only had to pick up kids whose parents didn't come already. Her own four children were usually already here, waiting patiently inside after coming in early with their daddy, but her husband had sent them all to East Haven Bible Camp, down in Georgia, so the group was small today. There were the Campbell twins, then a boy and a girl without a daddy whose mommy gave them her own last name of Dotson, and then her sister's three kids—Lonnie, a preteen boy just itching for trouble, Simon, sweet but scared of his own shadow, and Brandi, a girl who had to be in third grade already and still didn't know how to sit in a dress.

The children's Sunday School classroom was an addition on the side of the church that had a separate door to the outside so they wouldn't have to interrupt the adult service, which started half an hour earlier on account of business meetings. Joyce led the children into the addition, flipping on the lights and taking in the splendor of the room, which her husband had only three days earlier recarpeted in a deep burgundy and repainted with white walls. It still smelled new, fresh, evidence that their work was changing the world. The children did not seem to notice, instead piling into their routine seats on the benches opposite her. Even though they were only kids, Joyce still expected them to have at least noticed the work he had put in for them, the hours spent away from his own family, but they just sat staring at her, waiting for the lesson to begin.

"Alright, young'uns. Today's lesson is important! I'm gonna need every last one of you to put on your thinking caps for Jesus. Okay?"

Some nodded their heads. Some looked at their hands or out the window.

Joyce sat in a chair opposite them, with a whiteboard on a stand placed on the table to her side so she could instruct. She wrote numbers, 1 through 7, down the left side of the board, and then flipped it around so they could see.

"Let's start with this. Why do we pray? Can y'all give me some reasons?"

Silence at first. But Joyce was patient. It was one of her many gifts from the Lord. Patience, speaking in tongues, salvaging the lost, and a spirit of discernment. The Lord revealed these to her many years ago after a long night of prayer. She smiled at the children, held the marker firmly, and waited.

One of the Campbell twins spoke first. "If you're sick."

"Good! Yes. We pray for the sick."

She wrote *For the sick* in careful print on the little board.

"Who else? Everybody should say one."

A hand went up. She acknowledged it. "For helping people." It was Simon, her sister's middle son. He was the only one who raised his hand in Sunday School. Such a delicate little rule follower, always talking about helping people, always wanting to do something for others. The Lord bless that child. Yes, he would do marvelous things for the Lord someday if she did her job right.

"That's right. For helping people. Good. Why else?"

The others gave quick answers. For food. For mommy and daddy. For weather. When you're scared. Six answers filled the board. Lonnie had by this point put his head down and wasn't even looking up at her. Joyce knew that he only came to Sunday School because her sister made him, so he had never wanted to contribute. She would have to work harder to bring him to God.

With her softest voice, trying to sound more like a teacher and less like an aunt, she addressed her student. "What about you, Lonnie?"

"I don't know." His head stayed down.

One of the Campbell twins started bouncing on the bench. "I know one! I know one!"

Joyce exhaled. "Thank you, Ray, but I really want Lonnie to give us a reason. Come on, Lonnie. What's a good reason to pray?"

"For this to be over."

One of the Campbell twins put his hand over his mouth in shock and looked up to Joyce. The other started laughing. The rest of the class was split evenly among the same two responses.

"Well, I am sorry if this ain't exciting enough for you, if God is boring to you! But I'm trying my best. We put in this carpet just for you and painted these walls just for you, and here I am trying to help you see the Lord. Now you listen to me, Lonnie, I ain't putting up with no more of this."

Lonnie's eyes held her with a look she couldn't make out. Was it disgust? Hatred? Judgment? She knew he was a troublemaker, taking after his daddy, just like all the other men from over at the head of their holler, but how could that young'un look at her with such a god-awful expression? What had she ever done but try to make his life better?

Lonnie put his head back down, and a small part of Joyce was relieved that she wouldn't have to keep seeing that face he was making. She felt the blank space beneath the other six answers growing whiter and bigger, almost glowing in its emptiness. One of the Campbell boys, when granted to speak, said, "Peace. You can pray for peace."

How the Lord was with her. "Yes. That's nice. Peace." She wrote the word below the others on the list, filling the emptiness with something godly and good.

Joyce moved the lesson forward. Lonnie kept his head down.

She had asked for the Lord to help her build this lesson, and he had delivered. Oh, the Devil was using Lonnie, that was sure, but she was strong. She asked the Sunday School students what their listed items had in common, and while they tried as hard as children might to answer, they couldn't tie them up.

Perfect. She was ready.

"Well, everything everybody mentioned is asking God to do something for *us*. But what about God? Shouldn't we be doing things for *him*?" The kids crinkled their little foreheads, shrank their eyes in seriousness, and nodded their heads. Brandi, her niece, even rubbed her chin in thought, like a man might do if he had a beard. Joyce thought it was an obscene gesture on a little girl, but, of course, no one had ever taught her any better. At least she was thinking about God, sitting in a church, and staying quiet. Praise the Lord for that.

A low rumble came thumping against the wall. Then discordant shouting. The Spirit had taken hold of the adult service! A shiver of tambourines clanged and a rush of consonants spat out like the bursting of fireworks in sorrowful, muffled wailing.

The sound roused Lonnie's head from his crossed arms, causing him to sit up and actually look at the board ahead. The Campbell twins looked nervous. Joyce remembered they'd never been to a full service at night, and it was rare for the Spirit to move so strongly in the morning during Sunday School, which was usually just people sitting around taking up precious time talking about their own problems instead of asking questions about the Holy Word. But the Lord is mysterious and his ways are unknown. She said, "It's okay, boys. That's just the Spirit moving over there with the grown-ups. That's the love of God. It's a good thing." Shouts and moans of hallelujah rubbed across the panels of the walls. Thumping blasted in unpredictable spurts like muffled shots from guns. Joyce looked straight upward, like God was looking down at her, then hugged herself with both arms to show the children how good she felt. The other four children, having attended Holy Ghost–filled evening services before, were unbothered by the noise and seemed still lost in the question about what we do for God.

Joyce wished she could be with the other adults, receiving communion in Spirit and feeling the Lord wash over her body until she was free of it, drowned for a moment in his love, liberated of expectation, want, need. But she had work to do, here, now, with these seven little souls. She would deliver unto him his flock. She lifted her voice over the jubilation spilling in from the adult room. "So, what can we do for him? What can we do for God?"

Moving at a gentle pace, the children gave their responses. From the Campbell twins, say our prayers and don't tell lies. From the Dotsons, play nice and mind your mommy. Poor little things. They didn't even say parents, or, love their little hearts, mommy and daddy, them not even knowing where they came from. Brandi said no cussing, which is not something that should tempt a child in the first place, but Joyce had to be in the world and not of it, had to acknowledge that not everybody, not even her own sister, raised their kids like she did, hers down right now at a Bible camp in Georgia, spending days and nights dedicating themselves to the Lord's teachings. Her younger nephew, the middle one named Simon, said, "love everybody?" He even said it like a question, too scared to say it like he knew it. She added each child's contribution to the whiteboard. Lonnie was the only one who hadn't spoken yet, but his eyes remained focused ahead, the sounds from the adult service having roused him. Perhaps the spirit of God had set him straight, too.

"Lonnie, what do you think? What's something the Lord wants from us?"

Lonnie turned his head from the unfinished list and stared at her, and there it was again, that look—that bitter face of disgust, that ancient light of judgment burning from behind his twelve-year-old eyes. He said, "He'll not have us be hypocrites."

Joyce felt the breath pulled from her lungs and her face stung like she'd been knocked back by a log. She stood up and her chair fell back against the floor, landing against the carpet, its legs jutting out between her own. Her response was louder than she meant it to be, flooding with accusation. "And what is that supposed to mean?"

Lonnie spoke calmly. "Ain't that what you're always saying? He'll not have us be hypocrites?" His voice was steady, but Joyce was sure she could discern the pure disgust boiling behind his eyes.

Joyce tried to move toward Lonnie, forgetting the legs of the knocked-over chair fallen beneath her. She tripped, tumbling forward and onto the table, flipping the little whiteboard over and smacking it with her weight, sending a piercing clap across the room. The crashing board sounded like a slap, like an angry hand making contact with a face. She'd attempted to brace herself with her two hands but instead had landed on them as her stomach hit the table, both arms folding together underneath her abdomen, one over the other. She appeared to be bent in prayer, leaned against the table, but her legs were no longer on the ground.

She wrestled herself upward and a rush of cold trickled against her leg. Fearing blood, she looked down. Her white pantyhose had been torn by the legs of the chair, a large rip now bringing the skin of her calves into contact with the air. The children looked scared, except for Lonnie, whose face had lost all expression. Just an empty page looking back at her.

Her voice trembled as her heels touched the ground. "And who are you anyway? Who are you? You don't come in here and plan the lessons, or oil the pews, or make the food! You didn't lay the carpet or paint the walls! You come in here like God's just supposed to give you something you already earned. Well, that ain't it! Who the hell are *you* to judge *me*?"

The door connecting the classroom and the sanctuary whipped open, and in rushed Joyce's husband followed swiftly by three lady members of the church, racing together like they were fleeing a burning room. Lonnie stood up. Joyce was now crying, as were most of the kids. The widows from the church auxiliary were fast upon her with hands, a sudden shield of interlocking arms, praying without even asking what had happened. It looked like at any minute the flock might just sprout wings and fly her away to safety.

The pastor, Joyce's husband, looked around the room like he could see the past and make out what had transpired. "What happened here?" He said it like he was only asking to see if whoever answered would lie or tell the truth.

Lonnie spoke first. "I ain't did nothing. She's crazy. She went crazy on me just for saying not to be a hypocrite."

Joyce did not respond to him, but her crying began to soften, and she started praying with the women laying hands on her. The pastor picked up the chair, pushed it back under the table, and looked out the window toward the parking lot. He said, "You know what, Lonnie? Looks like Jimmy's back in the van. Why don't you go on out and sit with him till church is over?"

Lonnie didn't waste a second, his face glowing red in anger. "Fine by me! I'd rather sit with him than you two any day." Lonnie pushed the whiteboard, knocking it off the table. One of the Campbell twins gasped in fear at the noise. Simon sat on his hands. Lonnie circled past the praying women, slammed the door that led to the parking lot, and was gone.

The women took the slamming of the door as a sign to say Amen, like it was the pealing of a bell to call their prayer to a close. The pastor tapped the Bible he was holding against his waist with his right hand. "Are we good to finish the service?"

Joyce stood straight, smoothed her skirt, and faced her husband. "Yes, sir. We're good. In fact, we are blessed. Thank y'all for coming in to check on us. The Devil is among and tempting us today."

Nodding, her husband returned to the sanctuary, followed by the three women who had been praying. Joyce looked at the prayer-covered whiteboard sprawled on the floor, its back turned to them all. The lesson was ruined now, but was she not given the gift of salvaging the lost? "You know what, young'uns? I think we can just watch a movie. Yes. We might still have time to finish it today." She turned on the corner television and pulled an old and beaten VHS tape out of a small storage cabinet. A film about the rapture. Clearly, Lonnie was proof that the End was coming soon. She couldn't have even imagined a world where a child would speak like that to an adult, let alone in church. And such an ugly thing to say! God was coming soon, there was no doubt, and these poor heathen kids were not ready. They needed to know what they were up against, what the Lord had in store.

True that the movie was old, but it was more accurate than some of the newer ones that strayed too much from the Bible just to tell a story. Those might be entertaining and popular, but this one was plain. Truthful. Terrifying.

Joyce turned to her remaining students. "If you watch and don't go to sleep or close your eyes, we'll go down and get us some ice cream at the Dairy Queen afterwards." She turned on the movie, and with the six children watched a film about the end of time: saw Christians beheaded, blood flooding the streets, the wrath of God pouring down on the wicked, his dark skies inhaling the stars themselves as the unraptured fled the burning cities with nowhere to run.

After church, Joyce had Jimmy drive her and the children to the Dairy Queen. She'd forgotten, when she made the promise about ice cream, that she had a rip in her nylons, but she wouldn't be made a liar, not even if people in town saw her in such a state, not with the Devil loose and prowling like a lion. Everything was at stake.

They piled out of the car into the parking lot, Joyce following. The movie had clearly gotten through to the kids; they were standing in a quiet line, their backs held straight with respect. She noticed Lonnie standing with them. "No. Not you. You didn't watch the movie." Her eyes held his unflinchingly.

She watched his face fall in disappointment. Any look was better than the one he had been giving her earlier. The Lord had restored balance. She continued to stare Lonnie down as he climbed back into the van and closed the door behind him. She and the other children then walked toward the city-facing door of the Dairy Queen, the one between the inside dining area and the busiest part of the parking lot. It was Sunday, so folks were either already inside eating or in the parking lot after their own church services. She stopped the congregation of children a few feet from the door, directly in front of the dining room window, and gathered them into a circle. "Okay. Let's remember to say grace and pray our thanks to the Lord for the food we're about to eat."

The circle of children bowed their heads, joined hands, and began to pray so fervently, and with such sincerity, that even those inside stopped eating to watch. Joyce prayed, too, zealously asking God that each of these children might someday have their eyes opened to the ungodliness of the world.

YOU KIDS BE QUIET

Before my mamaw said *now hush*
and we might just hear the stars
I had never known
the holy whisper rolling in
a chorus of a thousand baritones
yellow pinpricks of light
ripping the skin off the sky
tearing it from hill to hill
its fresh wound trilling down
in drenching bursts of buzzing life
calling up chords of lightning bugs
harmonies slipping in drunken flits
echoing between the trailer and creek
drawn west in the husky undertow
of the dense rumble of the darkness

STORING CABBAGE

Big Branch. Ice Plant. Summer 1987.

Vicky Case looked out the thick glass of her old four-paned window and cussed. The brown waters of Big Branch Creek was spilling up over the edge of the culvert and running over the paved part of the road at the front of her property. The water looked mad, like each little wave was pushing the wave in front of it, like every wave was trying to rush the next down the creek. But there weren't nowhere to go.

She was thinking that she might should've went with the Jenkins yesterday when they left outta here. Everybody had been talking floods all week, what with all this rain and the threat of more, and the whole holler knew she didn't drive, even though she was only in her early seventies. But she'd never had need to get behind a wheel before her husband, Walt, up and died in a rock fall five years before, and besides, her neighbors was good people. They would run her to the store ever few weeks, take her to the doctor if she took ill, so there weren't no real need for her to drive herself nor nobody else nowhere. And she was getting on in her years, so people just naturally wanted to check in on her.

Yesterday evening, the Jenkins feller from up the road had opened her little chain-link swinging gate and come plodding up the sidewalk in his mining clothes. It was sprinkling out, and each step he took left a streak of coal where he'd just been, marking his path as he approached her. His woman and boy was still in his truck, which he left running, the windshield wipers squeaking against the glass. He was still covered head to boots in coalblack. Vicky was on the ground in her side yard cabbage patch, the fanned outer leaves of a large head of cabbage protecting her knees from the dirt, her right hand and knife obscured by the roundness of the large vegetable. She began pulling herself up with her cane to greet him, bringing the head of cabbage with her to toss into a pile of another dozen or so stacked into her wheelbarrow.

"Don't you get up for me, now, Vicky Case. You need some help?" The path from her swinging gate to her porch was long, since her property was long, backing up two or three times more than most folks nearby on account of the curve of the hill behind her house. He picked up his speed as he said it, throwing his voice over the yard and the rain so she could hear him before standing up. But she got up anyway. He was young, maybe twenty-five soaking wet, which he currently was, so striding down a sidewalk was still possible for him. The mines would take care of that soon enough.

"No, young'un, I'm about done here. Good to stand." She tossed her cabbage toward its kin, brushed her hands down the side of a flower-print housedress, and squinted at him from behind a thick pair of glasses with black horn-rimmed frames. They ended under a gray-and-red bandana wrapped around her white hair to keep the rain out of her eyes.

"Getting up all your cabbage?"

"Yeah. Well, truth be told I hate to do it this early. Them heads ain't as round as I'd like, it barely summer." Her sinking voice waved like the hills themselves as she talked, the consonants clucking against each other in the telltale cadence of an old-timer.

"Shew. Gotta do what you gotta do." He kicked absentmindedly as he talked and a slug of blackness from his boots sloughed off into the grass. The rain immediately began washing it away.

"Why, you still got your helmet on, Jerry Jenkins! You just get off work?" He nodded and she continued. "Well, shit. Holler at that woman and young'un a yourn over yonder in ye truck and y'all get on in the house and grab you something to eat. There's almost a whole pone a cornbread in the oven and a big mess a soupbeans. I can fry y'uns up some of this cabbage fresh, too. Got more in the house."

"Nah, I don't wanna go taking your food, now. We was just heading over to my mommy's up Ice Plant and was gonna see if you wanted to ride over there to your boy's house in case this rain gets any worse. Sparky Messer over to the radio station's calling for flooding." While he talked, Vicky pulled the wheelbarrow toward the remaining heads and the soft rain continued to rebuke the both of them and the cabbages they stood in.

"I just got this dozen or so left to pull. I'll lose em to the rain if'n I don't."

"We can wait on you."

Vicky grabbed the edge of the wheelbarrow and motioned to Jerry. She lifted the side of it toward him, putting both hands on the edge of the cart, butting it against the yellow flower-print housedress covering her knees and the thick men's rubber boots on her feet. "Here now, help me a second. Hold em cabbages steady while I drain out some of this water."

Jerry grabbed the wheelbarrow. "Here. Let me do that."

"No, now." It was less chiding and more declaration. "I already got it lifted. Hurry, grab em fore they start falling out."

Jerry held on to the cabbages with his palms, the only parts of him not covered in coal, his thick and stubby fingers splayed open wide. It looked like he was laying hands on their white and green heads, like he was about to start praying. Vicky tilted the wheelbarrow toward him and clear water rushed out and fell onto his boots, clearing them and revealing the blue tinge to the grayed leather underneath. She eased the wheelbarrow back down and nodded a thanks at him.

"So? You gonna come with us? We can drop you off at Dan's place. That trailer a his'n's small, but ain't no water getting up his side of Ice Plant."

"Nah, I appreciate y'uns. But I been here since me and Walt bought this land back in '31. Built the house ourselves. Foundation's twice taller than most. I've seen real high water, but in all them years it ain't never even got across the yard cause Walt knew what he was a doin. He laid the foundation back far from the road on purpose. Course back then there wadn't a road like this'n here. Was all dirt."

Jerry scratched the back of his hairline under his mining helmet. "Ain't no arguing Walt Case didn't know what he was doing if he married you."

"Don't you go a flirting with me, Jerry Jenkins." She smacked him light on the arm. "At least not when your woman's twenty feet away. Come back without her next time and try." They both laughed.

Jerry gave her a nod and smacked one of the cabbages like it was a work project he was done inspecting. "Well, alright, then." Vicky Case was such a stout and strong-willed woman, he almost reached out to shake her hand like he would a man's. He pulled his right hand back, then put both in the pockets of his mining jacket. "We're gonna head out. Now, there's room if you wanna come. I'd hate for you to be stuck out here if the water—" Jerry's sentence was cut short by some squalling and the creaking of the gate at the end of Vicky's property. Jerry's woman was hollering at their toddler, who was now running the length of the fence. He was fast, a wild streak of mushmelon skin and bare feet barreling through the rain and arching toward the far end of the cabbage patch that had already been cleared.

Jerry started after him, causing the child to stop dead in his tracks. He was shirtless and shoeless in a little pair of overalls. Standing in the middle of the garden with the rising creek roaring behind him, he looked just as mean and smart as old Huck Finn. Jerry eyed the young'un, daring him to move. "Get your ass back to you Mommy! Now!" The boy stared back, his eyes narrowing, visibly weighing his options. He took off again in the direction of the unharvested vegetables, jumping headfirst toward the cabbage closest to him. He landed on his knees and immediately started trying to pull it up.

Jerry pulled his right hand from his pocket and grabbed his belt buckle. "Get yourself up outta that mud fore I whoop your ass. Them ain't your cabbages, by God!" The child, by this point covered in dirt, reeling in the ecstasy of gardening in the rain, was sitting flat on his behind, leveraging the weight of his entire body to pull up on the cabbage with both hands. It was taller than him, and shirtless in his overalls with both hands on the rounded head, he looked like a grown man caught in a fight against a vicious, otherworldly monster.

Vicky threw her head back and laughed, the rain puddling onto her large glasses. She removed the bandana from her white hair and wiped her lenses. "Now, hush, Jerry Jenkins. You leave that baby alone. There's a hell of a lot worse things than wanting to help do some work." She put her glasses back on, then lowered herself slowly, using her cane, to the dirt beside the child. She showed him her knife and his eyes widened, half with delight and half in respectful awe. She then eased back the outer leaves, pushing them away until she could grasp the head. She cut across the root, showing the toddler how to dislodge the cabbage. She turned to Jerry. "What you call this young'un?"

"Name's Michael. But we all call him Mud. I reckon you can see why."

Vicky laughed again, this time toward the child and not the rain. She handed him the head of cabbage, which he wrapped his little arms around like it was a stuffed bear. "Here now, Mud Jenkins. Take this for your payment for helping me. Go on, now, little farmer, and give it to your mommy." The boy took off back toward the truck in a flash, like he was nervous she might change her mind and take back his cabbage.

He dropped it twice in his excitement. Vicky leaned forward and cut the next cabbage out while she spoke to Jerry. "You got a little worker there. And he sure ain't scared of the rain. My mommy always said the rain'll baptize you as good as a preacher if you're humble enough to feel God in the drops."

Jerry gave her a nod like she had preached Bible and he knew the passage. He said, "You ain't gotta give away your cabbages."

Vicky rocked back onto her knees with another leafy head in her lap and kneeled, looking to the truck, where Mud was now sitting in his mommy's lap and holding his cabbage like it was a month's wages. "Take it. Hell, I might not live through summer. I'd hate to think of that cabbage and me both a rottin and that young'un a wantin it."

Jerry tipped his helmet and left. Vicky watched them pull away, then pulled up the rest of the cabbages, brought them in the house, and dried them.

That was yesterday, when the creek was just up. Now it was today, and the water was over the road and climbing up her yard.

She'd usually store her cabbages in the basement, which was little more than a hole dug under the kitchen running the size of a large closet, but the water was already collecting and pooling down there, so she had them all laid out in the kitchen, alongside some potatoes and onions she'd been storing. They was high enough to keep out of the water, she reckoned, but the moisture was a threat to their longevity.

Now her counter was covered in produce. The kitchen looked like a makeshift farmers' market.

She picked up the phone. Line was still out. Probably not coming back any time soon. She'd wanted to call her son, Dan, and let him know she was okay. He lived over on Ice Plant Holler with his wife, Marie, their four-year-old, Patrick, and their girl, Rayeanne.

Patrick and Rayeanne was her only grandbabies she saw on any regular basis. Vicky and Walt had six children, five girls and then, finally, a boy to carry on the name. Each of the girls was hard-working and smart. Each married fast and took to having babies of her own. They was too busy to make it over to see Vicky too often, and two of the five lived out of state, one in South Carolina and another whose man took a job in Ohio. Her youngest child was a boy, her son, Danny. Well, now he went by Dan. Dan worked for the same mining outfit Walt had worked for. Marie worked, too, so they'd leave the kids with Vicky from time to time.

Rayeanne was a unnaturally easy child to watch. You could plop her down in front of a TV and she'd be quieter than a field rabbit all day. Just giggling at the cartoons ever little bit or so. And little Patrick was just full of life. He'd wanna run up and down the yard, catch lightning bugs, pick flowers, and play all the games Vicky had played as a child, all the games she taught her own kids, like making out cloud shapes or listening to the stars. And the questions that child had! He was full of questions, and, lucky, for him, she was full of answers, having spent her fair share of summers on the planet. *What is that? Why is the corn so small? Why does the corn have hair? What is rust made out of?* That baby seemed to wear questions everywhere he went, and, best of all, he took the time to listen when she told him the answer.

And he loved being found! The pure delight that young'un felt if you found him in a game. He absolutely rejoiced at a match of hide-and-seek, but, bless his little heart, he always went to the same place, down the stairs behind the curtain and into the basement, where he'd hide behind the shelf with the jams and pickles.

The jams! Vicky hadn't moved them cause she reasoned they were sealed, but the water would rust their seals if it was to rise more. Vicky started down her little steps below the kitchen only to realize it was too late: the flood water was now standing above most of the basement, sloshing across her shelves of preserved food. Food that was now ruined. Food she had grown under suns now lost to history, food she had canned with forearms stronger than those she now possessed, food canned with hands that still knew the warmth and comfort of her husband. Food that was full of her life, her history, her story, a story that was now inedible.

And gone forever.

Vicky rushed back up to the window, where she had stood less than half an hour ago. The rain was pelting the water in angry thuds, and the water was brimming over her front steps, now only inches away from getting into her home.

The whole bottom was flooded.

Vicky stepped to the backside of the house facing the hillside. The water was already climbing up the hill. The current was pushing through faster than she'd ever seen it move. Twenty years before, maybe even ten, she'd have risked the flow and took to high ground. But she could barely walk without her cane. She'd never make it to the hill.

As she turned back to face the kitchen, the electricity snapped out in a slow and foreboding moan. Good. If the lines had went down somewhere down the holler from her, then there wadn't no juice in the wires around the house. She wouldn't need to worry about getting electrocuted. She took a step forward and felt something bite against her feet. Wet. The water was now in the house, seeping above her floorboards.

She sat on a kitchen chair, pulled back on the rubber boots, and tried to formulate a plan. She was not leaving the house. She couldn't if she wanted to; the water was sure to get up even higher, so she would need to start stacking furniture. She could get her couch onto her bed if she had to.

She got between the couch and the wall and started pushing it. She regretted getting that solid wood couch with the brown windmill pillows as a gift to herself when Walt died. It was heavy as sin. But she was sturdy. She pushed. It sloshed as it lunged forward. The water had already come up another inch above the floorboards. She didn't have the strength to pull, and she could only push by using her whole body, exhaling and shoving with all her strength. Inch by inch, the couch scooted across the room. The rising mud made it slide, therefore making it a bit easier to move, which was no comfort to Vicky. Just as the couch slowly made its way across the house, so, too, did the water rise.

Luckily, there was no halls or corners. It was a straight path into the bedroom. Still, it took a good half hour for Vicky to bump the couch to the edge of her bed. She had to lean against the arm and rest before hoisting it up. Her breath was coming in heavy. Too heavy. Still, she didn't give herself long, what with how fast the water was now coming. She grabbed her cane, wedged it under the couch, used it to lever up the edge of the frame, and pulled with all she had. Once she got it off the floor, she laid the cane against her body, the frame still resting against her hip, and plunged her hands under the edge of the couch.

The water was tepid and her hands slipped through mud and silt that slid, grainy and sludgy at the same time, across her skin. The combination felt like death to Vicky, cold and yet soft and wet. Despite standing in the middle of her flooding bedroom in a pair of rubber boots, she found herself thinking of the time Walt had brought home oysters on ice that he bought off a man with a truck who'd stopped in Battersburg on his way north from the Gulf of Mexico. They, too, felt like death. Slick. Cold. Lifeless. She refused to eat them and let the men slurp them by the dozen with moonshine while she fried herself some red tomatoes.

Lifting it took her only one try. She flipped the couch up onto its side, then pushed it over onto her bed. It crashed down but stayed solid atop the mattress. It was the highest point in the house now, adding at least a few more feet of time.

She would need it. The water was halfway up Vicky's boots and starting to lap against her house dress.

The final act would be saving the cabbages. They were lying on the counters, but the kitchen was lower than the rest of the house on account of the rise of the land. If the rain climbed at this rate, it would cover them in a couple of hours. She decided to move them on top of the upper cabinets. One by one, Vicky retrieved a head of cabbage, climbed onto a kitchen stool, and hoisted them up as high as the kitchen would allow, onto the empty space above.

She couldn't reach the cabinet tops well, so she would tip the cabbages and let them roll backward. She noticed that the wood was dusty as she pulled her fingertips away. On the one hand, given the rising water swelling across her home of fifty years and the wetness in her boots, Vicky felt relieved to discover that there was a place in the world still dry. On the other, she felt a burning shame that any part of her home was this dusty. The shame made her feel old, like she was past something and hadn't realized it had happened. The shame also made her work all the faster to find spaces for the remaining cabbages.

Three. That's what was left that wouldn't fit above the cabinets. She grabbed them, folded them in her dress, and stomped toward her bedroom. This was it. The water was now spilling over and into her boots. Despite being inside the house, somehow the current was slithering fast across the living room.

One, two, three, she hoisted the cabbages onto the couch laid across her bed. Then she grabbed onto the metal headboard of the spring bed and started to consider the easiest and safest way to get up onto the couch when she heard something faint that, unlike every other sound, wasn't rushing, angry sludge. A hum.

It grew louder, and Vicky worried it might be electricity in the water. She released the headboard and tried to put her boot on the bed. Damn it. It was too high. She had Walt put the bed up high so she could roll out of it easier in the mornings. Now she couldn't get on it unless she rolled into it—but she couldn't roll onto it fully on account of the couch.

She turned around, hastened by the electric buzzing, and threw herself onto the mattress. There was a thump. Only it wasn't her. Something had hit the house. And the hum wasn't electric. It was a motor.

The yell entered the room in wavy bursts as it cut its way across the flooding house. "Mommy?"

"Dan?" Vicky's skin released a wall of tension into the flooded murk climbing up the bedroom walls. Only then did she realize how anxious she was. "Danny!?"

Splashing, and then her son was standing in the doorway. "Mommy! Shew. I've been tore all to pieces. Jesus, we figured you was dead." Dan was wearing a pair of jogging pants and a white T-shirt. He rushed to her side to help her down.

"What are you wearing?"

"Are you shitting me, Mommy? Here I am standing in a flood rescuing you and you're worried about my clothes?" He lowered her down and back into the water.

Vicky tapped his pants with the end of her cane. "I's just asking. How'd you even get here?"

"Only way I could. A boat. Heard Big Branch was covered and tried to get up here in the Ranger. Couldn't even make it past the Opportunity School. So I called over and fetched Doug McCoy's speedboat."

"Well, damn. I never imagined the day a man'd bring a boat to my door."

Dan kicked floodwater as he moved toward the bedroom. "Anyway, Mommy, we gotta go. Rain ain't stopping no time soon."

"Here." She handed him the first of three cabbages. "Take these on out."

"Mommy. I got food at the house. Come on."

Vicky ignored him, making her way to the kitchen. She got on her stepping stool, which was only a foot itself out of the water, and began to reach for the heads of cabbage from the tops of the cabinets.

Dan was standing in the floodwater on the other side of her kitchen counter, still holding the cabbages he'd been given. "Mommy! We ain't got time for this."

She reached her hand back and rolled one of the cabbages closer, then lowered it down and onto the counter. "Help me and it'll go faster." She moved to the right and then pushed her hand, trying to knock the next one back. As she leaned, her whole body shook, and she lurched forward and fell against the cabinets.

Dan was immediately at her legs, his free arm around her waist. She said, "I was just dizzy."

He lowered her to the floor. "No. That was the whole house moving. We're going. *Now*!"

Her boy had never given Vicky an order like this before. Few men or women had. She grabbed the cabbage she had just lowered and trudged toward the front door, the brown mud sloshing into her boots. Outside, the entire world was gone. Brown water rose up and buried everything in a new sea. Vicky had many times imagined Noah and the Great Flood. She had always pictured a wooden boat full of animals of every color floating on pristine blue waters cleansing the earth and shining back the color of a clear sky. But in that moment she knew—the flood was dark and muddy. The cleansing was messy. It was sloshing with dirt and grime and life and death. The hilltops now looked like distant islands and everything else—her garden, her fence, her two burning bushes on cement planters on either end of the yard, and even the roses of Sharon her and Trussie had planted by the road—was now thoroughly submerged.

Dan had tied the boat up against one of the pillars on the edge of the porch. She tossed her cabbage in and turned. Dan followed behind her, his three cabbages still in his arms. "Let me help you down, Mommy." He grabbed her arm and she lowered herself into the motorboat. It had a shiny spray-painted exterior, a crimson color with flecks of chrome. Against the primordial waters and her four saved cabbages, the boat felt almost like an alien presence, like some Old Testament flying saucer.

Dan began to untie the rope fastened to the pillar. He was wearing tennis shoes that barely climbed above the water. He handed her the three cabbages she had placed on the couch. Vicky said, "Can't you go and get them other'ns?"

He stepped down into the boat, moved behind her, and neared the motor as she spoke. She looked tiny and ancient in the wideness of the makeshift rescue vessel. "Mommy, I ain't never heard you this tore up about no damn cabbages."

She didn't respond. He started the motor. Black smoke choked through the air as he backed the boat up, then started away from her house. They floated over her sidewalk, down the length of her yard and across her cabbage patch. Dan temporarily stopped the motor to safely move over her chain link fence, scraping the gate as they pushed across and into the space above the road. They were now almost exactly where the Jenkins feller's truck had been just a day before, only they were suspended a foot above where the top of his truck had been.

The waters, now cold, were rocking hard and fast, and a creaking noise was throbbing across the whole flooded bottom in a rhythm, like the pulse of a living thing being measured. She realized it was coming from her house itself. It was waving with the water, the walls pushing against themselves with each tumble of the newborn rapids. Before she could get the words out to tell her son, the entire house lurched forward and fell inward, the outside walls caving and crumbling in like they were made of cardboard. Her house had collapsed into itself under the force of the water. Instinctively, she reached out for the cabbages around her and pulled them to her side, like she was grabbing her children to save them from drowning while the boat sped away downriver.

She didn't have a home anymore.

Dan reacted first. "Holy fucking Jesus Christ! Shit!" He was yelling over the sound of the engine. "Mommy, you okay?"

She wanted to say yes. She wanted to say no. She wanted to say that they were alive and there wasn't nothing in that house that she didn't have in her memories. She wanted to say that they had good insurance cause they didn't technically live in the floodplain. She wanted to say she had lost everything and didn't know how to live with the loss. She wanted to cry and scream like people do on television.

But all she could actually do was think about her lost jams and cabbages, about the time she had spent tending to them, nurturing them, encouraging them, and picking them. About how the sun felt on her back on the cold mornings she went out to the hothouse Walt built to get them started earlier. About how much more effort it took to dig the holes to plant them outside than it used to take. About how she weeded and then washed the dirt out of her clothes afterward. About how much time and energy and life went into coaxing them out of the ground. About how she might never grow another one again.

She wondered for a second if she might be going crazy, sitting there thinking about cabbages while she had just lost the house her husband built, but then thought the better of worrying. Worrying didn't do no good. And worrying about worrying? Well, that was just pure luxury, and she couldn't afford luxury. She was homeless now, after all.

The boat's motor was too loud for them to talk, and Danny was never a big talker noways, so, exhausted, they sat in silence as her son guided them down the foreign terrain of a holler she had known all her life. They passed submerged homes and cars. They avoided powerlines that she could have reached out and touched. Finally, the boat came to a stop at the edge of the Opportunity School, which sat on a hillside against the last part of the road that led into Mosely. Dan helped his mother up out of the boat and over into the passenger seat of his pickup. He started it. He turned on the heat. They didn't speak. She watched from the safety and comfort of his heated truck cabin as he backed up, got out and loaded the boat back onto the trailer, a boat that still held the four saved cabbages, and then climbed back in.

As he started to pull out, she told him to turn the engine off. He complied. "What is it? You okay, Mommy?

She rolled her window down. A faint whiteness poked through the trees. It was a dog in the hills, looking down at them.

"You reckon that dog's okay?"

"Shit, yeah. Dogs ain't like us. They don't try to figure stuff out. They just know. I betcha he took to the hills a week ago. He's probably doing a hell of a lot better than us."

He started the truck and pulled out toward his house, where they both already knew, though would never say, that she would live the rest of her life.

Vicky was showered, dry, and warm, wrapped in a thick bathrobe belonging to Marie. She was breathing calmly, and the smell of soap was floating off her skin and hair. Her son's trailer was on the side of the hill up Ice Plant Holler, on a little lot they had made. They had plans for a double-wide someday and would need to cut off more of the mountain to accommodate it.

It had been two days since she arrived at her son's house, and she was still getting used to the idea that she would be staying here for the foreseeable future. Though she had seen her exterior walls crumble against themselves, some part of herself, deep down, held a belief that when the waters finally receded she might find her house still there, exactly as she had left it, photo albums, books, bed, couch, and vegetables waiting on her. She knew this wasn't true, but her skin, as much as it now smelled like her daughter-in-law's soap, held tight to the belief.

Today was the first day Sparky Messer promised there'd be no rain at all. It was morning. Dan was still asleep from his late shift, the young'uns hadn't got up yet, and Marie was gone to work. She took a towel and stepped onto the front porch. She laid it across the steps and sat down on it. It felt nice to be outside and warm. The sun was drying up the parts of her that were beginning to imagine the entire world outside the trailer as a damp, cold flood.

She was totally absorbed by the sunshine and trilling of birds on the hillside when she heard the screen door rasp itself shut, followed by the soft thrumming of tiny steps. She didn't have to turn. "Is that my baby, Patrick?"

Small chirps of laughter responded to her, and she felt his hands on her back. A tiny embrace. He came to her side and sat beside her on the towel. He was wearing one of his dad's T-shirts as a nightgown. He lay his head across her lap. She moved her hand across his hair in a sweeping comfort.

"Sad mamaw?"

"No, baby. I ain't sad. Just letting the sun love on me."

"Your house got a flood."

He wasn't lying. "Yeah, baby. It sure did."

"And I cain't see it."

"Yep. We gotta wait till the water is down, baby. It ain't safe."

"Floodwaters?"

"Yeah. The floodwaters."

"The floodwaters is bad."

Vicky felt the sun slip out from behind the clouds and grow brighter. She was aware of the softness of her grandbaby's hair, the dryness of the towel, the faint and verdant wisp of summer making its way back after a year gone, like it had done every year.

"No baby. The water didn't know. The water don't know. Water don't know bad. Water don't know good. The water don't know nothing. It just is."

Patrick pressed his face against her legs and sighed.

THE WATER DON'T KNOW

2005

My beautiful Patrick,
I wanted to speak at your service. I wanted to tell everyone there what I couldn't tell you. What I couldn't tell myself. But I couldn't say it. I couldn't do it. I was never as brave as you. But I did write it. And maybe silent words are enough. And maybe you will hear it even if I don't say it.
Chris

They found your body
in the darkness of the lake
hours after I called the police.
They took a statement and I told them
that I thought you were on more than beer
that I was worried because you'd fought with your dad
that I was worried because you wanted us to swim in the lake
and I said no because it was late and you were drunk and I was scared
and you walked off my porch and said not to worry about it and you were fine
and you drove your car at three in the morning in one of your affirmations of life
and maybe you swam nude under the stars and for a brief moment were the freest man alive
and maybe you slipped on rocks and were afraid and called out my name and I wasn't there.
Only the water knows.

But the water don't know
that my ache for you wakes me
that it shushes my skin when I want sleep
that I saw you changing at the pool in tenth grade
and I was wanting to look but I turned away from you

because I hoped that you would someday give me willingly
what I wanted to take.

But the water don't know
that I drove to the bookstore in Battersburg
to get that comic with the doodles on the cover
cause you said something about them felt like home
and I just wanted to be a part of you feeling like home
and I kept it for months in my glove box wanting to give it to you.

But the water don't know
that your smile is twisted on the left
and only moves when your eyebrow does
and as your face disappears behind my closed eyes
the last blurs of you are the hook of your eyebrow and smile.

But the water don't know
that I only found the courage to tell my mom
that I was gay and this was never gonna change
because it might make it easier for me to tell you.

But the water don't know
that I would have followed you anywhere
just for the chance to know more of you.

But the water don't know
that without you

I
can't
be
in
this
place.

STORIES THAT DON'T GET TOLD

Mosely. Winter 1956.

Edward was waiting

his hope like a new fire

the threat

the snow was feathers

made his way.

the breezeway they built against the hill

Harold said it softly. "We

the entire house

not even knowing

again?"

How could they?

would by now

against his boots.

the length of the holler

"Don't ever

having placed the quilt his mamaw had

Harold's jacket

like oil and aftershave

a home

Edward holding on

ladled into two bowls

voice ascending, feet planted

the ripped sleeve, exposing

just one time

a faucet dripped

blistered hands

"What if

Harold steadied the

together.

UNTO THESE MEN DO NOTHING

we all returned to ancient Sodom
did heed its brimstone beacon
time after all just a construct
my brothers and I agreed to keep
ticking away
and were greeted at the gate
with wine and whores and sand
and Lot came by with men
we already knew were angels
and they looked upon
my sweet cousin Robby
who even back then they knew
would in 2009 be murdered
and stuffed into a plastic box
in some suburb of Louisville
when he fled the closeness
of creeks and hollers and hills
for some form of sodomite freedom
and the angels said unto us *we are sorry*
for what you have all been through
cause that's not what this story is about
but we had already been through
what we had already been through
because of what this story would be
and we joined the angry mob
and called out with them to Lot
to bring down the men that we might know them
that they might speak to the fullness of blazing ruins
whose smoke rises beyond time like a cracked furnace
and Lot stood at his door, already drunk, and said,
No, my friends. Do not do this wicked thing!
but weary of being clutched between verses
we named this a time for gathering stones
and cast them till thunder shook the earth with ink.

THE WORTHY

Ice Plant. Late Summer 2023.

Dan Case dabbed the outer section of PVC pipe with purple primer, enjoying the chemical scent laying itself across the air like an invisible veil. The thin gasoline burn loosened his brain cells for a few seconds, dissolving the jarred edges of some memories, softening the stories of light, color, and pain his firing synapses could tell after decades. After a few seconds, Dan smothered the same section of pipe in glue and slid onto it a plastic coupler like he was offering it a wedding ring.

It was warm enough for the glue to dry fast. It was Sunday afternoon, early September, but still hot. A good couple of hours and the glue would set enough for what little water might pass through during a church service.

Dan leaned back against the wooden door of the little church bathroom, which he had propped open to let the smell of solvent and glue escape into the main sanctuary. The bathroom was narrow and only a few feet deep, little more than a closet tucked into the rear corner furthest from the main entrance. He was holding the glued piece of pipe, giving it time to dry before reinstalling it under the toilet, when the scrape of opening church doors startled him.

Sitting on the floor, he couldn't see who had come in, so he wasn't sure if they could see him. Not wanting to scare anyone who wouldn't know to anticipate his presence, he called out a greeting. "Howdy! Don't mind me, just doing a little plumbing."

Within moments, a pair of well-shined dark shoes appeared atop the plush burgundy carpet that blanketed nearly the entire building. They stopped just outside the bathroom door, and standing in them was David Sizemore, the preacher of the Old Time Mountain Pentecostal Church, the husband of Dan's first cousin, Joyce. David's hair was slicked against his scalp and parted at an angle that rose sharply toward the crown of his head. Dan thought it looked like the barbs of a dark bird's feather.

David looked at the sections of married pipe in Dan's hand. "What you got there, Reverend?" Dan was not a reverend, and his nickname felt strange coming from an actual preacher's mouth. Like a melted word. David wore pressed gray slacks and a long-sleeved white dress shirt. It was entirely too hot for either.

Dan's denim shorts and faded *Pigeon Forge, TN* T-shirt were suitable for his plumbing work. "Joyce called me about a leak in the bathroom she saw, said you was over to Hindman between services and couldn't get no phone signal, so I told her I'd come over. Your toilet connector was stretched too tight for the dual stop valve is all, so I'm just lifting this pipe here a bit for y'all, then I'll hook the sink and commode back up."

As Dan spoke, David closed his lips against his teeth, almost as if he were trying to manipulate a toothpick without using his hands, breathing in through his nose. "Well, now, it's a kind offer of you to come out over here. We appreciate it. But she shouldn't a done that."

"It ain't no trouble. I was home and ain't no place in Mosely open on Sunday nohow."

"Well, see"—David scratched the length of his left forearm and put both hands in his pockets—"problem is you ought not to be doing no work on the church. I appreciate it, but it just ain't right, on account of you not being saved." David spoke calmly, but he kept his eyes on Dan.

Dan jerked backward. The door smacked the wall in an overreaction to his sudden movement. "Well, David, I didn't know I wadn't saved, now. What was Eugene Mullins a doin when he held me under Big Branch of Beaver Creek back in the summer a '72?"

David brought his hands together in front of his stomach, palms facing each other as if in meditation. He spoke calmly. "I ain't trying to offend you. But, now, truth is what it is. We work to stay saved, and you ain't been to a church in a long, long time. Bible says it clear: work out your own salvation with fear and trembling." He lifted his hands up and all around him, as if the words were written on the walls. A pause, and then he lowered his eyes again to Dan. "Course you're *welcome* here. All are welcome in the Lord's House. But it wouldn't be fitting for you, what with you being backslidden and all, to *work* on the church."

Dan rocked forward, lifting himself to his feet using the small sink in front of him. His face reddened with the struggle. He was in his early sixties, and his years in the mines had taken the best of his health. He stood in shorts and faced David. Dan's knees bore the imprint of the gray bathroom tile he had been kneeling against for the better part of an hour. "Here, then. Finish it yourself." He stepped into the sanctuary and thrust the pipe and connector at David. "You wadn't here, and I was just trying to make sure y'all had toilets that can flush."

David looked at the glued pipe as if Dan were a child offering him a toy. "Like I said, I appreciate it. But the church is the Bride of Christ. Only Christian hands can serve the church. Otherwise, wouldn't be right in the eyes of the Lord."

Dan's eyes flew up in wild anger. For a split second, they landed on a wooden statue of a crucified Christ draped in long purple strips of cloth, hanging above the pulpit. A river of colors flowed in from the window to the right. It wasn't a stained glass window. The church was too small and poor for such. But there were colored sheets of painted plastic that children had made in Sunday School, depicting Bible stories, and the light flowed in, bathing the dying Christ's body in greens, purples, and yellows their hands had mixed.

Dan brought his eyes back to David. "Are you kidding me!?"

David did not respond. He pulled his lips together as if he had no more intention of speaking on the matter.

Dan smacked the pipe against the sink and left it. "Do what you want. You won't have no toilets tonight."

Dan stormed past David, stumbling through the empty worship hall. He marched down the middle aisle that separated the wooden pews of the still country church and slammed the door as he left the building.

David did not turn to watch his wife's cousin leave. The slamming door echoed across the sanctuary, and David felt the vastness and emptiness of the building in the weight of the echo.

Yes. God was good. God was vast. But in the world of men, God was lonely. Few truly wanted the Lord. Few truly sought righteousness, and in their confusion, they were angry at God. How disappointed our Father must often be in his creation.

David tossed the sections of pipe into a trash can robed in a white lavender-scented liner. He wouldn't use them. At home, they used old plastic bags from the store for this purpose, but the liners were a humble way to honor the dignity of this place. One of many small prices that added up.

They could not be of the world. And so the world would hate the church.

This was the price John the Baptist warned about.

This was the price the church paid.

A sign would be put on the door to close the bathroom. Folks could make do; the men could go into the woods behind the church, if need be, and the women and children could walk over to the Pack-n-Save.

David walked to his office to write out a sign. His office was really just a converted boiler room behind the pulpit, but the builders of the church had given it its own door to the outside leading toward the hill. Back in the old days, when this church was new, the Reverend Ernest Spurlock had lived just on the hill's other side. He'd certainly have walked across it Sunday mornings to come in to light the boiler, then walk through the church and open the front doors to the congregation. It must have seemed to them that he lived in the church or simply appeared when the Lord wanted him.

People were thoughtful back in those days. They knew how to show respect to the Lord. They understood the sanctity of this building, what Timothy meant when he said thou oughtest to behave thyself in the house of God, which is the church of the living God.

The boiler had long been nonfunctional, replaced by central heating and air-conditioning, which David only turned on shortly before church began. No point paying to keep an empty building cool. The boiler room office was unbearably stuffy, so he opened the back door to let in some of the air whispering down the hillside.

David tipped over the cement block he used to prop it open with the sole of his shoe, thinking of Dan slamming the front door on his way out. People were too quick to anger and so easily blamed the preacher for holding up the standards of the Lord.

In the short year he had pastored the Old Time Mountain Pentecostal Church, he had already seen many take out their anger on the building, the congregation, and even himself, due to his upholding the Lord's commandments. There was Loretta Hamilton, who tried to bring her boyfriend to church while she was still divorcing her husband. The Lord rebuked her in the sermon, and she tore out of the building in a screaming fury, spinning gravel in the parking lot and taking out one of the new Sunday School windows. There was Marvin Maynard and his wife, who refused to hear the Lord about their son, Caleb, a known homosexual. David's wife, Joyce, was filled with the Spirit and weeping in tongues, and Sister Gail stood and interpreted the Spirit's word: God wanted them to rebuke his unnatural sins and ask for healing. The Maynards refused, and Marvin's wife got so mad she threw a hymnal against the wall, which had to be replastered. Even David's own brother, Jimmy, when rebuked in the Spirit for his drinking, took on a kicking and dancing spirit and knocked over a speaker box, jerking the cords loose as he thrashed about. He walked out of the church and never came back through its doors.

And now, his cousin by marriage, Dan Case, had slammed a door to the very sanctuary of the church. Mercifully, he had broken nothing.

It was a surefire sign that you were filled with a devil if you were destroying the church on account of your own wrongdoing.

David wrote out the sign explaining the toilets, found some tape, and with assurance guiding his steps returned to the bathroom that Dan Case had been squatting in. The church would survive the evening, they would use righteous money and its faithful servants to make changes, and this would be resolved.

The front door to the chapel creaked open. David turned, expecting to see Dan Case back and ready to give him an earful.

It was Joyce, her arms draped with plastic store bags. She lifted the bags toward him. Their smooth rustling, audible from across the sanctuary, was softened by the carpet. "Just some wood polish and freshener. What you doing here?"

"Dan Case come by. Said you sent for him. I put him out. Ain't right for him to work in the church." He paused and watched her retrieve her keys from her purse. "Not with him not being saved."

Joyce slowly removed the items from the store bag and placed them into the small cabinet at the far end of the sanctuary, behind the empty coat rack.

She spoke calmly. "You're right. I didn't mean to cause no trouble. I figured it was good to get Dan into the church for any reason." A line surfaced across the flush skin of her forehead. David couldn't tell if it was from the heat or the shame of her error.

"Dan does need the church. We all do. Let's pray for him during tonight's service."

"Well, what about the commode?" She closed the cabinet door, turning a key in an antique pewter hasp lock original to the building that she kept on a chain.

"God'll provide."

As he spoke, David watched his wife shake off the shivers. She said, "Shew. Somebody just walked right over my grave."

David nodded. "Let's go get something to eat before church."

They left. David carefully locked the doors from the outside. It being Sunday, Joyce would have left a chicken roasting in the oven at home for their supper. It was his favorite meal of the week.

That evening, the church was packed, at least beyond any recent memory. Joyce took attendance as her husband opened the service with a prayer. There were twenty-eight souls in the building, including the two of them. While he prayed, Joyce adjusted the wooden church register of weekly attendance and offering total. Last Sunday, there were nineteen in attendance and the church had taken in $380. If they really compelled the flock, if the Lord truly moved, they could get well over $600 tonight.

With that kind of money, they could do so much for the church, could do so much to save the souls in these hills.

Joyce positioned the register on the wall, leaving the slot for today's offering blank, and then silently joined the widows of the church auxiliary, who took the first row on the left, opposite the deacons on the right.

After the opening prayer, David lit the two evening service candles, opened the large King James edition Bible kept at the pulpit, and asked the congregation to share their praises and burdens.

The pews percolated with testimonies of pains and hopes:

A drunkard from over on Cow Creek had given up his beer only the night before and had come to find the Lord again.

A woman's mother was diagnosed with lady cancer so bad they were having to treat her up in Lexington.

A man's oldest girl had come home and begged him to put her in rehab.

God was moving people to the church to find their salvation. They could surely sense the End Times were coming, the impending judgments awaiting those not right with God when the trumpets would sound.

Joyce thought immediately of Dan, her own cousin not even clean enough in the eyes of the Lord to bring water to a toilet. She whisked her right hand far into the air.

Her husband acknowledged her. "Yes, sister?"

"I praise the Lord and thank Him for being here tonight and thank Him for saving my soul. I know the Lord is powerful and real."

A low rumble of amens rolled through the pews. The air conditioner kicked on, groaning against the evening's heat.

Joyce continued. "I've got so many lost in my family, Lord. So many who don't know the sweet rescue a God. I ask that the Lord bring them into His light a mercy. I ask that the Lord save them, that we might stand before Him in His grace and glory for all eternity."

The amens grew louder and Joyce began to weep. Sister Londa, standing to her right, placed a comforting hand on her shoulder and called out, "Bless her, Jesus! Give her strength!" Londa's Spirit-filled anointing caused her denim skirt to sway in waves of love.

Joyce felt the Holy Ghost seize her shoulders; it wept in rounds down her back. She convulsed slightly, her waist jerking forward. She gave into the pull and proceeded to the front of the sanctuary, turning to address the congregation. Twenty-six people faced her, with David standing behind, elevated, by the pulpit.

Joyce rolled her voice across the church. "Y'all please join me in praying for my cousin Dan Case. He's faced his share a trials in this world, so much sorrow in this life. Lost a boy to darkness. And in his own sin, he turned away from the Lord. Pray that God might move His hand a mercy over my cousin, just up the holler, that he might come back to the fold. Oh, please, Jesus! Hana-na Shana-na!" She broke out in tongues, her sharp ululations flooding the tiny church house like the sound of many waters. A rush of bodies rippled forward, all laying hands on Joyce and each other. Tears and prayers rushed around the praying throng, who began to dance in the Spirit and speak in tongues with her.

David had never witnessed such a mighty outflow of the Spirit so early in a service.

The preacher looked down as he turned to face the church.

The body of Christ.

Pleased, he stepped away from the pulpit, stood behind his wife, then began to pray with his congregation. He laid his open palm against the back of her head, and she fell to her knees and wailed out songs in the language of the angels.

Tambourines chattered.

Kinfolk and strangers wept and cried out with joy.

Bodies shook across the space separating pulpit from pew, pews that only an hour before his wife, after serving him dinner, had faithfully polished.

David closed his eyes and prayed to the Almighty that his wife's cousin might indeed see the error of his ways and come home.

The service was so loud that David didn't quite hear the slamming, didn't quite hear the sudden cries and broad yelps that gashed the harmony of the service, didn't quite hear the rhythmic panting behind him.

But someone finally screamed his name. "Brother David!"

He opened his eyes to see a dozen congregants staring past him, all pointing, some yelling in shock.

He spun round from his still praying wife to face the rear offering table.

A large brown dog stood directly behind him, mouth opened, eyes bright with confused excitement.

The door to the boiler room office was nudged free. The back door! He had left the back door open, and a dog had gotten in.

David spoke over the people still praying. "It looks like the Spirit is so strong tonight that even the animals are moved to bear witness!"

A few people laughed, and most prayers drew to their close as people shifted their attention to the interloping canine, but Joyce and the auxiliary widows continued silently speaking to God. She was still kneeling on the floor.

David approached the dog, and its bright eyes grew frightened. It wore no collar, and some bald patches on its legs gave it the telltale signs of some abandoned mutt. It started to turn, saw a group of men approaching, and spun back to David, who lifted out his arms as if to grab the creature.

Recoiling, the dog dashed toward the back wall, trying to hide under the offering table, and in doing so pulled the tablecloth, knocking over the collection plate and the two service candles.

The cloth immediately caught fire.

People began to yell. The men on the other side of the pulpit rushed to reach the dog and table. David instinctively turned and sprinted for the bathroom, flung open its door, and twisted the faucet handle.

Nothing. Then he remembered—Dan. The pipe!

He ran back, expecting the men to have put the fire, and the dog, out, but the flames were already devouring the tablecloth and reaching to touch the feet of the wooden Christ above it.

The men stared, transfixed by the blazing light climbing to reach their savior. Jesus did not flinch, staring out with the same expression of pain and mourning even as his purple loincloth, which he had worn every Sunday before this one, now flickered fire against his torso.

David rushed forward, but the dog, taking in his speed, spun out from under the table and into the Sunday School room, its side door into the sanctuary left open for ventilation.

David faced the burning statue. He tried to pull the fabric away, but the flames were hotter than he anticipated. They licked at his hands, singing at his fingertips. He slipped them to his sides, wincing, then tried again to clear the searing fabric from the wall.

But the fabric was gone.

Christ, and the wall behind him, was engulfed in flame.

The church was on fire.

Congregants began to run from the building, spilling out the front door.

Joyce stood up, squared her shoulders, and quickly began to help the elderly women on walkers down the aisle, women who had moments before prayed for her cousin Dan to repent of his sins.

A man called out from the other side of the aisle. "I called 911. They're a comin, Brother!"

A dark flood of smoke washed down from the ceiling and tumbled over the faithful, below, as they fled. David followed behind his wife, who had already started a count. He was the last out the doors. His flock crossed into the small gravel parking lot as sirens wailed beyond the mouth of the holler.

Joyce breathed in deeply and looked at David. "There's twenty-eight here, including us. That's everybody. I counted twice."

David staggered to the edge of the lot, near the church van at the side of the road, where people had begun to cluster. It was still an hour from sunset, but even this close to town the hills blocked out what remained of the sun, its fading glow spreading out like a thin, dark broth. David raised his voice across the waning light and frightened congregation: "God will deliver us. God will save us. Let us pray."

But even as he prayed, there was a scattering. Some stayed. But most folks were already in their cars, moving them to the safety of the other side of the road. Some turned either to the left or the right, up or down the holler, abandoning the church service and fire entirely, trying to get away.

The Old Time Mountain Pentecostal Church sat at the mouth of the holler, which ended in downtown Mosely; the fire station was scarcely a mile away. A fire truck appeared in front of the parking lot, its weeping siren and flashes of red and blue welcome intrusions into the prayer. Four men descended as David ran to meet them.

One thundered, "Anybody inside?"

David said, "No. My wife counted. Ain't nobody in there. I was the last out."

A firefighter spoke rapidly in jargon to another as they grabbed equipment from the truck. David stood mere feet from the firefighter he had spoken to.

It was the Maynard boy, Caleb. The homosexual. He was the firefighter who first spoke.

David threw his hands up, like Moses parting the waters. He positioned himself in front of the responders. "No, son. No. The Lord won't have it, not unless you've asked for forgiveness for your sins. *Please.*"

The Maynard boy was, in fact, a man in his mid-twenties. He towered over David.

"Buddy, I don't give two shits what you think. I gotta job to do. Get outta my way."

David turned to the other men, a solid wall behind their squad leader. He implored, "Are *y'all* born again?"

None spoke. Caleb yelled sharply, "They're my men. Not yours." He was already gathering gear as he gave the call over his left shoulder: "Secure the scene. *Go.*"

David bolted back to the church doors, opened them, and frantically looked inside. Already, the entire pulpit and back wall were consumed. Smoke collapsed from the ceiling in thick columns of rolling anger.

He spit as he pulled the doors shut, bolted the locks. He did not look at the approaching firefighters, nor the onlookers beyond them, but instead seemed to direct his attention to the trees at the parking lot's edge. Panic bubbled from his throat, his tongue thick, but his words were clear as his eyes tried to reach their branches. "The Lord will not deliver us through unholy hands. He won't! We must pray!" Orange pulsing bled through the sliver of space between the ancient doors, showing, even in the anemic light of dusk, the wind that lifted his oiled hair in flat plates from his head.

The armed firemen hovered at the bottom of the stairs leading to the door. Caleb yelled "Axe!" and another lifted one into the air. He turned to David. "Outta my way! *Now*!"

David's eyes touched the men. He stabbed both arms forward, his palms facing upward like they held a wall. "You shall *not* go in!"

Though the congregation was too far away to see or hear what was happening with full clarity, the scene was nevertheless unmistakable: the preacher had locked the church doors and was trying to prevent the firefighters' entry.

One of the churchmen broke from the crowd. "Brother David, what's happening!? Let them in!"

David's gaze tightly held the firefighters, who stood like granite statues at the foot of the steps. "I can't let them. The Lord will not have it! The church is the Holy bride!"

The man yelled back, "But we prayed and they came. The Lord sent help! *Let them in*!"

Another yelled, "Brother David, don't do this!"

A woman yelled, "Sister Joyce! Where are your keys?"

David's eyes jerked to see his wife clutch her purse close to her side. She didn't answer the call.

A teenage girl was the next to yell. "There's a dog trapped in there! Please! Help him!"

The Maynards' son took a step closer to the preacher. "I will knock your ass down these goddamn steps if you don't move, *right now.*"

David, eyes shut, hardened his face as if ready to receive a direct hit. He was mumbling a prayer: "I will hold fast that which is good. I will abstain from all appearance of evil."

Caleb was now inches from David's face. "I'm not the one burning down a fucking church."

Just as he grabbed David's collar, the girl called out again, her panic piercing the steady rumble of flames. "The Sunday School's back door! There's another way!"

The other three firefighters flew to the side of the building as Caleb released his grip on the preacher and followed suit. The sound of an axe chopping wood climbed up the side of the hill and fell back down the parking lot. A crash.

David swallowed and looked as though he might choke. He gathered himself and slowly walked to the side of the building in measured steps, like Christ walking on the surface of water. A firefighter kept the crowd pushed back toward the road, ignoring the approaching pastor, as the other two, one with axe drawn, stood guard by the opening. Caleb Maynard was already inside the Sunday School lean-to.

The crowd gasped as a cloud of light exploded across David's face. Flames lifted out of the roof and into the darkened sky, lighting the overhanging branches of trees from below.

A firefighter at the door hollered inside. No response. A low, rumbling creak sighed out from the hillside as a portion of the roof fell in, sending burning chunks of splintered wood and sheets of crinkling ember screaming into the heavens.

The throng howled in fright as the church began to fall in on itself.

Everyone looked up. The entire hill was in flames.

Wanda was listening to her police scanner and sipping coffee. It was a warm evening, so she'd opened her windows to let in the air while she sat on the small front porch in the one chair it could accommodate.

She lit a cigarette and felt her muscles flatten into the cushion of her chair. Night had shifted the air from hot to warm, and her bones were thankful for it. She was beyond the years that welcomed the cold.

The last of the cicadas were croaking love songs of crescendo zips in her front yard. They were interrupted by a mumble on Wanda's police scanner inside the house. Sitting on the porch, she couldn't make out everything. Some church over to Mosely being on fire. Ice Plant Holler. Police backup. That wasn't too close to the school, but it was almost downtown. Close enough.

She wondered if they might call off school the next day. School closings usually happened in the winter, when snow or freezes came. But fire?

She took a sip of coffee. Lukewarm. The exact temperature of the air. It was good, how she wanted it.

She wondered what she would cook if she was free.

The firefighter who had pushed back the crowd was now dragging a hose to the side of the church. The dry brush had taken on fire quickly, which spread up the hill with a rapid hunger. Streams of yellows and oranges flickered up the growth of the slope on either side of the trees, looking like exposed veins of light.

Katie Tackett and her husband, Henry, had waited until dusk to go sow two lines of bush beans. They wouldn't plant much, since they had a hard time getting any help to pick them, but it felt good to grow their own vegetables when they could.

It also helped with the cost of food.

Katie had already covered the seeds with some fresh dirt and told Henry they should wait until it was cooler to give them their first douse of water. Her mother had always said it was bad luck to water late bush beans in the heat of the day. But now it was time.

Though it was dark, she knew the land by memory, and pulled the water hose across the front yard, toward her side garden. She set the nozzle to a low mist and made sweeping gestures across the two rows of beans that ran between the outbuilding and the woods.

In the distance, she noticed a glow in the sky. Henry stood beside her, leaning against the fence, smoking his pipe.

"Henry. What is that?"

His eyes were better than hers, even if the rest of his body was worse. He looked off in the direction of the light. "Shew, I hope it's finally them aliens come to get me and take me to that planet a virgins like I've been praying."

Katie considered spraying him in the face with the water hose. Then didn't. She said, "Buddy, I wish they would! Your luck, it'd be a planet a virgin old men."

Henry smiled at her gumption. "Looks like they're burning the hills."

Katie stared and tried to get a closer look. If she squinted her eyes, she could just make it out. "Why do they do that, anyway? Burn the hills. Just seems dangerous."

Henry pulled in quick tiny puffs of air to keep his pipe burning. "All kinds a reasons. Some people's just clearing off their own land. Some people think it thins the brush to keep bigger fires from doing damage later. But usually, it's just accidents or ignorance."

Katie said, "You know, a burning's kinda beautiful, though, once you really look at it. Just so big and unexpected. And alive. Sorta makes me think a God."

Henry started coughing. Katie expected him to make fun of her, to make another joke out of everything, like he always did. But as his fit subsided, he raised his gaze and fixed it upon the burning mountain in the distance.

Henry said, "Yeah. You're right. It does."

The trees behind the church were incendiary. They cast smoldering cinders like stones, and embers were floating across the gravel parking lot where so many had prayed only minutes before. They landed on the scattered believers, who, unable to see, felt like they were being snowed upon.

The sharp plastic angles of the taped packet tucked into his underwear poked into the soft flesh of Jamie's groin. It was likely an unnecessary precaution, but the cops in Mosely were always overstepping the rules and searching people without warrants. Most of them dealt, too, anyway.

He wouldn't travel with a bottle of pills without his name on it, let alone pills with no bottle, unless he was careful. The cops had it out for him.

He was supposed to meet his customer in the parking lot of the old Martin's Department Store, empty and abandoned now for nearly ten years. Kids in town would park there and play music when they had nothing better to do, which was every day.

He was turning onto the main road into Mosely when he heard sirens. Police cruisers and ambulances were turning up into Ice Plant Holler. Panicked, he felt a quick slosh of sweat pool around the package in his briefs. Something was going down.

Jamie eased his truck into the Fast-n-Fill, quickly deciding to stop for gas. He calmly pumped a few dollars into a mostly full tank, then sent a short text.

"Sorry. Can't make it."

He pulled back onto the road and away from town. They wouldn't catch him today.

The thinned congregation prayed as the remains of their church blanketed them in soft wafers of ash and fire tore up the hillside and swept back down the holler. Service vehicles of all sorts now swarmed the parking lot like locusts, bathing them in artificial lights screeching in riled, skyward cries.

Tammy was only feet from a group of teenage boys in hoodies, vaping in front of the pop machine. She was sitting in a plastic chair, itself the top chair of a display stack of plastic chairs put outside for the Dollar Store's end-of-summer sale. Closing time was coming soon, and she was on her last ten, studying for the first exam of her final semester of school. One of the kids tried shaking the machine. One held up a phone. The other two snickered with teenage noises.

She waved her notebook at them, annoyed. "Y'all get the hell on out of here. I ain't got the energy to do CPR if that pop machine falls on one of y'all heatherns. And I'm on my break. Go on, now!" She smacked the plastic arm of the chair for emphasis, but it folded down impotently upon contact with her hand, like the chair was refusing to agree with her. The boys didn't respond, but the one with the phone put it in his pocket and nodded at her, a show of respect for her unambiguous way of telling them to leave.

She watched them file down the parking lot toward the drive-through cigarette store. Something was wrong. Behind the store, way off in the distance, she could just make out a tower of black smoke climbing up into the sky.

"What the heck is that?" She wasn't speaking to anybody in particular. A faint glow flickered in town, far away from the cut-through. A fire. She couldn't see where it was coming from, exactly, but a thick stroke of blackness was rolling up like it was escaping some angry furnace.

"Damn it to hell." She crawled down from the stack of chairs with four full minutes still left on her break. Employees weren't allowed to buy anything when they were on the clock; she had to do it now. She knew her asthma was gonna be acting up, and she'd need some Zyrtec. Smoke always smothered her to death.

The three firemen held their position, working to ready their hose at the Sunday School door as police began to run tape across the parking lot to keep the crowd behind a line of safety. Officers questioned the members of the Old Time Mountain Pentecostal Church, taking statements on clipboards. Ambulance workers handed out bottles of water and checked the oxygen levels of the congregation's elders.

Keesha was sitting beside her mommy on the bed of a pickup truck. It didn't run, but Mud Jenkins said he knew a feller who had a motor that'd fit it, so they parked it in front of the trailer time being.

Keesha figured Mud wadn't ever gonna get it running. He was already asleep, and it was only barely past dark on a Sunday. All he did was sleep.

She was glad. She liked him better sleeping.

A old red car pulled into the driveway. It was Big Jason's. He rolled down his window and waved at them both.

Mandi said, "Well, damn. Church ain't out for another hour. What you doin here already? They done run you off?"

Big Jason was kinda white in the face. "It's crazier'n heck, Mandi. Like I told you, I was only gonna go to that church over on Ice Plant cause I heard they was good people. But the dang church caught on fire!"

Mandi showed shock in her voice but remained firmly seated on the back of the tailgate. "Do what, now?"

Big Jason continued. "You wouldn't believe it. That preacher, you know him, David something-or-other, married to Joyce Case, he tried to bar the doors and wouldn't let the firemen in."

Mandi hopped down. "We-ll"—she said it in two syllables—"you picked a damned awful time to quit drinking."

Big Jason pointed behind him. "Ain't that the truth. But I wanna keep kicking, you know? Doctor said my liver cain't take no more. Shew. But here, take these two cases a beer. Even if I'm gonna quit, I ain't wasting em."

Keesha hopped down, too, in case her mommy needed help carrying the beer. Her mind was dancing with pictures of a church fighting a preacher while it was burning. She imagined them both in boxing gloves and the fire grew out of the church roof like ginger hair.

Mandi opened the door and lifted the first case out. "You sure you don't want one? Just this one last time. I'd feel guilty not offering, what with everything you been through."

Big Jason sighed, then cut the engine. "Yeah, I reckon. Just one more. Mud around?"

"Sleeping."

He stood up out of the car, stepping around Keesha, and grabbed the second case. They all walked back to the truck. He lifted Mandi up onto the tailgate and she giggled while he did.

Keesha said, "I can get myself back up."

Big Jason said, "Course, Keesha-Bug."

Two cans of beer clicked open. Keesha stared down at the creek, trying to imagine what it would look like, and sound like, and smell like, if her trailer was on fire, too.

They heard the barking first. Intense, guttural cries rising from a place of pure fear. Then clashing. The axed Sunday School door, still loosely coupled to a single hinge, crashed downward as a brown dog shot itself from the side of the church like it was barreling from a slingshot. It didn't go toward the lined-off crowd; it instinctively ran up the holler alongside the hill, flying down the rounded dip where the flat land started to curve up.

Following behind was Caleb Maynard, who fell out the door opening and then pushed forward at a steady speed, as much of a run as was possible in such heavy gear.

He circled back to join his men in an instant, who now had the hose fully extended and set. Caleb had been in the Sunday School addition not even a full minute, but the fire had already climbed the entire hillside. He yelled to his squad over the blaze as they steadied the hose for aim. "Dog's out, now. Was hiding, couldn't find the door. *We gotta go*!"

The men unleashed a torrent that shot through the air.

The preacher and his fractured remnant, bound on the opposite side of the road, bowed their heads in witness.

As the water fell, Caleb tried to imagine what they might be praying for.

The door barked open and Rayeanne threw her pocketbook on the couch positioned opposite her dad's recliner. She had just finished a double shift at the Fast-n-Fill and was desperate to take her bra off and get a pop. Dan was stretched out in his chair and flipping aimlessly through television channels.

"You hungry?" He didn't look up from the TV.

She grunted in response, leaning against the couch to remove her left shoe.

"You're home late. Thought the evening shift ended half an hour ago."

"Yeah. Whole a Ice Plant's backed up to Mosely cause a fire trucks."

Dan looked up at his daughter as she continued. "Joyce and them's little church—it's on fire."

Dan's channel surfing came to a sudden stop. He lowered the remote control to his lap. Rayeanne walked past him and opened up the fridge, leaning over to check the contents of some old Cool Whip containers. She said, "We got anything to eat?"

Dan watched her remove a lid and place the small tub on the countertop. He lifted his remote back up, turned once again to the television, and continued pushing through a muted chorus of neon pixels. He said, without looking back at her, "Yeah. Your mommy left some pork chops in the oven."

The hose fought against the fire, but the entire building was engulfed. The firefighters fixed their efforts on the hillside behind it, too. The wind thrust life into the flames, which blushed orange in thick harmony with each gust of air.

David crossed the holler and approached the four men, his hands to his side.

One yelled a warning. "Hey, now, get back. This ain't a safe place."

"I have a right to know what's happening! This is my church!"

The men looked down as they turned to face the preacher.

"Buddy, you ain't got your church no more. It's gone."

Little George and his sister Pauline was drinking pops and playing Rook on the back porch of his house. Pauline was a known cheat. It was a four-person game, but it was harder and harder to get the young'uns in on a night a Rook, so they made do with two dummy hands, hoping to keep the ghosts happy.

Pauline took a sip out of her can and sniffed the air. "What is that?"

Little George eyed her. She musta knew he was about to clean sweep the rest of the deck. "Come on now. Play ye cards."

She sat her can down and stood up. "No, I'm serious, damn it. You smell that?" She stomped over to the edge of the porch and called out to her brother. "Get over here."

Little George pushed himself up by planting his hand on the back of his chair. He didn't feel real steady getting up or getting down, but once he was on two feet he was as strong and solid as ever.

He joined her at the edge of the porch.

In the distance, they could see a fire climbing up a hillside that stretched into their own.

Pauline spit off the porch. "Reckon that's Mosely? Ice Plant?"

Little George counted the dips in the hills. "Yep. Mouth a Ice Plant."

"You reckon it's gonna cause us any trouble?"

"I doubt it. I've got all this cleared out plumb to the line up there. It won't get close to the houses. But we'll watch it."

"I'm gonna call over to the station and see if there's anything we can do. You sound awful sure. Don't think this'll come down?"

"No. Hill burnt the year before you come up. Didn't get close. And that was before we cleared the brush. Closest it might would get's the toolshed or graveyard. Might take out Jesus, but we'll be fine." He dipped his cap in a deferential gesture to the statue on the hill, the reflective tape around its head just beginning to glitter back the light from the distant flames climbing up the mountain.

"Shit. I'd hate for us to lose another Jesus."

"Well—ain't no worry if we do. There's plenty more'a him where he come from."

POSTSCRIPT

Montgomery County. Summer 2024.

In 2022, when I was the Kentucky State Teacher of the Year, I wanted to interview Appalachian children in the mountains of eastern Kentucky, where I am from, for a column I was writing for an education-focused periodical. I partnered with a school district and spoke with twenty students randomly chosen from several schools. I assured the district that I would publish the column only if the administration valued and was comfortable with what I wrote because I am mindful of groups coming in to exploit narratives of poverty for their own gain. I wanted the administration to understand that my goal was to give the students full control and to let them say what they wanted to say to people not from where they were from, to people from outside Appalachia.

The interviews were a holy experience. These young people's acute sense of the world around them was beautiful and painful in its honesty and clarity. When I submitted my column, the school district suggested that I go speak with more students who might share more positive experiences of the world. I chose to shelve the column instead. These matters are complex, and while I honor the choice and respect the intentions of those administrators, I come to different conclusions about what it means for stories that are less-than-ideal, for voices in pain, to be shared.

I would like, however, to share just three moments of insight I was witness to during my interviews:

Boy, 16: "I want everyone to know about our community—it's not about being different from stereotypes, *it's about being much deeper.*"

Girl, 16: "We need to destigmatize how we're viewed. When we do the same things as other people, *their prejudice fills in the blanks.*"

Girl, 18: "People look down on me when I fit a stereotype, *but they're disappointed when I don't.*"

Appalachia is perhaps the most heavily stereotyped and stigmatized region in the United States. When I was younger, a lot of older people worked hard to help us see that we were *more than* the stereotypes, as if the stereotypes revealed the worst of our stains and through hard work, we might talk, might dress, might act, might *be* in a way that is presentable to the rest of America.

In some ways, their approach worked. I can comfortably talk, walk, dress, and act like "presentable" folks from somewhere else. But the desire to be who I am and not change, to honor the accent, food, challenges, and culture, remains. The question also lingers: what about the "stereotypes" was wrong in the first place? Would a refusal to talk like my mamaw or eat the sorts of food she lovingly prepared not be a condemnation of her, a suggestion that there is something about her that is less or worse than others?

Progressive America, by and large, seems to tell me that I should not diminish my queerness to make non-queer people comfortable. Rise up, it says, and do not conform to the heteropatriarchy. Why, then, is it okay with me being less Appalachian? Why are my roots and my people still mocked in otherwise politically "woke" or academic spaces? Why should I change my speech patterns, my grammar, my beliefs about not taking life too seriously, my resistance to hierarchy, my aversion to snobbery, my taste in food, or my postal code?

This collection starts with those questions.

It aims, to borrow the language of the first Appalachian student I cited, not to be just different from stereotypes but to be deeper. It aims, to step into the words of the second student, not to remove those stereotyped parts of us but to remove the stigma placed on them by folks in power from outside of here. It hopes not to look down, as that third student worried, but to lift up, to hold in the light beyond where disappointment can touch.

And if some parts are just too uncomfortably and richly Appalachian . . . well, as my mamaw says, *Don't go getting tore all to pieces.*

ACKNOWLEDGMENTS

I am more anxious writing acknowledgments than anything I write. What a beautiful anxiety! I am anxious because I am so very supported in life by so very many people that there is no way I can list them all without making a mistake. Thank you, then, first and foremost, to those whose names aren't here. The absence is an indication of the vastness of my support and the failure of my mind. You, however, matter to me.

Thank you to my husband, Josh, for sitting with these stories and characters and caring about them as if they were his own—as he has done with all of Appalachia. And for literally driving in silence, from Prestonsburg to Asheville, from Birmingham to Lexington, as I quietly wrote parts of this book. I love you. Thank you to my choice-sister, Courtney, for being a constant spring of eastern Kentucky storytelling, imagination, courage, and humor. Give em hell, Courtney. Thank you to my family, friends, and neighbors for writing by hand in a world that would force y'all into some standard font.

Thank you to every reader who helped me see with their eyes—to Karen Taylor, who left the earth sure that I felt loved and seen; to Crystal Wilkinson, Frank X Walker, Robert Gipe, Chris Offutt, Wesley Bishop, Ann Kingsolver, Justin Wymer, Doug Van Gundy, J. Bradley Minnick, Chea Parton, Peter Parnell, Clint Waters, Misty Skaggs, Shadee Malaklou, Sylvia Henneberg, Glen Colburn, Andy Fogle, Chuck Reece, Amy Richardson, Jack Harrison, T. A. Inskeep, Erica Locklear, and my classmates and professors in the MFA program at the University of Kentucky.

To my cats and companions, Clayton, Dahlia, and Iris. You remind me that no one is too small to matter.

To every bookstore, library, nonprofit, book club, university program, or group of do-good reading folk that invited me to speak—I dare not list you all for fear of forgetting someone. This is how important you've been. Thank you! Thank you! Thank you!

To all the publishers and creative outlets who printed some part of this collection before this book existed—specifically:

Untelling and the Hindman Settlement School, for publishing "Gas Station Prologue" and for the continuous support of me and so many other Appalachian writers.

Harbor Review for publishing "Bathtub Faith."

Salvation South for publishing "Boys Saved from This," "Requiem for a Dollar Store Christmas Bear," and "Shortchanged"—and to Andy, Chuck, and Stacy for their dedication to the creativity pouring out of Appalachian and Southern writers.

Miracle Monocle and Sarah Anne Strickley for including "Blowing Dandelions" in the *You Blew It* microanthology.

Smoky Blue Literary and Arts Magazine for including "Sunday School Movie."

Young Ravens Literary Review for including "You Kids Be Quiet" among other poems and an interview.

Ghost City Review and John Compton for publishing "Unto These Men Do Nothing."

To Randi Weingarten and the American Federation of Teachers for lifting a burden from my shoulders while we all, from different angles and locations, fight the same fight.

To every person who encourages me, who sees me, who springs from the same dirt as me and keeps on going.

To the University Press of Kentucky for holding a microphone to voices that need heard.

To all those who ain't different from the stereotype, just deeper.

ABOUT THE AUTHOR

Willie Carver Jr. is a minoritized youth advocate, a Kentucky Teacher of the Year, and the author of *Gay Poems for Red States,* which was featured on *Good Morning America,* received the Stonewall Honor Award and the International OUR PRIDE Arts Festival's 2025 Rainbow Advocacy Award, was shortlisted for the Judy Gaines Young Book Award, and was named a Book Riot Best Book, a Top Ten Over the Rainbow Book by the American Library Association, and a Whip-poorwill Honor Book. He writes poetry and fiction from Appalachia. Willie believes everyone deserves to feel that they matter.